The Detective Esther Penman Series

The Art Merchant
Vengeance
Pentacle

For updates on all new releases and
promotional offers, sign up to the author
newsletter at **jkflynn.co.uk**,or follow author
J.K. Flynn on Amazon and Bookbub.

PENTACLE

A Detective Esther Penman Thriller

J.K. Flynn

ISBN: 978-1-7391797-5-5

www.jkflynn.co.uk

PENTACLE

PROLOGUE

SHADOWS SHIFTED AND danced as she ran, her naked flesh already torn to shreds on the brambles and grasping branches. It was as if the trees were coming alive to harry her in her desperate flight, the moonlit forest itself in league with the demon hunting her.

She stumbled on a hidden root. Picking herself up quickly, she staggered on. She had no idea where the thing was anymore, but it couldn't be far behind. She didn't dare slow, not for an instant.

Her breath was ragged now, her feet cut and bloody. It felt like her heart was trying to punch a hole through her chest. Broken scraps of distorted memory flitted through her mind. A campfire and the other girls, the naked dancing and the handsome boy with the dreamy blue eyes...

She knew him – the handsome boy – but she couldn't remember his name. Could not, in fact, remember any of their names. He'd taken her hand, wrapped her in a shadow. She remembered kissing him, his kissing her back, kissing his way down her body... down, down... The stars had fallen from the sky, and the trees had become dancers, pirouetting around the flames...

And then the creature had appeared.

She tried to ignore the terror that cut through her at the memory of it, just as she was trying to ignore the bloody gashes all over her bare skin. In truth, the physical sensations seemed far away; the pain and cold could have belonged to someone else.

She gasped when she stumbled into a moonlit clearing.

There it was.

Enormous clouds of angry breath wreathed its snouted features as it stood there, upright on two legs like a human. She heard it snuffling, inhaling the scent of her fear.

It lowered its horns and lumbered forward – its huge, dark eyes fixed on her as it came.

It was the sensation of warm urine running down the inside of her leg that stirred her from her terrified paralysis, and she found the strength to move again. Darting to her right, she forced her way through a web of thin branches. The forest was redoubling its efforts to snag her, grab her, hold her in place for the monster. Roots slithered up out of the ground to catch at her bloodied feet. Again and again she stumbled, somehow managing to stagger on each time. The moon was an evil eye throwing its spotlight upon her, banishing any shadows that might offer a hiding place.

When the ground fell away suddenly beneath her, she pitched forward – rolling, rolling, end over end until she didn't know up from down.

A sudden, intense pain was followed by darkness.

The falling had stopped.

She winced as she opened her eyes. A wave of horrible,

skin-prickling nausea swelled and rose from her gut, and suddenly she was puking up everything in her stomach.

It took her a few moments to figure out where she was.

How much time had passed? Seconds? Minutes?

Where was the beast?

She still felt queasy. The sting of a thousand cuts and gashes seared her flesh as she pushed herself to her hands and knees.

She was in a ravine, on the muddy bank of a small stream. The forest had lost its vengeful aspect. The trees were just normal trees again, swaying gently in a chilly wind, and the stars were back in the sky, as though they had never fallen in the first place. Squatting above the treetops was the moon, lifeless and benign once more.

Had she been dreaming? Had she dreamt it all? It was the drugs. She'd taken too many different things. Taken too much of the stuff the blue-eyed boy had given her. She knew his name. Why was she not able to remember his name?

When a dark shape detached itself from the trees on the ridge above her, she heard herself whimper.

The beast.

She hadn't dreamed it.

It was a grotesque parody of a human shape, its horns and bovine eyes glinting in the moonlight as it lifted its snout to test the air. When it spotted her, it dropped to all fours and began picking its way down the slope.

She attempted to drag herself backwards, but her flailing arms and bloodied feet did little more than rearrange the dirt around her. She couldn't scream. Her throat was so constricted it seemed as if invisible hands were choking her. A frantic keening escaped her lips, but nothing louder.

Meanwhile, the thing lurched closer.

She finally found a last reserve of strength. Pain lanced through her whole body as she scrambled to her feet. Turning her back on the monster, she plunged through the stream, the icy water splashing all the way to her thighs. She latched onto the desperate notion that maybe the creature wouldn't be able to cross water, that it would act as a ward against evil.

And then her foot caught on a jagged rock and she went under. The rush of the stream filled her ears, but the numbing cold leeched the last of the fogginess from her mind. Her fingers found purchase on the streambed and she pushed herself up above the surface, gasping for air.

It landed on her.

The water was no ward. It was a weapon!

With a vice-like grip, it forced her head back under. She twisted, bubbles pouring from her mouth as she tried to scream. Somehow, she managed to knock the monster off-balance and pull free.

Coughing and spluttering, she hauled herself out and staggered up the opposite bank.

A burst of hope. The creature – whatever the hell it was – could be defeated.

As she hobbled towards the line of trees, she risked a glance over her shoulder – and immediately wished she hadn't. The thing was out of the water now too, and closing the distance fast. With a growing sense of despair, she realised she wouldn't be able to outrun it. Her foot was too badly injured. Every step sent jarring shots of pain up her leg.

She was sobbing as she reached the treeline. She could hear it right behind her, snuffling and grunting…

With a desperate wail, she crouched down, snatched up a fist-sized rock and turned to face it.

But she was too late.

A silver talon flashed in the moonlight. She gasped and dropped her rock as the talon found her chest and sank deep. Out it came – before plunging into her stomach this time. Out and in, out and in it went – rapidly, over and over.

Falling to the dirt, the last thing she saw was the beast – its terrible horns and lifeless black eyes, its wet snout and matted fur. It was standing like a human again, looming above her, oddly slender in the fleeting moonlight.

The pain was excruciating, but it was already becoming something other, something apart from her.

Something she didn't want to feel any longer.

And so she closed her eyes, exhaled, and let it go…

1

ONE HUNDRED AND fourteen days. Esther watched a bead of condensation roll jerkily down the side of the glass and soak into the coaster beneath. She could taste it already, the sweet sting of the vodka, mellowed by the dash of tonic water. She could feel its fiery progress through her chest and stomach, warming her, comforting her. That's how she remembered vodka. Like a warm hug on a cold day. The effort of not reaching for it was starting to make her feel dizzy.

She hadn't ordered it. She'd just been sitting here, innocently sipping her lemonade, when one of the junior detectives from Spencer's team had plonked it on the bar in front of her.

"Vodka tonic, wasn't it, Sarge?" he'd said, with a drunken grin that was clearly meant to be charming. "I remember," he'd added, winking.

Esther had opened her mouth to reply, but the protest had died in her throat as the detective drifted back into the party. He hadn't meant any harm. How could he know?

One hundred and fourteen days.

She still held her glass of lemonade in one hand. The other was in her pocket, clutching at the small token, a flat alloy disc, about the size of a casino chip. She didn't need to run her fingers over the engraving to know what it said. She'd stared at it so often she could picture the words declaring she was three months sober without looking at it. But she traced them with her thumb anyway, as much to occupy her free hand as anything else.

One hundred and fourteen days and counting, and yet she couldn't take her eyes from the highball glass. Couldn't make herself get up off the bar stool and walk away...

"A pint of your finest bitter, please, my good man!"

At the sound of the familiar voice, Esther finally wrested her gaze from the drink.

Detective Inspector Jared Wilcox stood at the bar next to her. A tall man – well over six foot – with broad shoulders and a wild mane of white hair, his gruff features could make him seem intimidating to some, but not Esther. They knew each other too well. To her, he was more like a big, grizzly old teddy bear, more of a friend than a boss. It was clear from his stance and expression that he had imbibed more than his fair share of fine bitters already this evening. He glanced sideways at her.

"You look like you're having fun," he quipped.

"Not in the party mood, I guess," she replied and, with a disorientating combination of relief and regret, pushed the vodka tonic away from her. She spun on the barstool to face him.

As if to punctuate her statement, a raucous cheer rose from the other end of the room and they both glanced over.

Jared wasn't the only one who'd left sobriety behind an hour or two ago. The crowd of drunken detectives gathered around the tables at the far end of the room appeared to be coaxing one of their more cavalier young comrades to lick a mess of cake cream from Detective Inspector Samantha Vimes's fingers. DI Vimes – who was behaving completely out of character after the couple of bottles of red wine she'd consumed as part of her retirement dinner – appeared to be rather enjoying it.

"That'll be you soon," Esther said to Jared, nodding at the spectacle.

"I hope you don't mean that Detective Constable Fred Benson is going to be licking cream off my fingers, Sergeant Penman?" he replied drily.

Esther sniggered. "No, you twit. I mean a retirement party."

She almost suggested finding Helen Simmons from the local neighbourhood team to do some finger-licking but thought better of it. Had she still been drinking, it was the kind of silly thing she'd have blurted out. But with Jared's marriage all but over after a misguided fling with the woman, it probably wouldn't have gone down too well.

Jared paid the bartender and took a large swallow of his beer. He smacked his lips in satisfaction.

"Maybe next year," he conceded. "Still got colleges to pay for. Race is on now, though," he added, nodding towards Calvin Brett, the odious little detective sergeant from financial crime who'd ensconced himself with a group of senior officers in one corner, laughing along to some story Detective Chief Inspector Brian Small was telling.

"That boy has his eye on Samantha's job," Jared said, "or so I'm hearing. He's already kissing arses left, right and centre."

"Calvin Brett is always kissing arses," Esther grumbled. "The man's a cretin."

"Maybe, but if he gets the promotion, there's every chance he could be your boss in a year or two."

The thought of that greasy little sycophant becoming her boss was enough to make Esther shudder.

"Over my dead body," she muttered.

"Well, there's a less dramatic way to avoid it," Jared remarked, and Esther knew what was coming next. "You get the job yourself," he finished.

Bingo! And they were back to this again.

In truth, promotion was something she'd been thinking about more often recently, if only because Jared kept raising the subject, and always with the suggestion that she get herself lined up to take over from him. Whatever he said about college fees, she knew he'd been to a retirement seminar already. It made her realise that he was seriously looking at exit timelines. Much as she would hate to lose him, he wasn't going to be in the job forever.

As for the promotion, she'd taken his advice and sat the legal exam last month, and it turned out that she and Calvin Brett were the only two detective sergeants from Belfield to score a pass. Anyone at all who got through the next stage of the process – the board interviews – would become eligible to get shuttled into Central CID to fill Samantha's post, or Jared's when it came to it. But the fact of the matter was, as detectives with experience in the department, they were already in prime position, and DS Calvin Brett would be well aware of it...

She watched Brett laugh uproariously at something one of his cohort of chief officers was saying. The man seized any opportunity to wriggle his way into the company of the top brass.

"I've been chatting with Superintendent O'Halloran," Jared went on. "She's keen to help you if she can, Esther. She's not shy about pushing the idea of having more women in the upper ranks, and it's all about the boards now. And having good contacts. You can be guaranteed that that little toady over there is working every contact he has in his efforts to climb higher."

"Calvin Brett has spent his whole life brown-nosing," Esther retorted glumly. "He's got about ten years' head start on me. Besides, I'm no good at that schmoozing shit."

As if sensing their attention from across the room, Brett turned to them. He said something to DCI Small, patting him companionably on the shoulder, stood and sauntered to the bar.

"Jared, Esther," he slurred by way of greeting. Brett was another one with a skinful in him. "What are you two conspiring about over here?" His tone was mocking; Brett managed to inflect all his remarks with a touch of condescension. Or maybe that was just for her. God, she loathed him. "You two are always thick as thieves."

"Oh, we were just talking about Samantha's post, and who might take it now that it's coming vacant." Jared said it conversationally, but Esther detected the hint of mischief in his voice.

Brett, oblivious to the twinkle in Jared's eye, drew himself up and took on a more serious cadence: his self-promoting tone, as Esther thought of it; the man was a shameless self-promoter.

"Well, actually," he said, "Brian and I were just discussing that. It should be someone from Central, in my view. Someone who knows the dynamics of the place. No point shoehorning some outsider in when there are eligible candidates right here."

"Did you use that word?" Esther asked, putting on a show of incredulity. "'Shoehorning'? To *Brian Small*?"

It seemed to only dawn on Brett then that DCI Small was himself an outsider, one who had been shoehorned in to cover for the last chief inspector. He reddened and glared at her.

"He knows what I meant," he snapped.

"I'm sure he does," Jared murmured.

"And he's delighted with the fraud investigation I'm running with the NCA," Brett went on. He addressed Jared, but his eyes kept cutting to Esther as he spoke. She sat there, trying not to scowl at him. "We've got the French Gendarmerie onboard now. This people-smuggling business is still rife, Brexit or no Brexit. Our team have detained fifty-two trafficked people these past two months, and we're finding grow-houses all over Belfield as a result of the operation. A little icing on the cake." He smirked. "I was playing golf with the chief super the other day and he was saying how well it's all been playing out in the national press, and with the Home Office. He's keen to see our team take more of a role. He's already spoken to…"

Esther zoned out as Brett nattered on about his big achievements with the NCA. The National Crime Agency was a bit like the UK's answer to the FBI; working with them at a countrywide level was bound to make headlines. Watching Brett's fat head grow sweatier and redder as he spoke, Esther considered what he would be like as a boss. She quickly decided that, personal enmity aside, he would be awful to work for, and she needed to do whatever she could to avoid it. Unfortunately, Jared was right: the only obvious way to accomplish that was to get promoted before he did. That, or move district. And she wasn't about to let a slimy little prick like Calvin Brett chase her out of her city. There was no doubt the man was positioning himself to pounce on DI Vimes's post. If he succeeded, he would be her superior, and when Jared retired, he might become her direct line manager…

She shuddered again.

"Does that kind of thing bother you, Esther?" Brett sneered.

Esther quickly rewound his last few comments and realised he'd been talking about brothels and sex slaves.

"No, Calvin," she replied calmly, "just your unhealthy interest in it."

Brett's sneer deepened; he wasn't about to bite. He changed tack instead.

"What about you?" he asked spitefully. "Got anything big on?"

He knew very well that she hadn't. Two idiot brothers just released from prison who'd carried out a string of armed robberies – she'd already got them arrested and remanded at His Majesty's pleasure again – and a travelling gang ripping off elderly people with door-to-door sales frauds. Those were her biggest cases at the moment, and neither of them held a candle to Calvin Brett's NCA gig.

"Thought not," Brett remarked when she didn't reply. He glanced around the room, abruptly seeming to decide that their company was no longer doing it for him. "I need to take a piss," he announced, and wobbled off towards the restrooms.

"There goes soon-to-be Detective Inspector Brett,"

Jared murmured.

"He's right, though," Esther said. "My investigations are no match for his people-trafficking op."

"Ah, but you have a commendation from the Faraday case in your back pocket," Jared replied. "That's one more commendation than Calvin Brett has. And there's the Peter Darren case. That'll be a big one, and it'll be making headlines again soon, with the trial coming up in a couple of months."

"Don't remind me," she muttered.

Peter Darren was a local drug lord she'd managed to put away a few months back. His defence counsel were playing silly buggers and had recently managed to wangle yet another adjournment. Although, in truth, the term 'silly bugger' was not one you could reasonably apply to Francis Unwin KC, Darren's barrister and one of the best criminal defenders in the country.

"Besides," she added, "those headlines won't be very helpful if the verdict doesn't go the right way."

"He'll get convicted," Jared said. He was trying to sound reassuring, but Esther could hear the doubt in his voice. Sure, Darren might get convicted of *something*, but the murder charges were already looking dicey, and if the Crown Prosecution Service weren't able to make any of the bigger stuff stick in a jury trial – and there was no guarantee that they would – there was every chance Peter Darren would walk out of the courtroom with time served. She was about to say as much when they were interrupted by the trilling of Jared's mobile. The DI set his pint down and pulled out his phone.

"Detective Inspector Wilcox," he answered, sounding remarkably sober for someone who was so evidently *not*.

There was a long pause as he listened to the voice on the other end. "On-call DS tonight?" he asked, frowning.

With a sigh, Esther raised her hand.

"You're in luck," Jared told the person on the phone. "As it happens, she's sitting right next to me." Another pause. "Okay, I'll tell her." He hung up.

"What is it?" she asked.

"A missing person," he replied, picking up his pint again. "Teenage girl, missing three days. Just been bumped to high-risk. Duty inspector wants CID to review the case tonight."

Esther stood and grabbed her bag and jacket.

"I'll call in to the station and take a look at it on my way home," she said. "Think I've had enough of this party anyway." She avoided looking at the vodka tonic still sitting on the bar counter. "Drunken robbers, amateur conmen and runaway teens," she muttered wryly. "Not going to get any promotions on the backs of cases like these."

"Chin up," Jared told her. "You're ten times the police officer Calvin is. Play your cards right and you'll beat him to the promotion if you give it a go."

Esther smiled, grateful for his attempt at cheering her up. "Goodnight, Jared. Go easy on the bitters. Don't forget you're on duty tomorrow."

Jared frowned at the pint in his hand as if only just remembering his offer to cover Samantha's last weekend for her.

"And behave yourself," Esther added.

He gave her a sheepish smile, no doubt pondering his recent follies. Another pint or two and he'd be good for nothing anyway, Esther thought, as she threw her bag over her shoulder and headed for the door.

2

IT TOOK ESTHER twenty minutes to walk from the pub to Belfield Central Police Station. A queue of patrol cars outside the custody gates told her the uniform crews were having a busy Friday night. The CID offices on the fourth floor were dark and empty by comparison; Esther's arrival tripped the sensors, and the lights flickered on as she made her way across the open-plan detective's workroom to the pokey office she shared with two other detective sergeants.

Firing up her computer, she scanned the whiteboard on the wall for the number she needed and dialled it.

"Duty inspector," a warm, sing-song voice answered. Belinda Pickford. Esther had dealt with Inspector Pickford a few times this past year; she was a motherly woman who had a reputation for coddling her team.

"Inspector? It's Esther Penman. I understand you have a misper for me to review?"

"Esther, how are you, dear? I'm glad it's you!" Esther could hear the smile in Pickford's voice, but then her tone grew concerned. "Yes. A teenager. She's not quite hit the seventy-two-hour-mark, but I've decided to raise her high-risk now and notify the National Missing Persons Bureau."

Risk levels were how the police graded missing persons, and consequently spoke to how many resources they should deploy and how much intrusion they could justify in their efforts to find the subject. Medium-risk was pretty standard, and all medium-risk misper investigations remained with uniform police. Low-risk mispers got very little attention. High-risk, in contrast, was a whole other matter, often involving detectives from CID.

"Okay," Esther replied, "what's the background?"

Pickford's briefing was meandering and long-winded, but she got there in the end. Mila Rose was sixteen years old. Her original name was Mila Rimkus, her mother having been a Lithuanian immigrant who died shortly after their arrival in England; it seemed that she and Mila had fled a terrible domestic situation in the Baltic state and severed all ties. If the girl had any relatives in Lithuania, no one knew who they were. Pickford's team had made some enquiries with the Lithuanian police, but feedback from EU forces was slower than it had been before Brexit, and nothing useful had come back so far. The authorities there did have records of domestic disturbances, but the man who'd terrorised Ms Rimkus had been knifed to death in prison two years prior, and he wasn't believed to be Mila's blood father in any event. Rimkus had led something of a chaotic life in Lithuania, with drugs and drink a significant factor. The more Pickford spoke about Rimkus, the more the woman reminded Esther of her own mum.

After the death of her mother, Mila spent a couple of years at one of Belfield's less savoury children's homes, before being adopted by a Baptist minister and his wife four years ago.

Police had very little information on the girl, Esther could see, from scanning the system while the inspector spoke. If Mila Rose, aka Mila Rimkus, was a graduate of the English care system, it seemed she'd managed to avoid the worst company it had to offer. In fact, her adoptive parents – Pastor Timothy Rose and his wife, Vera – appeared not to have had any trouble with her until she'd failed to return home from Belfield Grammar on Wednesday afternoon. Once they'd learned that Mila hadn't even arrived at school that morning, they'd phoned the police.

Uniform officers had quickly tracked Mila's last movements as far as a suburban bus stop, where she'd disembarked, calmly and in no apparent distress, a half-hour before her first period at school. The stop was several halts short of her usual one, which was just around the corner from Belfield Grammar. Door-to-door enquiries in the vicinity had proved fruitless, and there was no CCTV, apart from the footage on the bus. Mila was wearing her normal school uniform in the video – a navy blazer and grey skirt – and carrying her black canvas school bag over one shoulder. Although it was confirmed that the girl had her iPhone with her, all calls and texts had remained unanswered apart from one message yesterday, which had simply stated that she was fine and to leave her alone. There was no way to verify the message had come from Mila herself, since she wasn't picking up calls. There'd also been no activity on any of her social media accounts. Until this evening.

"Tonight's social media post is why she's going high-risk," Pickford explained.

"What's in the post?" Esther asked.

"It's the oddest thing, Esther. It's in *Latin*. Her parents have told us Mila doesn't do Latin in school. They've never heard her express any interest in the language."

"What does it say?"

"'*Terrestria effundam et transcendam.*'"

"What does that mean?"

"'I will shed the earthly and transcend.'"

"Oh."

"Exactly," Pickford replied. "A potential runaway teen is one thing. A runaway teen sending cryptic messages in Latin about shedding earthly possessions is quite another. I want CID running this case."

"No problem, Inspector, we'll take this on. Is there a uniform crew assigned to Mila right now?"

"I have one crew dedicated to her, and I've told the despatchers not to divert them unless it's a life-or-death call. PCs Imelda Fisher and Brendan Garfield. Brendan's a rookie, but Imelda is one of the best on my team. She's Brendan's Field Training Officer, and more than capable."

"I take it they have a recent picture of Mila?"

"They got Mila's school yearbook photograph from the parents."

"Can you send them up to my office?" Esther asked. "And tell them to bring the photo," she added.

"I'll send them straight up to you."

"Thanks, Inspector."

Esther hung up, then read through more of the investigation log while she waited for the uniform crew to show up. Three days' worth of tick-box entries made it repetitive and tedious reading, and there wasn't much more to be gleaned apart from what Pickford had told her.

Esther's attention began to drift while she waited; she

found herself playing with her sobriety chip again. The dark green disc was made from some unidentifiable alloy, the words *To Thine Own Self Be True – Unity – Service – Recovery* engraved around the edge, and a big, bold 3 MONTHS stamped in the middle.

Three months. If she could do three months, she could do four. If she could do four, she could do five. She could keep going…

The sound of movement from the open-plan workroom next door brought Esther back to the present, and the lights that had winked off out there shortly after she'd slipped into the sergeants' office flickered back on again. A moment later, two uniform officers appeared in the doorway.

"DS Penman?" the female officer asked. She was in her early twenties at most, with dirty-blonde hair in a short bob and a pale, sharp-featured face that made Esther think of a fox. She seemed very young to be doing FTO duties; she couldn't have been long out of probation herself. On the other hand, the big, heavy-shouldered fellow hovering behind her was clearly the rookie; even if Pickford hadn't told Esther he was new, it would have been obvious from the way he glanced about uncertainly and let PC Fisher do all the talking.

"Come in," Esther said.

Fisher did as she was told, and the rookie – Garfield – lumbered in after her.

"What can you tell me about Mila?" Esther asked. It never hurt to get a briefing from more than one source.

"Missing since Wednesday morning," Fisher replied, handing over the photograph of their misper as she launched into her spiel.

Esther studied the photo as Fisher spoke. Mila Rose was

young and pretty-looking, with dark hair and eyes, and a trace of baby-fat on her cheeks. It was an official school photograph, posed and well-lit. Mila wore her school blazer, which was helpful, since that was what she'd been wearing when she went missing. She sat with her hands folded in front of her, smiling sweetly for the camera. The cynical part of Esther – the part that remembered her own days on patrol duty, endlessly chasing missing kids – insisted that young Miss Rose wasn't nearly as innocent as she looked in this photo, and that she was probably off getting wasted with her mates. But Esther also knew that sometimes – every now and again – bad things *did* happen to missing teens. Looking at Mila's dimpled smile, she fervently hoped this was not one of those times...

"What about a phone trace?" Esther asked when Fisher finished speaking. The constable's briefing was far more concise than the inspector's, but there was nothing significant in her account that Pickford hadn't covered. "Inspector Pickford mentioned a text message yesterday, and I noticed a request in the investigation log to have a trace done."

"The trace was requested, yes," Fisher replied uncertainly, "but it wasn't authorised until she went high, an hour ago. Nothing's come back yet, and to be honest, the guy in the telecoms department wasn't all that hopeful we'd get anything useful. Mila's phone's been switched off since that social media post earlier. I've been ringing it every twenty minutes or so."

Esther shuffled through the sheaf of printouts that Fisher had set on her desk: screenshots from Mila's public social media accounts. One was a shot of the Latin message that had set off alarm bells and elevated the girl to high-risk.

Terrestria effundam et transcendam

And scribbled below the printed image in ballpoint:

I will shed the earthly and transcend

"Is the translation accurate?" Esther asked.

Fisher gave a slight shrug. "I put it into Google Translate. I don't know Latin – no one on duty tonight does – so I can't say for sure if it's written properly or she just did the same thing I did and stuck it into the search bar. Could mean she's, you know... thinking of ending things, maybe..."

"That's if Mila was the one who sent it," Esther murmured.

The date and time on the screenshot declared that the post was put online two hours ago.

"Nothing since this?"

Fisher shook her head. "All her accounts have gone dormant again. And, like I said, her phone is going straight to voicemail."

"What about her bedroom at home?" Esther asked. "It's been searched?"

Fisher nodded. "A crew from the late shift did it on Wednesday," she replied, "when the Roses reported her missing and they went to the house. I haven't been in there myself, but there was no mention of suicide notes or anything in the handover. There's a bag and some clothes missing, according to the mother, so it kind of looks planned. That's why she's stayed medium for so long. Looked like a runaway, before that post went up."

Esther set the print-out of the Latin screenshot and Mila's school photograph down on her desk and studied them while she digested all the information. As the silence stretched, PC Fisher became fidgety. Clearly, she was a woman who liked to keep busy. Her rookie was the opposite; after his initial glance about, he stood there silently, no indication he was even listening. Like a big rock.

At last, Fisher broke. "What should we do next, Sarge?" she asked, unable to remain still or silent any longer. She was practically bouncing on her toes. Pickford had said she was competent; Esther wondered if the inspector had simply meant 'eager'. "Should we just wait for a signal from her phone, or...?"

Esther looked at Fisher and found herself thinking about Triona. Her girlfriend was on a nightshift at the hospital. There was nobody waiting for her at home.

"Let's go visit the Roses," she said, putting the printouts and photograph into her handbag as she stood. "I want to check the girl's bedroom myself, and speak to the parents. I assume you have a patrol car?"

Fisher produced a set of keys from her pocket.

"Okay then," Esther said, as she pulled her jacket on and slung her grungy leather handbag over her shoulder. "Let's go meet the parents."

3

THERE WAS PROBABLY no hour that was too late to call on people in Timothy and Vera Rose's situation. They must have spotted the patrol car pulling up to the kerb in front of their house – a semi-detached in a cluttered, middle-class suburb of southern Belfield – because they were both standing at the front door as the officers alighted and made their way up the drive. Esther couldn't help but notice their searching looks, and the disappointment in their tired, hollow eyes when Mila didn't climb out of the car with them.

Fisher introduced her, the officer having developed a kind of rapport after two shifts of dealing with the case. The three police officers were ushered into the house, and Vera insisted on making a pot of tea. Esther wasn't a big fan of tea, but she indulged the woman, knowing that the mechanics of routine tasks were exactly the kind of thing that helped people to cope at times like this.

While Vera went to put the kettle on, Esther asked

Timothy if she could take another look through Mila's bedroom, and the pastor led them upstairs. He was a short man, hardly much taller than his wife, wearing pressed chinos and a thin turtleneck tucked into his trousers.

"This is Mila's room," he told them, stepping aside at the door to allow Esther and her colleagues inside.

Esther surveyed it for a moment. It was unusually neat and tidy for a teenage girl's bedroom. She began going through the desk drawers, and Fisher followed her lead by sifting through the wardrobe. Garfield just stood in the middle of the room, looking confused and immobile, until Fisher explained to him what they were searching for – diaries, notepads, anything that might contain a clue as to where Mila had gone, or what she was thinking when she disappeared – and he joined in.

"The other police officers have already gone through her things," Rose said from the doorway.

"Just being thorough, sir," Esther replied.

She knew the initial officers on the case had searched the room already – even without Fisher's confirmation, it had been recorded on the investigation log – but they'd done the search when the girl had been missing for only a few hours. It would have been a routine rummage, the searchers fully expecting a text or a call and a shamefaced return later in the day. Now that Mila had been gone for days – and now that strange Latin messages were appearing on her social media – it made sense to give the place another check.

"She had her regular schoolbag with her when she left?" Esther asked, flicking through a set of text- and copybooks stacked to one side on the small desk.

"Yes," the pastor replied. He was hovering in the doorway, watching them work. "She has to swap out the books most days. You'd think in this day and age they'd be using iPads or tablets or whatever, but all together those books weigh a tonne. No space for lockers at the school, apparently. I've been trying to raise the issue through the Board of Governors for months now."

"So, these books here are for classes she didn't have on Wednesday?"

"That's right. Vera's checked them to make sure."

The margins and inner covers of the copybooks were festooned with doodles in pink and green ink. Mila liked to write her name, over and over again, with little hearts in place of dots over the *i*. There was another name too, similarly heart-crowned, sprinkled in amongst all the *Mila*s.

"Who's Naomi?" Esther asked.

"That'll be Naomi Hawthorne," Rose replied. "Mila's best friend. Lives a few streets away, over on Elmwood. Her parents, James and Gail, are part of our congregation. Naomi hasn't heard from Mila since Wednesday either."

Esther glanced up at him. "Do you believe her?"

The pastor looked slightly wrongfooted by the question. "Yes, of course. She seems as worried as the rest of us. The Hawthornes are good people. I thought you folks had already spoken to them?"

"We've been out with Naomi and her parents," PC Fisher confirmed, for Esther's benefit as well as the pastor's. "I've spoken to Gail Hawthorne and Naomi twice today. They still haven't heard from her."

Esther nodded, tucking away the names for future reference, but meanwhile something else had caught her attention. The bottom corner of the last scribbled-on page in one of the copybooks had been torn away. She squinted as she held the paper up to the light, turning it first one way and then the other. When she was sure she could see indentations on the page below the missing part, she plucked a pencil from the desk. Sharpening it until the tip was as long as she could get it, she leaned in close and, very gently, used the side of the pencil's elongated tip to shade the page exposed by the torn-away paper. When pale impressions of letters and numbers started to form, she applied a little more pressure, careful not to press too hard. PC Fisher had stopped her searching and was watching with interest.

Once Esther was done with her pencil-shading, she switched on the desk lamp and held the page at an angle below the bulb. A line of writing had been revealed. Older doodling had left a mess of indentations which obscured the end, but Esther could make out the first part clearly enough.

Anita! 44 D

No heart this time.

"Who's Anita?" she asked.

There was silence from the corridor. Esther glanced up. Pastor Rose was looking at her blankly.

"I'm sorry?" he replied. "Who?"

"Anita," Esther repeated, flourishing the copybook. "She's written the name 'Anita' and torn it out. 'Anita 44 D'. Does that mean anything to you?"

Rose shook his head. "I – I'm sorry, but I've never heard her mention any Anita before. I don't know who that is."

Was it concern that made him shift uncomfortably?

Esther held his gaze for a moment, then lifted the copybook. "Mind if I hold on to this for a bit?" she asked.

He nodded. "Of course," he said. "Whatever you

need."

She had probably ruined the page for any further analysis, but she wanted to see how the good pastor reacted to the request. And besides, who knew what the science department guys were capable of; they often surprised her with what they could do.

Esther and Fisher went back to their rummage search. Esther found a short stack of diaries under the bed, but they were old – nothing since the year before last – and none of them held mention of any Anita. The entry dates and contents suggested they would have little bearing on her current disappearance.

After another five minutes of systematic processing, Esther decided there was nothing else in the bedroom of any significance.

She allowed Pastor Rose to lead them back downstairs to the kitchen, where Vera had set out teacups, a matching teapot and an impressive array of biscuits on a platter. Enough biscuits for twenty people, Esther thought, murmuring her thanks and taking a seat along with the others.

She began by asking Vera if she could remember Mila ever mentioning a girl called Anita, explaining about the torn-out note on the copybook she'd found.

"No," the woman replied, looking confused and concerned, "I've never heard Mila mention anyone called Anita. Could it be a girl from school? Naomi might know, mightn't she, Tim?"

Her husband nodded and said something noncommittal.

"This would be Naomi Hawthorne?" Esther confirmed, jotting in her notebook. If Naomi didn't know any Anita, an enquiry with the school might yield some results.

"Naomi Hawthorne is Mila's best friend," Vera offered tremulously. "Mila doesn't have a big circle of friends. Just Naomi, really. She's such a good girl normally. Always does her homework and chores and keeps her room tidy. I can't... I just..."

She began to sob quietly. Her husband put a comforting arm around her.

Esther moved on to the subject of the social media message. They were already aware of it; it might have gone some way to explaining Timothy Rose's harried expression and Vera Rose's shaky grip on her teacup.

"Is it biblical?" Esther asked the pastor.

He frowned and shook his head. "I'm not familiar with the phrase."

"It's not something Mila might have picked up from a religious text or anything?"

"Latin is the language of the Roman Church," he replied tightly. "All our Bibles are in the King's English. Besides, Mila wasn't... wasn't feeling particularly religious lately."

There was a subtle shift between him and his wife then. Vera stopped crying and dabbed at her tears, and the pastor seemed to be sitting a little more stiffly all of a sudden.

"Was that a source of friction?" Esther asked.

Vera half-glanced toward her husband, but he kept his arm around her, his expression wooden.

"Mila had been questioning her faith for some time," Vera answered. She spoke slowly, as though picking her words carefully. "It wasn't something new. We aren't tyrants. She's entitled to have her own views." The way the woman said the words, Esther thought it sounded like a well-worn refrain. "Besides, she's a teenager. Teenagers rebel. They question things."

Esther studied the pastor.

"But it *was* causing some tension in the house?" she pressed.

Her gaze seemed to make him even more uncomfortable. He opened his mouth, then hesitated. A guarded look came over him. Vera answered again.

"It wasn't something that would have driven her to run away," she replied firmly. "Mila had her own views, and I respected that. Tim has been trying to lead her back to the fold, but this is nothing new. Why would she suddenly run away now? It just… it doesn't make sense. Besides, this internet message – it isn't like her. Not like her at all. I'm worried, Officer." The woman's trembling grew more pronounced as her fears bubbled. "I'm worried that she didn't send this. Or that… or that if she *did* send it, someone with her made her write it."

"I want to assure you, Missus Rose," Esther replied, "now that I'm looking into your daughter's case, I'll be giving it my full attention. I'll do my very best to get her back safe and sound."

She knew that it was an optimistic pitch, but she was keen to give them some hope while she still could. Cryptic post or no, the possibility that Mila had absconded voluntarily was still very real. Besides, it was clear that Vera Rose needed to hear something reassuring, with her hands shaking so much Esther was worried she was going to slop tea all over herself. Her husband noticed and placed his own hand gently on her wrist, steering the cup back to the surface of the table.

"What about school?" Esther asked. "Has Mila been having any difficulties there recently? With her studies, or other students? Has there been any suggestion of bullying?"

Vera shook her head. "I don't think so. Mila would usually tell me about things like that. Although…"

Esther looked at her questioningly. "Although?"

"She'd become more withdrawn recently. She wasn't… she wasn't talking to me as much as she used to."

"What about Naomi? Have there been any fallouts between them?"

Vera frowned at her tea. "Naomi told us Mila was avoiding her these last few weeks. She couldn't say why. They haven't had a fight. She says Mila just seemed to be drifting away." She looked up at Esther. "Naomi seems very upset over it all. If I'd known, I'd have spoken to Mila about it. I'd have found out what was going on between them. Naomi is a good girl, a good friend for Mila."

Pastor Rose nodded. "The Hawthornes are good people," he murmured again.

Esther could see Vera was growing more upset, so she moved on to more stable territory, asking questions about Mila's local hangouts, shops she liked to frequent, any other associates they could think of, giving Vera the opportunity to contribute some information and feel helpful, even if it was information they'd largely gleaned already. Esther scribbled it all down dutifully, irrespective of whether it was old information or new.

Pastor Rose's face remained impassive while Vera spoke and Esther jotted her notes. He gave his wife's arm a brief squeeze every now and again, but whenever Esther caught his eye, he looked away quickly.

Esther made a note of this too.

At length, she told them about the next steps in the enquiry, including the possibility of a national media appeal. She spoke about checking airports and ferry terminals the length and breadth of the country, although they did confirm Mila had no passport; her Lithuanian one had long since expired, and she'd never renewed it or applied for a British one.

When Esther felt she'd covered most of the ground she needed to, she explained to the Roses that she wanted to go speak with Naomi Hawthorne before it grew too late to visit. Assuring them that she would be in contact if she learned anything new, she gave them her card and told them to call her if they heard from Mila, or if they had any questions.

Once they were back inside the patrol car, Esther checked that PC Fisher had the Hawthornes' address.

The officer nodded. "It's just a couple of blocks away."

"Then let's go and see what Naomi has to say."

4

NAOMI HAWTHORNE SAT at one end of the kitchen table, her parents on either side of her, looking guarded and uncomfortable. A diminutive girl, she was made to look smaller still by the oversized hoody she was slouched inside of.

Esther and Fisher sat at the far end of the table and Garfield stood by the door; he had resumed his impression of a disinterested boulder.

"I understand that you and Mila were drifting apart recently," Esther said. "Is that right?"

Naomi nodded, eyes darting about as if she had been accused of something. She kept glancing at PC Garfield warily, although he seemed oblivious to the attention.

"It's okay, Naomi," Esther said. "You're not in any trouble. I just want to get an idea of what Mila might have been thinking when she went missing. It may help us find her. Was there any reason you two fell out?"

Naomi shrugged. She began picking at the edge of the

kitchen table until her mother reached out and tapped her hand gently, then the girl heaved a sigh and shrugged again. "It wasn't like we had a fight or anything. She just, I don't know, started coming up with excuses not to meet up. Stopped replying to messages. Stopped calling around."

"Was there anything in particular that you think might have triggered it?"

Naomi shook her head. She may well have been upset like the Roses said, but Esther was finding it hard to tell.

"Did she start hanging out with other people at school?" Esther pressed. "Or outside of school?"

Naomi shrugged again. She liked shrugging.

"And you're sure you don't know anyone called Anita?"

Another headshake.

It was Esther's turn to sigh, though she managed to hide it behind a small cough. Christ, teenagers were weird. She tried to muster some sympathy; after all, she'd been a pretty weird teenager herself, and in far more dramatic style. But empathy and awareness of those years faded quickly once people left them behind.

She rephrased the question. "Did you notice her with any other people recently? In or out of school? Was there anyone new she was chatting with on social media? Anything like that?"

"She just seemed to stop talking to people generally," Naomi muttered. "Everyone I know, anyway. Just started turning into a bit of a loner." There was a sudden flash of defensiveness in her face. *It lives*, Esther thought drily. "I did try talking to her," the girl said, a touch of heat entering her voice. "I *did*. But she just... she just didn't want to talk to me."

"When did she start behaving like this?"

"I dunno. About a month ago, maybe?"

"And there's nothing you can think of that might have caused this change in behaviour?"

"I know she was having arguments at home, about Jesus and God and the Bible, but that was going on a lot longer. It wasn't such a big deal at the start, but her Dad's the pastor at our church and stuff and, I don't know, she said he took it kinda bad."

"Badly," Naomi's mother interjected, and gave Esther an embarrassed half-smile; Esther couldn't tell if the embarrassment was for interrupting or her daughter's poor grammar.

"Badly," Naomi repeated, with a grimace for her mum.

"Can I see the last messages Mila sent you?" Esther asked.

The girl shrugged. "Sure."

She fished her phone from somewhere within her voluminous hoody. Her thumbs darted across the screen in a dizzying blur before she passed it over.

Esther scrolled through the messages. Everything from the last few days was one-way from Naomi to Mila, asking her if she was okay, where she was, telling her everyone was worried. None of the messages had elicited a response, nor was there any indication that they'd been read. Scrolling further into the past, Esther could see that the traffic remained pretty much unidirectional throughout the last few weeks, just as Naomi had said, with Mila either ignoring the texts that Naomi sent or brushing off her invitations to hang out. The last message Mila had responded to was from three weeks ago, a reply to a suggestion from Naomi that they go to the cinema. She'd simply replied that she didn't feel like watching a movie, but perhaps another time. There were a few prior exchanges along a similar vein. Esther couldn't help feeling a little sorry for Naomi as she handed the phone back. Maybe the girl *was* a little sad under her fuck-the-world expression.

"So, she never mentioned any problems?" Esther asked. "Apart from some trouble at home over the religious stuff?"

Shrug. "Yeah, but I don't think the arguments at home had got any, like, worse or anything. They'd been going on a while. She'd laughed about the pastor getting all uppity about it."

Naomi's father made a tutting sound. It was at times like this that Esther lamented the rigorous procedures police abided by these days; speaking to Naomi with her parents present was the correct protocol in this kind of situation, but what Esther really wanted to do was get the kid on her own, to see if she might open up a bit more without her parents listening in. She was considering how big a deal a deviation from the rules would be – whether the Hawthornes seemed like the type of people who'd make a complaint to the department – when she became aware of the tinny sound of a transmission coming through PC Fisher's radio next to her. The words in the woman's earpiece were just beyond the edge of hearing, but all eyes turned to the officer as she pressed her transmit button and replied, "Yes, yes, all received. I'll let DS Penman know."

She leaned in to Esther and whispered, "They've got a result on Mila's phone. Last time it was on and pinged off a mast was three hours ago. Around the time of that weird post."

"Where?" Esther murmured, keeping her voice down, conscious of the curious eyes across the table.

"Norwick Forest," Fisher whispered back, "halfway up

the mountain."

Esther turned to Naomi. "Is there any reason why Mila would go up into the Norwick Hills? You guys ever hang out in the woods up there?"

Naomi looked confused and slightly alarmed by the question; it was the most expression Esther had seen on the girl's face since they'd sat down. Esther didn't want to start the rumour mill going, but she was keenly aware that if Mila's phone had registered the location three hours ago, she was working against the clock.

"No," Naomi told them. "We never go up there."

"What about any of the other kids from your school?" Esther asked.

"Some people hang out at the quarry, I think. Sixth formers. The ones with cars. But they wouldn't hang out with me or Mila."

Esther glanced at Fisher. The officer shook her head. Not the quarry.

"Anywhere else?" she asked Naomi. "She isn't into hiking or camping or anything? Didn't mention anywhere up there she'd like to go?"

Naomi looked completely nonplussed by the line of questioning now.

"Mila?" she asked. "Camping? Uh-uh. No way. She never mentioned anything like that. Mila's not... *outdoorsy.* Neither of us are."

Esther addressed both Naomi and her parents as she pushed back her chair and got to her feet. "I'm sure the other officers have already asked you to get in touch if you hear from her, but I want to reiterate that now. If Mila does make contact, it's very important you let us know straight away." She met Naomi's eye while she said it. She knew the parents would report anything; Naomi, on the other hand, she still hadn't quite figured out. "Anything at all, you understand?"

The girl nodded slowly, unable to hold Esther's gaze for long.

"Of course, Officer," Naomi's mother chimed in. "We'll call straight away if we hear anything."

"Thank you," Esther replied, as the Hawthornes accompanied her to the door.

PCs Fisher and Garfield were already outside and heading for the car. Esther handed her card to Gail Hawthorne and thanked her and her husband again for their help, before following the uniform officers down the drive.

As she slipped into the backseat of the patrol car, she saw that the two PCs had switched places; Garfield was in the driver's seat now, which allowed Fisher to fire up the onboard computer. She tapped at the keyboard and gave directions, while Garfield set off for the Norwick Hills.

"We just got this back from the telecoms department," Fisher said.

Esther leaned forward between the front seats so she could take a look at the computer screen. It contained a graphic – a map of Belfield and some of the surrounding county – pasted into the body of an email. Esther could see where the telecoms guys had marked out two arcs with dotted lines. The space where both arcs intersected was shaded in red. It covered a dismayingly large swathe of Norwick Forest.

They left Belfield behind, crossing over the Valley Bridge and wending their way up into the forested slopes of the Norwick Hills. Fisher continued to issue instructions to Garfield, checking their position on her phone's map against the graphic on the car's computer screen. About ten minutes into their journey, she told Garfield to pull over. He stopped at a layby overlooking the valley.

"We're inside the shaded zone now," Fisher announced. "Looks like it pinged within two square miles of this spot."

Esther stepped out of the car and stared around at the night-shrouded forest. They were quite a distance up the mountain here. A wall of trees marched steeply towards the stars behind them and fell away to the clustered lights of the city below. If the signal was logged three hours ago, there was no guarantee that Mila – or whoever had her phone – was anywhere nearby, but Esther still felt a need to do something. Despite the arrival of spring, the air on the mountain was frigid. Her breath formed white clouds in front of her face, and fog had settled in clumps across the dark forest below.

"Call in Air Support," she said to Fisher, who had joined her in her survey of the valley. "Get them to do a sweep of the whole area, concentrating on that shaded part of the map. If Mila is out here, maybe they'll spot a heat signal or something. Are you two on duty all night?"

Fisher nodded.

"Okay, I want you to patrol every road – every track big enough for a vehicle – on this side of the valley."

"Will do, Sarge."

Esther sighed as she stared out across the forested slopes again. "We're going to have to wait until daylight to search the forest properly."

It was deathly quiet up here. They hadn't met another vehicle in about five minutes, and even though it would be busier during the day, this mountain road wasn't a major route; it brought motorists to the other side of the Norwick

Hills and on to Hodderston, but the motorway to the east was far quicker. Esther didn't think the isolated nature of this place was a good thing for Mila. Standing here, in the cold and the dark, she suddenly had a terrible fear for the girl.

"Take me back to the station," she told the uniform officers. "I need to start getting things organised for a full search in the morning."

They returned to the patrol car. As Garfield started the engine, Esther looked out her window at the miles and miles of treetops all around. Unless the chopper found something tonight – and she wasn't banking on it – it would take coordinated teams of volunteers and dog units days to search this place thoroughly. Weeks, if they had to extend it.

No, Esther was under no illusions about how daunting a task searching this place was going to be.

5

IT WAS ALMOST one a.m. by the time Esther got home. The house was dark and empty. Triona wouldn't be done with her nightshift until six at the earliest.

After spending an hour discussing the case with the on-call search and rescue coordinator – a sergeant from a northern station called Mark Taylor – she was a little more confident about the prospect of combing the Norwick Forest. Taylor had promised her two units of police search teams, four sniffer dogs, and anywhere between twenty and fifty community volunteers to begin with. He had a long night of planning and organising ahead of him in order to hit the ground at six a.m.; he was mustering his key supervisors at Belfield police station at four to get things rolling, but there was no point starting the search itself until after sunrise.

Esther had offered to meet him at the station at four, but he'd convinced her there was no need; the search was his bit, he'd said, and she'd have other shit to deal with tomorrow. He suggested instead that they rendezvous at the coordination site – the layby where she, Fisher and Garfield had stopped – later in the morning. They would run the search from there. Esther, dead on her feet by that stage, hadn't put up much of an argument, although she had agreed to stop by before she headed to the station in the morning.

Pulling off her clothes, she crawled under the covers, and sleep found her fast.

It seemed to Esther like she'd only just closed her eyes when she awoke to the feel of Triona sliding into the bed next to her. But when she glanced at the clock on her bedside table, she saw it was almost 7:30 – she'd been so tired last night she had forgotten to set the alarm! Well, at least Taylor might have made some progress by the time she got to him.

"Sorry," Triona whispered, "I didn't mean to wake you."

She immediately belied her words by snuggling up to Esther.

"Argh, you're cold!" Esther gasped.

"You're warm," Triona replied, grinning as she moved in close and kissed her, hands slipping down between her legs.

Esther smiled, but then forced herself to pull away with a regretful sigh.

"I gotta go to work, Tee," she said.

"But it's Saturday," her girlfriend murmured, undeterred in her nuzzling.

"I'm on-call this weekend," Esther explained, closing her eyes and enjoying the feel of Triona's lips on her skin, "and I've got this misper case I need to go in early to oversee."

Triona worked her way down to Esther's chest, pulling her vest aside to kiss her nipples. "How early is early?" she mumbled between kisses.

Esther chuckled. "Are you not tired after running around a hospital for twelve hours?"

"Tired and horny."

Esther gave a gratified moan as Triona's fingers started to work their magic, but their antics were cut short when Esther's phone began to trill on the bedside table.

"Shit," she grumbled.

Triona's head popped up as Esther shimmied sideways to grab it, then rolled aside with a sigh when Esther put the phone to her ear.

"Hello? DS Penman."

"Esther? Esther, it's Mark Taylor."

"Mark, hi. How's the search going?"

A hesitation on the other end of the line made Esther's heart plummet.

"You've found her?" she said, unable to keep the dismay from her voice.

"No, it's not that," Taylor replied. "It's something else."

Esther sat up straighter. "What is it?"

"Hard to explain. I think maybe you should come see this for yourself."

Pulling aside the covers, Esther hopped from the bed. "Okay, I'll be with you in twenty minutes." Twenty minutes might be a push, but this early on a Saturday, she might just get there by eight.

"I'll meet you at the coordination site," Taylor told her.

"See you there," Esther replied, already pulling on her jeans.

She hung up and dropped the phone on the bed, then

headed to the bathroom.

"Sorry, Tee, gotta go," she said. "Duty calls."

"I'll just have to take care of myself, then?" Triona remarked.

Esther, already scrubbing her teeth, returned to the bedroom and leaned on the doorframe. "'Fraid so," she replied.

Triona was sitting up in the bed now. As Esther watched her, she straightened and adjusted the sheets about herself.

"I got a call from my da yesterday," she said.

"Uh-huh?" was all Esther could manage around her toothbrush. She went back into the bathroom to spit and rinse.

"My parents are coming to visit."

Triona's voice had dropped a touch, but the sentence carried; it was as if the world had gone quiet to usher those six words to Esther's ears. She spat, straightened and returned to the bedroom, toothbrush still in hand.

"When?" she asked.

Triona returned her gaze sheepishly. "Tomorrow."

Despite her best efforts, Esther's expression must have registered some kind of alarm, because Triona suddenly started talking very rapidly.

"I'm sorry, babe, I completely forgot they were planning to come over until my da mentioned it again last night! To be honest, I don't remember us *actually* ever finalising anything. Honestly! I'd have remembered." She hesitated, a slight frown wrinkling her beautiful brow. "I think," she conceded uncertainly.

Esther did her best to hide her nervousness at the prospect of meeting Triona's parents for the first time. She held Triona's gaze for a long moment. She could tell both of their minds were running along the same lines.

"How will they be?" Esther asked.

Triona sighed. "Well, I've told you about my ma," she replied. "She's still a little… uptight about my 'lifestyle choice'." She gave the words air quotes. "Da says she's trying to come to terms with it – hence the visit – but I think maybe he's being generous. I suspect he's pestered her into it." She dropped her eyes and picked an imaginary bit of lint from the bedsheet. "I'll understand it if you're not keen. My ma can be… *difficult*."

Esther crossed the room and sat down on the bed in front of her. "No, I want to meet them," she said. "They're your folks. Of course I want to meet them."

That comment made Triona light up, and Esther couldn't help grinning. She loved when Tee smiled like that, like a child at Christmas.

"Great!" Triona exclaimed. "You'll love my da. I really want him to meet you."

Esther wanted to meet him too. It was her mother Esther was worried about. The same thought seemed to occur to Triona, and her smile slipped a little. Esther leaned forward and kissed her.

"It'll be fine," she assured her, but she must not have sounded all that convincing because the frown crept back onto Triona's forehead as she spoke again.

"I hope so," she said. "At least with my da here my mother might behave herself."

Esther hoped so too, but she kept that to herself. She kissed Tee again and then went to get changed. She'd already lost five minutes, and she was anxious to see what Mark Taylor had discovered up in the Norwick Forest…

6

ESTHER PULLED INTO the layby where she and PCs Fisher and Garfield had parked the night before. Her tiny Fiat was dwarfed by the array of vehicles that now lined both sides of the road, including police vans and pickups emblazoned with the local authority's search and rescue insignia. There wasn't much traffic, but what little there was slowed in passing, curious travellers rubbernecking as they went by.

Esther zipped up her coat as she stepped from the car. Even in the bright sunshine, the air up here was crisp. Flashes of colour among the trees upslope resolved themselves into the yellow-and-red jackets of search volunteers, trudging north in a strung-out line. Esther could see more hi-viz coats downslope and, closer at hand, the white peaks of a large canopy. She headed for that.

The coordination tent was a roomy shelter, one side of it tied open to allow her a view of the interior as she approached. Along the back wall was a table lined with massive thermos pots and stacks of cardboard cups, trays of cling-filmed sandwiches and tubs of biscuits. Another foldable table stood at the centre of the tent, where two men were leaning over a set of ordnance survey maps. The first was in his sixties, with a ginger beard that was turning grey in patches, and a dark green woollen cap pulled low over his ears. The second was in his forties. He had a square, chiselled face and a salt and pepper crew cut. He looked like a caricature of an army man, with that thick chest and those broad shoulders – cast him in plastic and you'd have a life-size GI Joe, Esther thought.

"Sergeant Taylor?" she asked, as she ducked into the tent.

Both men looked up from their muttered conversation, but it was army-man who nodded.

"Esther?" he asked.

"That's me."

Taylor stepped briskly around the table to shake her hand – a firm pump. Esther felt her pulse quicken. Taylor was hot, there were no two ways about it; he exuded that same air of military efficiency she'd sensed from the late-night phone call, and she felt her knees weaken a fraction under his steely blue gaze.

"I'm glad you're here," he said. "Come with me." He glanced over his shoulder at the bearded man. "Rodney, we'll meet up again in three hours and see what kind of progress there's been before we make a decision on the upper slopes."

Rodney nodded and began rolling up the maps as Taylor led Esther from the tent. They headed downslope through the forest. The searchers she'd seen on arrival were already little more than distant yellow specks among the trees to the south. Taylor caught her looking at them.

"We rotate the searchers," he explained. "Divide the area into manageable portions and put supervisors in charge of each. It'll take at least two days to search the two square miles around the phone signal, and longer if we need to expand the search. It's difficult terrain, especially north of the road. But now we've found this…" He trailed off, frowning.

Esther was getting impatient. "What is '*this*'?" she asked.

"Better you see it for yourself," Taylor replied simply. "It's not so far."

Maybe it wasn't far for Sergeant Taylor, but to Esther it seemed like there was no end to their march. She was glad that they cut west after a hundred yards or so, traversing the southward gradient; she hadn't been looking forward to the trek back up the hill. Even still, she was out of breath by the time Taylor brought her to a clearing where a uniform officer stood guard in front of a stretch of crime scene tape. Beyond the tape stood an old cabin.

"I've taken the liberty of getting local police to set up a scene until you've assessed it yourself," Taylor explained.

"I'm assuming that if you'd found a body you would have said so by now," Esther replied. She was sweaty and out of breath, and irritable from her trek through the woods.

"That's correct," he replied. He signed the officer's crime scene logbook, and Esther followed suit. "No bodies. Just plenty of… *weird*."

The cabin was a dilapidated wooden thing, derelict and ramshackle. A buckled plywood door hung open in a crooked frame, and weeds sprouted in abundance from the sagging, rusty corrugated roof. The gutters and tin stovepipe were all askew, and the cheap weatherboard cladding was green with moss, where it wasn't rotten and

47

falling away altogether.

There was plenty of litter lying about, but even the litter looked old: rusted beer cans and crisp packets and plastic bags with logos that had long been discontinued where they weren't faded completely. Esther had been thinking it might be some kind of teen hangout as she'd approached, but any teens who'd left this garbage behind were probably well into their forties by now...

Being careful about where he set his feet, Taylor stepped up to the door. He pulled it wide and gave her a meaningful look. Esther picked her way towards him – although the carpet of leaves and pine needles were unlikely to hold any footwear impressions – and stopped on the threshold. The hair on the back of her neck rose as she studied the interior.

Despite its rotting façade, the cabin's single room showed signs of recent habitation. More trash and old rags lined the bottom of the walls, where they'd been swept aside to clear some space. The back wall had been painted white; compared to the layers of fading graffiti elsewhere, this wall almost shone, making the symbols that had been daubed in red stand out starkly. At the centre was a huge, inverted star inside a circle, and around this main symbol were painted an array of smaller ones, none of them familiar to Esther.

But it wasn't the weird symbols that had her hackles rising. In the middle of the freshly swept room stood a ring of fat black candles, all half-melted into puddles of wax. They were set around another circle-and-star symbol, this one chalked on the floor, and at its centre was a patch of what looked like...

"That looks like blood," she said.

Taylor nodded. "Think it might have something to do with your misper?"

"I don't know," she replied. "But it's all too fresh, and too much of a coincidence." She turned to him. "Have you called for forensics?"

He shook his head. "I was waiting for you. Thought you should see it first."

"Let's get CSI out here," she said, "and Mapping and Photography."

"I'll get the officer to radio a request to Despatch."

While Taylor headed back to the cordon to pass on her instructions to the uniform officer, Esther ran her eyes over the cabin's interior again. She shuddered.

Even without a body, this wasn't good.

* * *

It didn't take long for word to come back from the despatchers: CSI were short-staffed and it would take them over two hours to get out to process the cabin. As impressive as Sergeant Taylor's military operation was, Esther quickly grew tired of snooping about the woods, watching teams of searchers trudge back and forth from the tent. She was yearning for a cup of good, hot coffee; the lukewarm stuff in the dispensers wasn't doing it for her. Even Taylor's broad shoulders and blue eyes were starting to lose their charm. She decided to nip back to the station and check in with Jared. Maybe grab a warmer coat and some gloves from home. Springtime or not, the cold of the Norwick Hills was seeping into her bones.

After a quick detour to grab a couple of coffees from a drive-thru, Esther parked in the station yard and headed straight to Jared's office.

The door to the DI's office was closed, so she tapped on it gently.

"Yes?" came a growl from within.

She found Jared in the process of dropping a couple of Alka-Seltzer into a glass of water. A small towel sat in a steaming bowl next to it. His face was sagging and his eyes were bloodshot.

She couldn't help smirking. "Did you have a few too many last night, Detective Inspector Wilcox?"

"Musta been the curry on the way home."

"Of course it was. Here"—she set one of the takeout coffees down next to his fizzing antidote—"got you a coffee. Might help."

"Thanks," he mumbled. He looked pitiful.

"Anything juicy in the morning reports?" she asked.

He shook his head and immediately seemed to regret it.

He winced. "Nothing interesting," he replied. "Bar-room brawl in a riverside tavern down Yorkgate could result in some poor bugger losing his eye – that'll come our way if he does – but nothing apart from that. Thank God. Might just shut the door and get some sleep. Oh, there is this, though." He plucked an envelope from atop a pile of papers on his desk. "Found it shoved under my door this morning, with a note from Superintendent O'Halloran to pass it on to you."

The envelope was made from thick, creamy paper embossed with the watermark of some fancy stationery company. On the front, in simple ballpoint pen, was her name: *Esther P.* It wasn't sealed. She untucked the flap and pulled out a card emblazoned with the logo of the National Police Chiefs' Council. It was an invitation to some kind of dinner function, with guest speakers from a Canadian constabulary. Again, the space for the invitee was written in simple ballpoint: *Detective Sergeant Esther Penman, Belfield CID.*

Esther must have looked as puzzled as she felt, because Jared finished off his Alka-Seltzer, chased it with a slurp of coffee, and said, "I forgot to mention it to you. She suggested it a few days back. Said she could source you an invite. Get you rubbing shoulders with some of the top brass. Help with your promotion efforts."

Esther pulled a face and gave a dramatic shiver as she dropped the invite on his desk. "Sounds like hell," she said. "Not my scene."

Jared gave her an exasperated look. "She's gone out of her way to get you this, Esther. I think the least you could do is show your face. She's trying to help, and it's no bad thing to have a superintendent in your corner."

Esther sighed. "I know. I don't mean to sound ungrateful, but…" She trailed off. She did sound ungrateful, and she knew it. But she wasn't exaggerating when she said it sounded like hell. It really did. It sounded political and posh and… *ugh.*

Jared spoke into the silence. "If you need some motivation, just imagine Calvin Brett bossing you around next year, or the year after."

Esther grimaced and picked up the invitation again. It was clearly the result of some last-minute wrangling on the part of the superintendent; the event was tomorrow evening at 7 p.m.

"Okay," she said. "I'll make an effort. For O'Halloran."

Jared's smile looked more like another wince, with his pinched lips and bloodshot eyes. "Good decision."

He took his phone off the hook, then reached for the facecloth in the steaming bowl. After wringing it out thoroughly, he set it on his face and tilted his chair back until he was lying almost flat.

"Now, do us a favour and close that door on your way out," he said.

Esther considered telling him about the cabin in the woods, but decided to leave it. She hadn't found the missing girl yet, and that was all the update he'd be interested in right now.

"Lightweight," she chortled softly as she left, closing the door quietly behind her.

Back in her own office, she saw that neither Caroline nor Spencer was in. Usually only one of the three of them were detailed Saturdays, but even on weekdays the other two detective sergeants seemed to spend half their time in the canteen. It was amazing how many coffee breaks they could squeeze into a single shift.

She dropped the invitation onto the top of her in-tray – something to think about later – and then sat at her desk and turned on her computer. She'd run through her emails quickly before she headed back out to the search site. With any luck, CSI would have arrived by then.

Her computer was just coming to life when Calvin Brett sauntered into the office. He must have been covering the weekend too. That, or he was snooping about while most of the detective offices were empty. He seemed to find any excuse these days to pop into CID, each occasion an opportunity to see what she was up to or needle her about her promotion prospects. She wondered which it would be today.

"Well, Esther," he quipped, visage red and eyes glassy

from the late night, "how's your hunt for the hungover teen going? New career opportunities in the field of babysitting await, eh?"

Needling, then.

"How are you today, Calvin?" she replied neutrally, ignoring the barb and concentrating instead on her screenful of unopened emails. She was always amazed at the number of emails the police force generated in a single day, even in a small constabulary like hers. Perhaps if they went back to paper memos, people would suddenly realise how little of it was actually pertinent...

"I'm fine, Esther," Calvin replied. "Fresh as a daisy. Unlike the good inspector, *I* can handle a few pints." He sniggered.

Then his eyes fell on the invitation and the sneer slid from his face. Esther had to admit she took a little pleasure from watching his amusement turn to consternation as he plucked the card from atop her pile of files and read it.

"How did you get this?" he demanded, outrage warring with disbelief in his expression.

"Connections," she replied simply.

Brett stared at her, speechless. His gaze returned to the invitation, and when he finally looked at her again, he was glaring.

"You think you're so smart, don't you?" he snapped. His cheeks and forehead had turned a dark shade of purple. "Yanking someone's chain, are you? Who is it this time? One of the supers? Worked your way up the ladder, have you? Tugged enough of the old boys off to get a favour or two? Or maybe it's O'Halloran. Yeah, that's it. Someone did mention you'd turned dyke. Me? I don't buy it. Everyone knows you've shagged half the men in the station.

53

You're just trying to tick another minority box. That's it, isn't it? Tick another box to get your promotion." He leaned in close, voice almost a whisper – a nasty, rasping whisper. This close, she could smell last night's drink on his breath. "Well, sleeping with anyone with a pulse doesn't make you a member of a minority group, Esther, it just makes you a tramp. You want to know what I think? I think your little lesbo act is a fake, and I'm going to expose you. You're not fit to be an inspector. You're reckless and undisciplined, and you're far too much of a selfish maverick to be in charge of a CID division. I've worked too hard for too long to watch some gallivanting hussy pip me at the post. I'll expose your bullshit for what it is if I have to, however I have to."

He flung the invitation down on her desk and stalked off.

Esther sat there, mouth open, too shocked at the unexpected outburst to speak. She'd never seen Calvin Brett lose his cool like that before, and it threw her for six, but he was out the door and out of sight before she could conjure any sly retorts or angry rejoinders.

7

ESTHER WAS STILL mulling over Calvin Brett's diatribe two hours later. She was back at the derelict cabin in the Norwick Forest, doing her best to concentrate on a briefing from her head CSI, Carl Etebo, but it was difficult to focus with Brett's spittle-coated words encroaching on her thoughts. It stirred memories of DCI Small's remarks a few months back and had her wondering if everyone in the department thought of her that way. No. She wasn't going to let herself be derailed like that again. She was stronger than that.

Not for the first time, she wondered if she should have gone to paper on Small. The idea had made her feel even weaker back then: whinging and whining to the bosses about hurtful words. *Stick and stones...* But now here she was again, with another nasty, spiteful misogynist spitting bile at her. And even if she wasn't reaching for the vodka this time, the little prick was distracting her.

With an effort, she pushed thoughts of Brett and DCI

Small aside and forced herself to listen to Carl.

The CSI supervisor was a short man, an inch or so shorter than Esther. The son of Nigerian immigrants, he'd grown up in south London, and his accent was strong with the area's sharp inflections. Although he came off gruff and standoffish at first, it was easy to warm to him once you got to know him, and he had a lot of time for Esther. He stood now in his white forensic suit and overshoes; he had removed the mask and hood after he'd stepped clear of the cabin to meet her. Another CSI technician – an anonymous figure shrouded in white that Esther assumed was a woman, because she was even shorter than Carl – was organising bags of collected evidence, setting them out and photographing them with a chunky, big-lensed black camera.

"We've taken quite a few samples of the blood," Carl was saying. "It's relatively fresh, I reckon. A day or two, maybe. We've sifted all the rubbish in the corners of the room, but most of it looks pretty ancient. Junk food wrappers, beer cans and bottles. Used condoms." He grimaced and Esther made a face. "Although we did find the remains of these in the campfire ashes 'round back."

He lifted a sealed evidence bag that contained broken bits of melted plastic and scorched metal.

"Those look like pieces of a mobile phone," she observed.

"At least two mobile phones, actually," he replied.

"Either of them an iPhone?"

Carl frowned. "Hard to say. Lab should be able to tell us."

Esther took the bag from him and turned it over, studying the fragments through the clear plastic. She couldn't see any markings or serial numbers.

"Will we be able to get IMEI numbers off them in this state?" she asked.

"They're pretty much destroyed," Carl replied. "I can't see anything on any of the parts we've recovered. Again, maybe the lab guys will find something I've missed." He glanced around. "Not ideal conditions out here. That's why we've boxed up the candles. Took photos of everything in situ first, of course. We'll dust for prints at the lab."

He stayed quiet for a long moment, staring at the rundown old shack.

"What do you think happened here?" he asked. There was a touch of unease in his voice, a characteristic Esther would not normally associate with Carl Etebo.

She followed his gaze through the cabin door, to where his colleague squatted in her white forensic suit, sorting through the items laid out on the floor.

"Christ knows," Esther murmured. "Something fucked-up."

"You think that young girl was involved in it? The one who's missing?"

Esther shook her head to indicate she didn't know, but she was thinking about the signal from Mila's phone last night, and hoping that the fucked-up-something that involved candles and blood and weird symbols wasn't as bad as she feared it might be…

She turned when she spotted activity out of the corner of her eye. Two community search and rescue volunteers were running up the hill towards Sergeant Taylor, who stood just outside the cordon, having a conflab with a few of his search supervisors. From the harried expressions on the faces of the new arrivals, it was clear they'd found something.

Carl followed Esther as she trudged over to the gathering. The younger volunteer, in her late teens and hardly more than a girl herself, looked stricken. The older woman was doing the talking, breathless and animated as she gestured back down the hill in the direction they'd come.

"...left her just as we found her. Brendan offered to stay and make sure nobody else goes near her, and we both ran back as quickly as we could."

"What is it?" Esther asked without preamble.

Taylor's face was grim. "A body. Female."

"Mila?" Esther asked.

It was the woman who answered. The younger one just stood there, pale and silent. "I don't think so. Didn't look like her photo. This girl is older. Blonde hair."

"How far?" Taylor asked.

"About a mile, give or take."

"Show us," Esther commanded, and all five of them set out at a determined pace down the slope.

Even downhill, it was tough going in places, with random gullies and thick patches of undergrowth to push through. At their brisk clip, Esther soon began to sweat in all her layers.

After some time, they came to a mountain stream, babbling along on a bed of smooth stones. There were several fording points, so traversing it was easy enough. About twenty yards beyond the stream stood a man. Brendan, Esther assumed. He was in his sixties, tall and lean. He looked suited to his weatherproofs and boots; Esther suspected he would normally appear hale and hearty, but right now his face was almost as grey as his beard. He moved forward to meet them, darting glances over his shoulder as he came. Esther could make out a splash of colour between the trees, the flesh and blood tones incongruous among the drab browns and greys and greens of the forest.

"Sorry," Brendan said to Taylor, lifting the radio handset he held in one hand, "radio battery died. Did Beth and Jolene tell you?"

"A dead female," Taylor replied simply.

Brendan nodded. "I haven't touched her or gone near her. Could see she was… she's definitely dead," he said, swallowing, "and I thought, for evidence, it would be better just to stay back."

"You did the right thing," Esther told him, and he gave her a grateful look. She turned to Taylor. "Can you send out a message for more resources? We'll need a cordon around this clearing. Three officers minimum. And we'll need an FMO to attend."

Taylor nodded and turned aside to make the transmission on his radio.

Esther and Carl picked their way towards the body, both of them carefully scanning the ground as they went. There was little in the way of footwear impressions, the ground here as thick with pine needles as everywhere else.

Esther stopped a few yards from the victim and hunkered down to get a better look at her. She was, as Brendan had said, clearly dead. Completely naked, her pale flesh was punctured by multiple stab wounds and covered in the brown-red stains of dried blood. Glazed blue eyes, outlined in dark mascara, stared sightlessly up at the treetops. Esther could tell from her roots and eyebrows that she was naturally fair-haired. She was older than Mila too, maybe twenty or twenty-one.

"A frenzied attack," Esther murmured, only realising she'd spoken aloud when Carl, who was standing next to her, replied.

"And the animals don't seem to have had much of a go at her," he said, "so she's not been here too long either."

Even with the stab wounds and the bloodstains, Esther could make out a number of tattoos on the woman's thin limbs. One in particular caught her eye, although it was not the largest by any means. She pointed it out to Carl.

"Like in the cabin," he said, nodding.

It was, indeed, just like the symbol in the cabin. A pentagram, in plain blue ink, on the inside of the woman's left wrist. Unlike the other tattoos, which were elaborate and professional-looking, this one appeared simple and amateurish, even to Esther's untrained eye. The only thing the woman wore was a gauze bandage around her left palm. It was grubby and dark now, soaked in mud and blood.

"And this isn't the missing girl?" Carl asked.

Esther shook her head. "Definitely not Mila."

Standing, she looked around, but there was nothing else obvious nearby.

"So, who is she?" Esther muttered. "And what in God's name happened in that cabin?"

They turned at the sound of Taylor returning.

"I've sent Brendan and Jolene and Beth back up to the tent for a cup of tea and a sit-down," he said. "They'll be there for you to record statements from, but probably best they get half an hour or so to decompress."

Esther saw the three volunteers disappearing through the trees in the direction of the tent.

"Good idea," she said. "Can you radio up to see if we

can get a fingerprint scanner down here? If this woman's been through custody, we'll have her prints on record."

Taylor nodded and moved away to make another transmission.

"I'll get some more technicians out here," Carl offered, "and get a processing plan in place for when they arrive."

"Thanks, Carl."

Esther took out her mobile phone and dialled Jared. It rang four times before he picked up, his voice low and gravelly.

"Sorry to wake you, Inspector," she said sweetly, "but I need your help. My misper investigation has just turned into a murder inquiry. I need you to assemble an investigation team for me."

Jared cleared his throat noisily. She flinched at the sound. Jared didn't bother with niceties like phone etiquette with Esther.

"You found her?" he asked.

"Not her," she replied. "A woman. Don't know who yet, but we're working on that. Stabbed to death, probably within the last twenty-four hours. Pretty brutal. She's been left here in the woods, naked. And there's a cabin…" She trailed off.

"A cabin?"

Esther hesitated. "I'll brief you properly when I get back to the station. It's weird."

"Weird."

Esther grimaced. "Yeah. Weird. I'll explain later."

Jared sighed, but he clearly didn't have the energy to press the subject.

"Roger that, Sergeant," he replied tiredly. "I will let you know when I've got your inquiry team together."

"Thanks, Jared."

Esther thought she heard him let out a soft groan as he hung up, but her mind was already moving on from DI Wilcox and his hangover and back to the task at hand. She scanned the woods as she put her phone away, turning a circle to take in the trees all around. Although she couldn't see anyone else from here, she knew there were teams of police and volunteers stretched all across these woods, searching the forest systematically. If Mila was out here, they would find her. But right at that moment, with a glance at the blonde woman in the clearing, Esther was really hoping they didn't.

* * *

The walls of Naomi's room were covered in boy band posters. K-pop, for the most part. There was scarcely a square inch of the Disney Princess wallpaper still visible. At first glance, the placements looked haphazard, but Naomi had been meticulous about hanging them. She'd always been fastidious about the arrangement of her bedroom, from the fairy lights strung carefully along her shelves to the hanging plants that adorned her windowsills and desk. Naomi liked things tidy. She took great pleasure – solace almost – in rearranging her bedroom from time to time, in keeping it neat and orderly.

Right now, though, as she sat on the edge of her bed and stared at her phone, Naomi wouldn't have noticed if someone upended the entire laundry hamper or tossed the contents of her wastepaper basket across the floor. She was staring at Mila's profile picture. Mila had accounts on a couple of different social media platforms, but this one was her favourite. Not that it mattered. Her status was the same on all of them.

Not currently online.

Naomi had been checking them every ten or twenty minutes for the last two days, hoping for a message, or a sign that Mila was checking them too, wherever she was. But there was never any change. The words seemed sinister now, the lack of activity unnerving, and Naomi's fearfulness was made worse by seeing Mila's smiling face stare back at her from the screen.

She scrolled through the timeline of messages to the most bitter words she had sent, accusing Mila of being a stuck-up and shitty friend. Mila had not responded then, and as fears for her safety grew, Naomi had changed her tone, apologising, pleading with her friend to get in contact. The cops had seen all those messages, all of them unanswered. Mila hadn't actually responded to Naomi in weeks, but staring at that spiteful message – the one among dozens of caring ones – she felt ashamed.

It was only when a teardrop hit her wrist that Naomi realised she was crying. She set her phone down and pulled some tissues from the flower-carved box holder on her bedside table.

It wasn't just shame that had her trembling and crying. It was fear. Mila might have been drifting away for weeks, but something had changed in the days before she'd vanished. Her behaviour had been even odder than usual. And Naomi couldn't figure out what it was, no matter how often she would replay her interactions with Mila in her mind.

She blew her nose, took a fresh tissue, and wiped her eyes. It was no good. Whenever she thought about Mila, she started to come apart like this. She needed to do something, but she couldn't think what. Because whatever assurances the cops and other adults made to her, she could see the worry in their eyes. And that worry was infecting her, making everything so much worse.

Naomi didn't just miss her friend.

Naomi was frightened.

8

JARED STOOD AT the back of the room and tried to ignore the dull throb that seemed to fill his whole skull. He was getting too old for the late night boozing sessions, even if it was for a colleague's retirement. With a growing sense of despair, he realised that all he really wanted these days was a quiet night in with the telly for company.

At least Esther was on top of everything. He could always rely on her to run things whenever he was feeling under the weather.

He did his best to concentrate as she briefed the small team of detectives he'd assembled in the CID conference room. They numbered less than a dozen, but it was all he could do at short notice on a Saturday afternoon. Those recent budget cuts had the senior team jumping down everyone's throats at the slightest whiff of unnecessary overtime.

As he listened to Esther issue instructions, he thought about the promotion process, and the prospect of Calvin

Brett getting the DI spot instead of her. Esther was a far better detective than that snivelling brown-noser. Jared doubted Brett had done any work out in the field in years. He was a man more suited to conference halls and cosy offices. Samantha's old team would be miserable with him at the helm.

He wondered if Superintendent O'Halloran would sign off on making Esther official SIO for this murder investigation. Being on record as a Senior Investigating Officer in a murder case would put Esther ahead of Brett in the race for sure. She'd been acting as SIO in all but name for years, but getting a proper credit for it would boost her prospects massively. Jared was becoming a tad worried that she didn't really see how good this promotion would be for her, how it was exactly what she needed. Sure, a DI spot would expose her to more of the politics and bullshit of police management, but he was confident she could handle it. She'd be a great DI.

He forgot his headache and queasy stomach as he mulled the idea over, and decided he would speak to the superintendent about it first chance he got.

Esther was summing up now, dishing out tasks to those assembled. Nine detectives might not be many to start a murder inquiry with, but this team was the best in the district.

"Craig, you're on Mila," Esther said. "Pull together everything you can for me, back to her time in Lithuania, family history there, everything you can dig up."

Craig Browne nodded.

"Oliver," Esther went on, "same for our dead girl. We've identified her as one Katie Wilde from her fingerprints, but we don't have much on her. Juvenile cautions for shoplifting, criminal damage. Petty stuff. This girl is a product of our wonderful care system, but she's just turned twenty and we've had no known associates updated to her file since she was seventeen. Go through her history, speak to her old social workers, focus especially on anything you can find that might link her to Mila, or Mila's school. We need to find out if these girls knew each other, and if so, where and when they got in contact. Wilde might have only turned twenty, but if she's been hanging around with teenagers, I want to know about it. We have to identify anyone else at risk.

"Derek, can you get on to the Norwick National Park authorities and see what they can tell us about that cabin, and about that area in general? Find out if they have any CCTV we might have missed – illegal fly-tipping traps or that sort of thing. I'll need you to take charge of a wider CCTV trawl too. Anything up that mountain road, from traffic cameras to locally owned ones. Whatever you can find. Hopefully we'll narrow down the time of death at the postmortem tomorrow, but anything over the last seventy-two hours is crucial."

"Will do, Skipper," Derek Grant replied, jotting the instructions into his notebook.

There was no second-guessing. No sighs or yawns. Glancing about the room, Jared knew it was nothing to do with his presence. It was all Esther. The team liked her. She had real leadership qualities, the type you can't write up in a competency self-evaluation; hers was the ability to connect with people, to motivate them with her sense of purpose. It was a natural charisma, not the book- and conference-learned crap that Calvin Brett and most of the others relied upon. Brett could never command a room like

Esther.

"Okay, folks," she concluded, after detailing a few more jobs, including a door-to-door of the relevant neighbourhoods and a canvas of Pastor Rose's churchgoers. "I know the afternoon is wearing on, but we're going to be on late tonight, and it's overtime for everyone tomorrow." No groans or protests. Some people nodded. "I'll buy us buns." A few smiles. "Let's get to work. We have a teenager to find and a killer to catch."

Chairs were pushed back and conversation rose, everyone heading off to set about their respective tasks. As the room emptied, Esther gathered up her papers. Jared approached her.

"Good briefing," he told her.

"Sorry," she replied, "I didn't mean to step on your toes."

Jared chortled. "Are you kidding me? I have the hangover from hell right now. You do most of the work anyway. No reason you shouldn't run the meetings and briefings too. In fact, I've been thinking it's time you got some official recognition for all the work you do, maybe getting you credited as SIO on this thing."

Esther stopped and looked at him. "Senior Investigators are usually DCIs, or detective inspectors at the very least. I've never heard of a sergeant being an SIO."

Jared shrugged. "First time for everything. Besides, it should be about ability, not rank." He grimaced. "The two don't often correlate, in my experience."

Esther frowned. "But the policy—"

"Screw the policy. I'll speak to O'Halloran. If anyone can make it happen, she can."

Esther raised an inquisitive eyebrow. "Is this anything

to do with that DI promotion?"

"Are you saying you don't want it?" he asked.

Esther shook her head, her expression darkening as she finished gathering up her things.

"No," she replied vehemently as she headed for the doors. "I've decided that there is no fucking way I'm going to let Calvin fucking Brett get that DI job."

She shoved the doors a little too forcefully, and Jared had to hurry to keep up as she marched down the corridor towards their offices. There was a renewed determination about her all of a sudden. Maybe it had taken a murdered woman and a missing teenager to make her see sense; the idea of that young girl relying on Calvin Brett... Jared shook his head at the thought. Whatever it was, something had lit a fire in her, and Jared was glad of it.

9

IT WAS CALLED a pentacle. Esther had spent the last couple of hours scouring Wikipedia and a variety of other websites, researching the symbol daubed on the wall of the derelict cabin and tattooed on the inside of Katie Wilde's wrist. The buzz of activity in the open-plan office next door had faded to a distant drone long ago. Even the rapid clacking of Caroline Mulhern's ten-thousand-words-a-minute typing had ceased to be a distraction as Esther clicked from one page to the next, staring at five-pointed stars – right way up or upside down, inside circles and out of circles, with or without other odd symbols punctuating their spaces.

She'd learned that a pentagram with a circle around it was referred to as a pentacle, and that it was a symbol often used by a wide variety of groups and traditions, from British Wiccans to Mormons to LaVeyan Satanists. Esther was fairly certain that what she'd seen in the Norwick Forest that morning had nothing to do with Mormonism. So, was Katie Wilde into Wiccan witchcraft? Or had she and whoever she'd been with been involved in some kind of Satanic ritual?

There were hundreds of articles about occult symbols and magic, covering everything from Satanism to medieval witchcraft. She read about modern events and historical ones, from the Salem witch trials in the seventeenth century to the Satanic panic of the 1990s, when thousands of debunked or exaggerated reports of Satanic ritual abuse spread across the US and then the rest of the world.

But there were too many branches of research to chase up in one day. Esther was being pulled in so many different directions in the infinite realm of the world wide web that she was starting to get a headache. Candles and pentacles in a disused cabin way out in the woods... whatever it was, it was fucking weird.

She was ready to give up for the evening when she stumbled across a website promoting a local store, just off Marigate Street, offering services that included tarot card readings and reiki. It stocked all sorts of products – incense and herbs, healing stones and crystals – but it was the images of various pentacles, carved from metal and wood, that caught Esther's eye. The shop was run by a woman called Thelma Faye, a self-proclaimed expert in spiritualism, witchery and healing. There was a photo of the shopfront, a rather pokey, narrow little spot, its window full of books and candles and jewellery. Under the heading *Opening Times* was a message in bold red writing:

Closed for refurbishment. Online shopping still available. Please use the contact page for any other services and I will get back to you. Apologies for the inconvenience.

Esther clicked on the contact page. It was a standard form with spaces for a name, an email address and a short message. There was also a landline telephone number, but it just rang out with no voicemail facility when she tried it.

Taking a punt, Esther typed her name and police email address into the form, along with a few lines for the attention of Thelma Faye, explaining who she was and that she'd be interested in speaking to her about her knowledge of local witchcraft for a case she was working on. She clicked 'submit'.

Getting some insider information and understanding a few of the local personalities involved might be useful, and Faye seemed as good a place to start as any. Esther wondered if Belfield had a Church of Satan, or a Temple of Satan, or whatever they were called. That might be a stretch. She decided not to go hunting right now. Her eyes were stinging from staring at her computer screen for so long. Besides, one weirdo at a time would be quite enough. She'd wait to find out what insights, if any, Thelma Faye could provide and take it from there.

She was so lost in thought that when the phone on her desk rang, she nearly jumped out of her skin. She glanced across at Caroline to see if the woman had noticed, only to find she was alone. The sergeants' office was empty. She had been so absorbed in reading about witchcraft and Satanism that she hadn't even registered Caroline knocking off her desk lamp and leaving. She shook her head and picked up her ringing phone.

"Esther, it's Carl. We've processed both scenes as far as we can, but the light's fading. We could do with another couple of hours in the morning."

"We'll be holding both scenes until after the postmortem anyway," she told him.

Two crime scenes, even out in the Norwick Forest, were going to attract attention. It was for that reason that Esther had called out to the Roses again, to let them know what she'd discovered. Or some of it, at any rate. She had left out the part about the cabin and the symbols. There was no use in alarming them unduly, and until the investigation unfolded a little further, it would be prudent to keep some details back. Still, her insistence that the discovery of a young woman's body – in an area to which Mila's phone had been traced – didn't necessarily mean the worst did ring a bit hollow, even to her ears, and the Roses had been understandably distressed by the news. The fact that they didn't know anyone by the name of Katie Wilde, or recognise her face from old mugshots, only went so far in assuaging their concerns. Pastor Rose had seemed the lesser fazed of the two. He'd announced solemnly that he would lead a prayer service for the young woman at the church tomorrow. Vera hadn't said anything at all, standing quietly by his side with a worried frown throughout. Esther had wanted very much to get Vera by herself for a few minutes then; she wanted to know more about the friction between Mila and Pastor Rose.

"You find anything else significant?" she asked Carl.

"Footprints," he replied. "In the softer mud by the stream near the body. Two different sets. One shod, one not. Traces of blood, probably our victim's."

"The footprints… are either set male?"

"Hard to be certain. They're both about the same size, and our girl Wilde's feet weren't particularly small. I'm guessing a seven or eight, UK size."

"I'll take a look when the reports get uploaded," Esther replied. "Thanks for all your help today, Carl."

"There's one more thing. You wanted to know about any other tangible links between the crime scenes, apart from the pentagrams?"

"Apparently they're called pentacles."

"Whatever they're called, it doesn't seem to me like the blood at the cabin is a result of this stabbing down by the stream."

"No?"

"We haven't found any sign of significant blood trails leading away from either the body or the cabin, but there's plenty of blood soaked into the ground beneath our victim."

"So, she wasn't moved," Esther murmured. The FMO – the police doctor – had said much the same.

"Looks to me like she was stabbed right where we found her. With a bloody big knife."

That was something Esther had noticed too: the size of the stab wounds themselves. It *was* a big knife. Or something else.

"Okay, thanks for the update, Carl. I'll meet you back at the scene in the morning, after the postmortem."

"See you then," he replied, and hung up.

Esther set the phone down. The main detectives' office outside was half in darkness; there were still a few people working a late shift, but most of the desks were empty now. She checked her mobile phone and sighed when she realised the battery was dead. She'd meant to plug it in and forgotten, distracted by her journey down the rabbit hole of internet research.

All of a sudden she felt drained, as if the exhaustion had been lying in wait, finally pouncing now that she'd emerged from her digital dive. Last night's late finish and today's early start had taken it out of her. It was time to call it a day. Katie Wilde's postmortem was scheduled for the morning, despite it being a Sunday – there being some leverage when it came to violent homicides, even with the most pernickety pathologist in England – and she and Jared would have to be down there for ten a.m. They were still waiting on the superintendent's clearance regarding the assignation of SIO titles, but Esther realised she was keen to take on the mantle now that Jared had suggested it, even if it meant dealing with a grouchy Doctor Ventner all by herself.

After a quick call to the duty inspector to make sure that a crew had been assigned to Mila's case overnight and that they had Esther's number in case they needed to get in touch, she switched off her computer. Grabbing her coat and bag, she headed for the door, murmuring goodnight to the handful of detectives who were still at their desks as she left.

On the drive home, her mind wandered. She felt exhausted, but she wasn't sure how easily she would find sleep; her brain was still buzzing, flitting back and forth between the crime scene in the Norwick Hills and the webpages about witchcraft and Satanism. She needed to focus on gathering leads. She decided that, first thing Monday, she would have detectives canvas every tattoo parlour in Belfield; the pentacle on Katie Wilde's wrist may look like a DIY job, but her other tattoos weren't. Wilde had clearly been into her body art. Someone might know her, or where she hung out. Or if she'd been seen with a dark-haired, eastern European teenager recently...

She found a kerbside spot on the broad, tree-lined street where Triona lived. Where *she and* Triona lived, she corrected herself, and the thought made her smile. There were some days she hardly recognised herself, when Tee's presence in her life lifted her up to a floaty, blissful place she couldn't ever remember reaching before.

But then Calvin Brett's earlier remarks came back to her, and her smile slipped. Spiteful little prick. She would show him. She was going to beat him to that DI spot, just to see the expression on his face when she did it.

Schooling her features, she put DS Brett's remarks out of her mind and made her way up the terrace's porch steps.

"Sorry I'm late, Tee," she called out as she stepped inside, shouldering the door closed and hanging her coat and bag on the end of the banister. "We found a dead girl up in the woods – not the girl I'm looking for, another one – and then I got caught up with stuff at work and my phone died, so if you asked me to pick anything up for dinner, I haven't got it, but I figured maybe takeaway tonight anyway? I'm pretty beat, hiking up and down that mountainside all day, but that's what a dead body on shift gets y—"

The words died on her lips as she stepped into the kitchen. Triona was half-standing – too late to intercept her – with an apologetic look on her face. Esther recognised the older couple sitting at the table from the photographs around the house.

Triona's parents. She'd completely forgotten!

Triona's mother sat straight-backed and rigid. Her auburn hair was scraped back in a tight bun and her makeup was understated. Her coat was unbuttoned – revealing a gold necklace with a small crucifix that hung conspicuously out over her woollen sweater – but she was still wearing her coat, as though she hadn't yet felt comfortable enough to remove it. There was no missing the distaste in her sharp appraisal as she assessed Esther coldly, with eyes that seemed to weigh and measure her to the pound and inch.

Triona's dad, on the other hand, was smiling amiably. He was a portly fellow with thinning grey hair and broad, ruddy features. His cheap anorak had been cast off and slung on the back of the chair behind him.

"Esther, this is my ma and da, Áine and Cormac," Triona said. "Ma, Da, this is Esther."

"Hello," said Esther with a nervous smile.

"So, you're Catríona's new... housemate," Áine said.

Triona opened her mouth to speak, but it seemed her mother – without so much as glancing at her – sensed the coming rebuke and pressed on, softly and quietly, eyes fixed on Esther.

"I'm sorry, dear," she continued, "Catríona does go through so many housemates, it can be hard to keep track."

Esther stood, unable to think of anything to say. She glanced at Triona again. Her girlfriend's cheeks were flushed and her face was a storm, but her father cut in before she could respond, his tone suggesting that he was well used to interrupting these moments of conflict. It was clear that he'd mastered the trick of obliviousness too, ignoring the daggers his daughter was staring at his wife.

"My goodness, Esther, it's very nice to meet you at last," he said in a broad Irish brogue. "Triona has told us so much about you! A police detective, are you? That must be very interesting altogether!" His smile widened as he stood to shake her hand.

Áine didn't rise. She just sat at the far end of the table, staring at Esther, her mouth screwed up like she was chewing on a lemon. Esther decided to focus on Cormac.

"It has its moments," she replied, smiling back as she sat

down at the kitchen table across from him. "How was your flight?"

"Not bad, not bad," he said. "Bit of a queue at Dublin airport, but things are so much quicker when you only bring a bit of carry-on luggage, don't you find? Been a while since Áine and I were last on an aeroplane, isn't it, love?"

Áine murmured something noncommittal, but Cormac went on regardless.

"Been a while, alright, I'd say. Seven or eight years, maybe. Since we flew to Lanzarote that time. You remember, love? We brought the Irish weather with us – rained for the first three days! Luckily, we got a bit of sunshine before the week was out. Lovely and hot. You need a bit of sunshine now and again, don't you find? Don't get much sunshine in County Roscommon, do we, Áine? No, not much sunshine at all. Sometimes I think Ireland has her own blanket of cloud. Although it might just be out west, alright, because sure enough we have a few friends in Dublin, and they'd be telling us that the sun is splitting the rocks out where they are, and us looking up at grey skies at the same time, you know?"

Esther smiled and nodded. She was quickly warming to Triona's father, and not just because he was a nice alternative to the mother; he had a natural conviviality about him that made him instantly likeable.

She glanced at Triona. Esther couldn't remember ever seeing her girlfriend look quite so tense. She was watching Esther anxiously now; Esther gave her a reassuring smile.

Triona appeared to reach a decision then. With another quick glance at her mother, she muttered, "I'll make us some tea."

"That'd be lovely, Triona, love," Cormac replied, but his

attention was back on Esther. "So, Esther, are you investigating a body, is that what you said? A murder, is it?"

Esther gave him an apologetic smile. "I can't really talk about it, but yes, I'm investigating a suspicious death. What do you do yourself, Cormac, if you don't mind me asking?"

"I'm retired now," he replied, "but I was a contracts manager at Roscommon County Council, for my sins. Nothing as exciting as policing, I'm afraid. Although we did have quite a bit of dealings with the guards – that's what the police are called in Ireland, the guards. Well, *An Garda Síochána*, is their proper title in Irish, but everyone just calls them the guards. Some of them were right clowns, though. We had this one fella back in the day…"

And off he went again, chatting about the local cops in Roscommon town and all the antics they used to get up to. Esther found that Cormac was a man who was easy to relax around. By the time Triona set four mugs and a pot of tea on the table, Cormac had covered topics ranging from the Irish climate to some quarrel between the UK and the EU over fishing rights, and on to a book he'd read about the British psyche and the English civil war, and how stubbornness seemed to be a trait the people of both islands shared. Esther's head was spinning, trying to keep up with it all, but she found she was grinning and happily answering all of Cormac's questions about Belfield whenever they touched on the subject. Triona's mother hardly said a word, but Cormac talked enough for the both of them, his ready smiles and chatty nature countering the chill that Áine brought to the room.

"And, of course, you know our Triona served out in the Middle East with *Médecins Sans Frontières* for a couple of years when she was younger?" Cormac said. He had moved on to the topic of conflicts around the globe.

"I did not know that, actually," Esther said, turning proud eyes on Triona.

Triona blushed and shrugged. "It wasn't *entirely* unselfish," she said quietly. "I wanted some real experience. Get thrown in the deep end kind of thing. See the world."

"Still, love," Cormac said, "you worked in war zones. Your mother and I were beside ourselves, but we were very proud too. And your sister, of course, was always asking about you." He turned to Esther. "Sadie was only twelve when Triona flew out to the Lebanon. But she knew enough to be worried about her sister."

"You've heard that Sadie is engaged now, have you, Catríona?" They were the first words Triona's mother had spoken in quite some time. She was eyeing her daughter shrewdly over her mug of tea as she took a sip, searching for a reaction to the comment.

Triona grew tense again, her jaw clenched.

"Yes, Ma," she replied, "I know. We *do* talk."

Esther knew that Triona thought her mother was constantly comparing her to her younger sister, and constantly finding her wanting. Esther had spoken to Sadie once or twice on video chats – just quick hellos and pleasantries on Esther's part, nothing more as yet – but she knew Triona got on well with her sister in spite of Áine; Sadie and Triona kept promising to visit one another sometime, but it just never seemed to happen. A wedding date would take care of that, no doubt.

"Wonderful young man from Sligo," Áine added. "His father runs a very successful car dealership up there."

"Yes, Ma," Triona replied. She sounded like a sullen teenager. Esther was reminded of Naomi Hawthorne all of a sudden. "I *have* spoken to Ronan on the phone too."

"Yes," Áine said, and sniffed. "Well."

She seemed to think that was statement enough.

"What about some grub, eh?" said Cormac, in that way he had of trying to dispel the tension. "I don't know about anyone else, but I'm famished."

In the end, they ordered a delivery from an Indian restaurant a few blocks over. Cormac chatted the whole evening, asking Esther about her police work and Triona about her work at the hospital. Áine didn't say very much, and when she did speak her voice was a soft murmur, usually a direct response to something Cormac said. He appeared to be trying to bring her into the conversation, and not really getting anywhere with his efforts. Even after she'd divested herself of her coat and sat down to eat – small mouse-like nibbles; Triona's mum seemed all skin and bone, like she ate food under sufferance – she was withdrawn.

Esther steeled herself and, when the opportunity arose, she suggested quietly to Triona that if she wanted to get a bottle of wine or some beers for her and her parents, she would be okay with it; Triona had been so supportive when she learned about Esther's battle with alcohol that she had pretty much given up drinking herself – there was no alcohol in the house. But Triona shook her head.

"Da doesn't drink much apart from the odd glass of wine," she replied, "and my ma doesn't touch the stuff. We'll be fine without."

Esther was quietly grateful. Despite Cormac's chatty nature, Áine's presence was making her tense, like her every word was being judged. The iciness seemed to be rolling off the older woman in waves.

After the meal, Áine insisted on helping Triona with the

clearing up. It was the most animated Esther had seen her all evening. Esther and Cormac moved to the living room, where he began expounding on the benefits of national parks and nature reserves. Somehow, he ended up talking more about American ones; he confessed he'd never been to the States but had recently watched a lot of interesting documentaries on Yosemite and Yellowstone on the National Geographic Channel.

They all retired early, Triona's parents tired from their journey and Esther needing an early start. She was really feeling the last two days' lack of sleep catching up on her.

"Christ, Esther, I'm sorry," Triona murmured. Finally alone in the room, they slipped under the bed covers and snuggled up next to each other.

"That's okay, Tee," Esther replied. "It was me who forgot. With everything happening at work… it just completely fell out of my head." She paused. "You think it went okay?"

Triona pulled away to smile at her. "Yeah. You were great with my da."

Esther chuckled. "Your dad's easy to get on with. He does most of the talking."

"That's my da."

"But I don't think your mum likes me very much."

Triona sighed. "Don't worry about her. My da likes you. That's the main thing. My ma… my ma is a lost cause anyway."

Her words were traced with sadness. Esther pulled her close, kissed her head, buried her nose in her hair and breathed in the smell of her. Exhaustion was already dragging her down, though, and within minutes she was asleep.

10

ESTHER WRINKLED HER nose, wondering what combination of chemicals it was that made mortuaries smell so acrid. The place was spotless – cupboards and surfaces pristine, steel gleaming – but visits to this place were always accompanied by a sharp assault on the nostrils, undercoated by the scent of death. In spite of all the chemicals, it was the undertone that stayed with you for the rest of the day.

She realised her mind was drifting as Doctor Ventner droned on, the pathologist's shiny bald head gleaming like the stainless-steel table on which his subject lay. Despite his monotonous, unemotional expounding, he had imparted some useful findings already. For example, the fact that all the stab wounds were caused by the same blade. And the fact that the attacker appeared to be left-handed and relatively short, judging by the entry points and angles of the wounds. It might not sound like ground-breaking stuff, but these were exactly the kind of facts that helped build a profile.

"It was a wide blade," Ventner was saying, returning to the subject of the murder weapon. "Or, rather, it was tapered. Many of the injuries are clean lacerations – in that the blade went in and out quickly – and we clearly have a wide opening and a narrow point."

"Could it have been something other than a knife?" Jared asked.

Esther glanced at him. He was looking much fresher today. He'd told Esther on the way to the postmortem that Superintendent O'Halloran was keen on the idea of her taking the SIO role officially, but it was a decision that needed signing off right at the top. O'Halloran was going to put the plan to the District Commander to get his approval, but the likelihood was that Esther would have to settle for joint-SIO with Jared, in order to comply with policy and enable authorisations only someone at inspector rank could provide. That was why he'd tagged along to the postmortem this morning. Not that Esther minded. She liked having Jared around.

Ventner considered the DI's question with pursed lips, then shrugged. "It was a blade. It was sharp, probably metal, but beyond that I will leave the theories and surmising to you, Inspector. That's your job."

The man bent his bald head over the cadaver again. Jared gave Esther a bemused grimace, and she smiled. The pathologist's bedside manner was something of a legend among the Belfield police.

"When we removed the gauze bandage from her left hand," the pathologist went on, "we found a shallow incision, four centimetres in length, on her left palm. A poultice had been applied to the wound. Both wound and poultice were fresh and would have occurred shortly before death.

"The deceased also had sexual intercourse before she died," he added, moving down her body.

"She was raped?" Esther asked.

Ventner sighed. It was the kind of sigh Esther associated with disappointed teachers at school. He regarded her frankly over the rims of his glasses. "The stab wounds indicate a struggle. Examination of her vagina indicates sexual activity."

"Any bruising or contusions around her genitals or buttocks?" Esther pressed. "Was a condom used?"

Ventner hesitated, then shook his head, a small, birdlike twitch. "No bruising. No signs of injury to her vagina. And we have collected semen samples, so it is unlikely that a condom was used." He was already moving to the lower legs, pointing out scratches and cuts all over her calves and feet. "These are signs of a prolonged journey through rough terrain with no protection. Some of these wounds would have been painful to the average person under normal conditions, especially some of these deeper injuries to the soles of her feet."

"Another link to the cabin," Esther remarked. She'd already decided it was more likely than not that whatever had gone on in that cabin had involved Katie Wilde and at least one other person. Quite possibly her killer, or killers. A desperate flight through the woods tied in with that theory – a flight fuelled by such fear that the victim had ploughed on in spite of some very nasty cuts to her feet.

"What about the time of death?" she asked. "Have you managed to narrow it down at all?"

Ventner nodded. "Late Friday night or the early hours of Saturday morning."

Esther turned to Jared. "I'll need you to get the super to authorise road checkpoints. Two crews, one either side of the mountain should do it – there's only one main route over the Norwick Hills in that area. We'll do one today and another two next Friday night and Saturday morning. See if we can't get hold of some regular travellers around that time who might have seen anything unusual."

Jared nodded. "You're in charge, as far as I'm concerned. Whatever you need."

They were interrupted by the sound of Ventner snapping off his nitrile gloves. "You'll have to wait for the toxicology reports for the full picture, as always," he announced, ambling over to the clinical waste bin to dispose of the gloves, then moving over to the sink to wash his hands. "Drugs in her system, DNA profile from the semen samples. I'll email the report to CSI. Unless there's anything else?"

Clearly Ventner wasn't thrilled about having his Sunday morning disrupted by inconvenient murder victims. He turned, fists on hips, and regarded them levelly.

"Thank you, Doctor Ventner," Esther replied, giving him her most genial smile. It was an effort with this man. "You've been very helpful."

Ventner grunted in response, and Esther's smile became one of amusement as the pathologist turned away to help his assistant begin tidying up. It seemed he was keen to be away indeed; Esther had never seen him help any of the mortuary assistants before.

"I'll send an email to the lab," Jared told Esther as they left, "and get those samples analysed pronto. Our girl is on the system, which means her assailant might be too, if he's a partner or an ex."

"You think it's a domestic?" Esther asked.

"Don't you?"

Esther shook her head. "I don't know. Stats say it's the most likely scenario, but all that voodoo ritual stuff... I think there were more than two people in the woods the night Katie Wilde was killed. And I have a hunch that Mila Rose was one of them."

They made their way from the mortuary to the car. The sun was shining, and it was warm down here, off the mountainside.

"When I spoke with the superintendent earlier," Jared said, "she mentioned that event tonight. Says she got you a peachy seat. You're at a table up the front, a couple of chief superintendents and an honourable member of parliament for company."

Esther groaned. "Fuck, I forgot about that. Surely, she doesn't expect me to go right in the middle of a murder investigation?"

Jared turned and gave her a flat look over the roof of the car. "I'll manage the team while you're there. The super's done you a solid getting you that ticket. Give it a chance."

Esther sighed. "I know," she replied. "I'll go. I'm shit at those kinds of things, but I'll try."

"Just think about Calvin at home stewing while you're at it," Jared said with a smirk. "Should get you through the evening."

That did bring a smile to Esther's lips.

11

PASTOR ROSE WAS at his church. He went there more
often, Vera said, and stayed longer, praying for Mila with the
congregation and organising leaflet drops with those who
volunteered. He told Vera the flock – that's the word Vera
used, 'flock' – were like a wider family, whose love and
support would sustain both of them through these dark
days. She accompanied him whenever she could, but she
wasn't as strong as Tim. He was comfortable with all the
attention; Vera couldn't bear it.

She insisted on making tea again when Esther and Jared
called by on their way from the mortuary to the police
station. Esther wasn't sure if it was Jared's amiable presence
or Pastor Rose's absence that made the woman seem more
relaxed this time round. The DI munched happily on the
biscuits Vera provided along with the tea; Esther knew he
had a habit of skipping breakfast in advance of autopsies.

She herself took polite sips of her tea, letting Jared and
Vera chat for a few minutes. Only when the conversation

began to subside did she take the opportunity to start working through the stock of questions she'd prepared. She delivered them neutrally and without taking notes. They were just some clarifications, she told Vera. Details that might help the investigators, details like: did Mila have a particular way she wore her hair? Did she have a favourite type of high-street food, or a favourite shop? Was her uniform new and undamaged, or was there anything that might set it apart, like small stains, rips or frays? Did she walk with her back straight and head up, or did she slouch?

Was she left-handed or right-handed?

"Mila is right-handed," Vera replied. "Tim's the leftie."

Jared set his cup down. He didn't reach for any more biscuits.

If Vera detected the subtle change in atmosphere, she gave no indication. She'd been answering Esther's questions with increasing confidence, like someone who realised an exam they'd been dreading was actually well within their ability.

"There was something else," she said now. "Something I noticed this morning. I was going to phone, but it's such a small thing. I wasn't sure…"

"Anything," Esther said. "Anything you can tell us might be of help, no matter how small."

"Mila had a keyring," she said. "A flat, polished stone with a horse and knight on it. It had the word 'Lietuva' etched underneath. I think it was very special to her, something she'd taken from Lithuania. The thing is, she never kept it with her keys, or on her bag, or took it anywhere. Always left it in her room, as though she was afraid she might lose it. I would see it sitting on her dresser or on a shelf when I was dusting. But… I can't find it now.

I think she might have it with her."

Esther finally took out her notebook and jotted down the description of the keyring.

"What colour was the stone?" she asked.

"A pale sort of greyish. Smooth, with the horse galloping and the knight waving his sword over his head, and the word etched in tidy and precise letters. I asked Naomi whether she's seen it recently, or whether Mila mentioned it, but Naomi didn't know anything about it."

Esther concluded her jotting. Now, to the other reason for her visit...

"I got the impression that there might have been quite a bit of friction between Mila and your husband in the weeks leading up to her disappearance," Esther said, watching the other woman closely. "I understand it can be embarrassing, but I need to know everything if we're to have the best chance of getting Mila back. How bad was the tension between her and your husband? What's been happening between them?"

Vera remained very still for a moment. When her answer came, her words were slow and heavy, like they were being dragged out. Her eyes stayed on the tabletop as she spoke.

"Timothy is more used to people coming to him," she replied, "looking for help and answers. I imagine he felt it was some kind of personal failure not to have Mila engaged and active in the church. But you can't force someone to worship." She said that adamantly, as if she had grown accustomed to saying it recently.

"So, he was just pushing her too hard to get involved in the church?" Jared asked. "There was no other... acrimony between them?"

Vera shook her head. "No. That was quite enough as it was."

"You said you didn't think that's why she'd run away, but can you be sure?" Esther asked.

Vera gave a small, uncertain shrug. "I don't know. It seems I don't know half as much about Mila as I should."

Esther studied her for a moment. She didn't seem to be holding anything back, and Vera Rose didn't strike Esther as the kind of woman who would be good at lying.

At length, when it was clear Vera had said all she was going to say about the subject, Esther moved on. She asked a few more questions about Mila's habits and missing clothes, and at length they finished their teas and said their goodbyes, with the usual promise to keep in touch.

When they got back to the car, doors closed and out of earshot, Jared turned to Esther.

"Is Pastor Rose a tall man?" he asked.

Esther shook her head. "He is not."

"Left-handed? Small in stature?"

Esther nodded. "Noted, Inspector, but when I spoke to both of them yesterday, he didn't seem to recognise Wilde's name or picture."

"You sure he wasn't acting?"

Esther sighed. "How can I be sure of that?"

"Preachers can be good actors."

"Preachers, maybe. But I don't think Vera is."

Jared turned to glance at the Roses' house as he started the car.

"No," he conceded. "You're probably right there."

"I get the sense that if Vera Rose suspected anything, she'd have said. Or would have done a miserable job of trying to hide it."

Jared grunted in response to that, then pulled away from the kerb. All the way back to the station, Esther found herself reliving her conversation with the Roses the day before – their reactions to the news about Katie Wilde, to the revelation of her name, her photo. Memories became distorted with every recollection; Esther knew this, but she was fairly confident that if there *had* been anything in the pastor's expression that warranted suspicion, she'd have noticed it at the time.

12

THE MAIN YARD at Belfield Central Police Station was full, so Jared dropped Esther off and went to find a spot around back. Feeling lazy, and with a bagful of buns for the team under one arm, Esther headed for the lifts.

While she stood listening to the trundle of the elevator car, she turned to find Calvin Brett sauntering towards her. In again, on a Sunday. How very diligent of him. There could hardly be too much to do in Financial Crime on a Sunday.

She was about to give him a piece of her mind for what he'd said to her the other day when she noticed his expression. What the fuck was the little weasel smirking about? He looked like the cat who'd got the cream.

"There's a witch here to see you," he chirped before she could say anything.

"A *what?*" she snapped, slightly thrown by the unexpected announcement.

He gave a throaty chortle. "A witch, Esther! Woman

says she's a *witch*. Here to see *you*. She says you left a message for her, looking to speak to her about a case."

Suddenly Esther remembered the website, the contact form and the message she'd left for that woman, Thelma Faye.

Brett guffawed. He was clearly relishing this. "Bit desperate, don't you think?" he remarked. "Surely the investigation isn't going so badly you need assistance from the spirit world? What's this witch going to do for you? Contact the dead girl's ghost and ask who killed her?" He laughed outright. "Oh, this'll go down well, I tell you. Definitely the stuff of a detective inspector, this... Calling in witches and fortune tellers to solve your cases for you."

The elevator pinged and the doors slid open. Brett stepped into the empty car and turned to face her as he pressed the button for an upper floor.

"Well?" he said. "She's waiting in the enquiry office for you. You'd better go see her quick, in case your tarot session is on the meter!" The elevator began to close. "I hope you're not planning to claim it on your expenses!" he called out, just as the doors shut.

Bastard! Esther thought, not sure whether she was angrier at his gleeful ribbing or her foolishness for having sent that message on the spur of the moment. Fuming, she stalked off towards the enquiry office.

The normal receptionist – a woman called Pat who'd worked at Belfield Central for as long as Esther could remember – didn't do weekends; in her place sat a pale, watery-eyed young man with a shock of red hair and no shoulders to speak of. He looked at her nervously as she glanced past him at the trio of people in the waiting area on the other side of the heavy glass screens. Two men and a woman. One of the men, bearing an impressively dense pattern of tattoos across his neck and throat, had clearly just been released from custody, with a plastic bag full of his property clutched on his lap. The other was an older gentleman; he stood in front of the noticeboard, reading some of the various anti-crime leaflets pinned up there. The woman was in her middle years; she sat patiently a few seats down from the tattooed man. She was slightly plump, her hair tied in a fat braid that fell to her waist.

"Uh, are you, um, DS Penman?" the receptionist stammered. "I-I did put a message out over the Tannoy, but the other detective said you were out. He went to get in touch with you."

"Is that woman's name Thelma Faye?" Esther asked, leaving her bag of buns on a nearby countertop.

The receptionist nodded.

"The interview rooms all free?" she asked.

He nodded again.

Esther went out to the public section of the enquiry office to meet her visitor.

"Thelma Faye?" she asked as she approached and stuck out her hand in greeting.

The woman looked up and smiled. She stood to take Esther's hand.

"Thank you for coming in to see me," Esther said as they shook. "I could have come out to you. It would have saved you the trouble."

"It's no problem, Detective."

"Let's speak in private." Esther motioned her towards one of the interview rooms.

Inside, they settled themselves on either side of the small table.

Thelma Faye wasn't what Esther expected in a witch. She wasn't sure exactly what she had expected; not old and warty with a long chin and a pointy nose, certainly, but not this either. Faye was pretty. Plump as she was, she wore the weight well, and it didn't detract from her natural beauty. She wasn't wearing any make-up but, had it not been for the abundance of silver streaking her brown plait, from a distance the woman might have passed for late twenties or early thirties. She wore a purple woollen shawl, and her skirts and blouse looked like flax. A plain wooden bangle adorned her left wrist, and a leather thong around her neck held a white stone etched with some kind of rune, suspended above an ample bosom. She looked like an ageing hippy. An ageing hippy who was suddenly studying Esther very closely.

"That man bothered you," she said abruptly.

Esther blinked. "I'm sorry?"

"The man who came and spoke with me a few minutes ago," Faye replied. "He has caused you a bit of bother."

In spite of herself, Esther was impressed. And a little disturbed. She frowned, opened her mouth, but found she couldn't think of anything to say that wouldn't make her sound like an idiot.

Faye smiled. "No, it's not magic," she said. "Many people think witchcraft is a lot of nonsense about spells and brewing potions. In fact, it's mostly about herb lore and general wellbeing. Connecting the spiritual with the physical. Knowing a bit of human psychology doesn't hurt either. I majored in psychology at Uni. I noticed a tension in the way you're carrying yourself, a tension you're trying to hide. And that man who spoke to me – the other detective – he made a show of politeness, but he didn't make any real effort to hide his disdain for my vocation. With those things in mind, I took an educated guess."

Esther had hoped she'd shaken off her annoyance at Brett.

"What about rituals and occult symbols?" she asked, keen to move on from the subject of Calvin Brett. "Do you know much about those kinds of things?"

Faye shrugged. "A bit. It's not what I practice. The Wiccan community isn't quite as organised as traditional religions. My interest lies mostly in the area of organic practices, spiritualism and meditation. Not so much in the study of magic and occult lore."

Esther pulled her notebook from her bag and drew a pentacle.

"What can you tell me about this symbol?" she asked, sliding it across the table.

"It's a pentacle," Faye replied straight away. "A pentagram bound by a circle, the five points representing the five classical elements." She pointed to where the tips of the pentacle touched the circle as she listed them off: "Air, Fire, Water, Earth and Aether."

"Aether?"

"Spirit," Faye explained. "The element that binds all things."

"Is it something that's used in... rituals?" Esther asked.

Faye sat back and regarded her for a moment before answering.

"Pentacles are used in some rites, yes," she replied, "along with other things."

"Other things such as...?"

"Chalices, athamés."

"Athamés?"

"Ceremonial blades."

Esther frowned, recalling Doctor Ventner's analysis that the blade used on Katie Wilde had been wide and tapered to a point. "And what do these athamés look like?"

"Any blade can serve as an athamé," Faye replied. "Contrary to popular belief, a knife doesn't need to be any particular colour or shape, or be inscribed with sigils or runes, to serve as an athamé."

Esther hesitated. "What do the rites usually entail?"

The woman shook her head, a wry smile on her lips. "I can't tell you everything, Detective. Unless you'd like to join my coven?" Esther's expression brought a chuckle from her. "Don't worry, they don't involve lascivious orgies or summoning demons, if that's what you think."

Esther paused, then decided to take a chance. Hell, she already had Calvin Brett torpedoing her reputation upstairs; she might as well get as much information from this meeting as she could. She pulled out her work phone and found the file with the photos from the cabin in the woods. She brought up a picture of the cabin's interior before Carl and his colleague had started working on it, a wide-angle image that contained the pentacle and candles on the floor, and the symbols on the back wall.

She showed it to Thelma Faye.

"Would one of your rituals look anything like this?" she asked.

It was Faye's turn to frown. She leaned in to examine the picture more closely. Her lips tightened.

"That's no Wiccan rite," she replied. "That's a Satanic ritual."

Esther set the phone on the table so that they could both look at it. "How can you tell?" she asked.

"A Wiccan rite involves a circle drawn on the floor, not a pentacle. And those symbols on the wall are not associated with Wicca. This is the eight-pointed star of chaos. This one, the infinity symbol topped with the two-barred cross? That's the symbol for brimstone. These ones here, all around them... may I?"

Esther nodded and Faye took her notebook and pen and – glancing from time to time at the photo, which she tapped now and again to keep the screen from going black – recreated the symbols one after another in a line on the page. When she was finished, they made a neat row.

$$\text{ל . וִי תָ ןָ}$$

"It's Hebrew," she said. "Badly drawn Hebrew, but it's meant to spell out the word 'Leviathan', or sea serpent. It has various connotations in different religions but is sometimes considered as a form taken by the devil in Bible stories."

"So, this is the work of a Satanic cult?" Esther asked, a touch of dread beginning to steal through her again.

Faye didn't seem so sure. "More likely some kids who've looked up a few things online."

Kids. Teenagers. Mila.

And one murdered woman.

"You'll see these marks as part of symbols used by Satanists," Faye told Esther. "And the inverted pentacle. Here—" She used a fresh page from the notebook to sketch out two pentacles. "See the difference?" she asked. "This pentacle, point facing upwards, is Wiccan. Associated with Nature. Mostly good stuff." She smiled and winked. "This second one, though, is an inverted pentacle. Point facing down." Faye had drawn an elementary rendition of a goat's head inside the inverted pentacle, with the horns contained within the upward-facing points, ears to either side, and a snout in the downward-facing one. Even poorly drawn as it was, it gave Esther the creeps. "Symbol of Baphomet," Faye said, following her gaze. "The Sabbatic Goat. Church of Satan."

"Satan worshippers?"

Faye shook her head, frowning again. "I'm not an expert on Satanism, Detective, but I do know most Satanists don't worship the devil, per se. They don't believe in a devil the way Christians do. As far as I understand it, their philosophies are based around the rejection of traditional Abrahamic faiths – Judaism, Christianity, Islam – and a belief in the fundamental chaos of the world, in following humankind's basic instincts of carnality and enlightenment. Most mainstream Satanic groups are just about individualism. Almost like a worship of the self, it seems to me, but I'm not a Satanist, so I'm probably not doing them justice. And of course, we're not talking about one big, cohesive organisation. I'm sure there are some Satanists who believe in… darker things."

"Would you know of any groups in Belfield, or the UK more widely, whose members might have a pentacle tattooed on their wrists?" Esther asked. "Here?" She pointed to the inside of her left wrist.

Faye gave her an apologetic headshake. "I'm not a big fan of tattoos, myself," she replied. "And I don't personally know anyone who has a pentacle tattoo. Not on any part of their bodies that I've seen, anyway."

Esther was quiet for a long moment, staring at the page with Faye's sketches.

"I'm sorry I can't be of more help," the other woman said at last, "but here"—she jotted a number on Esther's notepad in the space below the Baphomet symbol—"this is my mobile number, in case you come across anything else you think I may be able to help you with. Honestly, you might be as well off doing what these kids have done and hunt around on Wikipedia and Google for a bit."

"Thank you, Miss Faye," Esther said, as they both stood. "I appreciate your help."

"And if you need a potion to make that man's bits shrivel up, call by the shop," Faye added, adjusting the shawl on her shoulders. "I have all sorts of wonderful recipes."

Esther's face must have been a picture, because Faye laughed.

"I'm joking, Detective. I have no potions that shrivel men's bits. But I do have herbal remedies that help with stress and pain relief. Feel free to pop by. I'll give you a discount. Law enforcement discount. Just for you." She smiled warmly. "You have a good aura about you."

Esther couldn't tell whether that was a joke too, but the woman seemed serious as she said goodbye and left.

Esther looked down at the page with the two pentacles drawn side-by-side. The upright and the inverted. The Sabbatic Goat.

Sure, it might be kids, she thought. But kids could do a lot of damage.

Teenagers could commit murder too.

13

ANITA JESS STARED at the small pentacle tattoo on her wrist. It had hurt when Jason had done it, but not any longer, and the redness on her skin had long since faded. It was a bond. The symbol of her new family.

She flexed her left hand where the cut to her palm was only starting to heal. She'd replaced the bandage and rubbed more of her herbal salve on it, but it was still stiff and sore. It made her think of Katie, and she felt a pang of loss, but only for a moment; she reminded herself that what happened to Katie was simply what happened to a sister who betrayed a sister.

She'd never had one of those when she was a child. A sister. Never had a real family of her own. She'd envied the other children at school. None of the various fosterers she'd been placed with had ever felt like home, and some of them hadn't been good places for a child. Some of them had made her want to fly away as soon as she'd arrived. Some of them...

She closed her eyes and breathed slowly. She had to do that now and again, when too many thoughts entered her head too quickly. Or too many feelings filled her up.

What had she been thinking about?

Oh, yeah. The pentacle. The bond.

Katie. Sisterhood.

She opened her eyes.

Anita had learned long ago that the world didn't give people like her anything. What she wanted, she had to take.

Things like family.

Things like sisters.

Had Katie been her real sister? Not *real* real, obviously, but blood-bonded by magic. Anita couldn't be sure. She was losing track of the rituals. They were becoming a blurry mess of sensations in her head.

Fire and flesh.

Fear and love.

The sunlight was streaming through a gap in the bedroom curtains in such a beautiful way, swirling motes of dust giving the shaft of light substance. It looked as if she might actually be able to touch it, to feel it, if she reached out...

Something Jason was saying caught her attention. She blinked and let her hand drop. The sunshine was nothing more than a shaft of light again. Untouchable.

"What?" she asked, glancing over her shoulder at him.

"Katie," he muttered. He lay back against the headboard, wearing only a pair of jeans with the top buttons undone. He was rolling a joint in that dextrous way of his. He could roll them with one hand – he'd shown her once. His left wrist was bound in white bandage. Anita had wrapped that for him, swaddling his forearm in about ten yards of dressing. He'd been showing off, cutting his wrist instead of his palm. The idiot could have bled out. He'd just laughed it off, though. Said he'd been demonstrating his commitment.

"I told you," she said, shifting her position on the edge of the bed to turn and face him. "She took some of her stuff and left. Said she'd had enough. Wanted TV and shit again."

Jason frowned as he licked the edges of the paper and sealed it.

"Weird. She wasn't putting out those kinds of vibes on Friday."

Anita bristled. "What kinds of vibes was she putting out?"

He hesitated, half-glanced at her, then lifted a candle from the bedside table and lit the spliff. He inhaled deeply, holding it in as he passed her the joint. She took a more modest draw.

"How did she get out of the mountains?" he asked, his voice croaky from the smoke.

"She was talking about hitching a ride or something."

"Have you heard from her?"

She gave him a flat look as she passed back the spliff. Exhaled. "How? We burned our phones in the ritual. Severed our 'electronic leashes'. Remember?"

Jason didn't reply. He took another long pull on the joint as she turned away and glanced around the bedroom. It wasn't finished yet, but it was coming along. Transforming. While Jason fixated on burning modern technology, Anita focused on their home. On taking back her life. Banishing the evil, room by room. Controlling her destiny by confronting her past.

One with nature.

Mother Nature.

Mother. Sisters.

She shook her head. She was drifting again.

The little cottage had such potential. Her memories of it might be tarnished, but Anita was strong enough to look past those. The wife had been dead for too many years, which meant it needed a *lot* of work. But Anita was willing. She'd already started her organic vegetable patch in the back garden, in the perfect spot for sunlight, away from the edge of the woods. They were going to have to get rid of that horrible plastic patio set – ugly olive-green stuff – and replace it with something natural. She was sure Jason could drag some pieces out of the forest. Wood that had already given up its life force. Anita could picture it now: thick logs set around a fire. She smiled. It would all be perfect in the end. She was building her own family now, here in this beautiful refuge, far away from the city.

It was true, what the teachings said. No one should allow themselves to be subjugated by the patriarchal hierarchy. It was all an illusion – a fix, to keep people like her down.

You just needed the courage to take what you wanted.

It was there for the taking.

14

ESTHER WAS ALREADY starting to sweat through her knickers. As she meandered through the black-tie crowd, she was just glad she'd layered on the antiperspirant. Triona had lent her the dress, a slinky black number with thin straps on the shoulders and a skirt that stopped a risqué couple of inches above the knees. She'd told her it made her look sexy as hell, but Esther simply felt exposed. High heels and girly clothes weren't her thing. She was trying hard to avoid the bar – to avoid even *looking* at the bar – and not think about her sweaty ass crack.

And it wasn't just the bar. She was getting plenty of lingering stares too, some from men old enough to be her grandfather. God, this was awful. She was seriously considering doing a bunk. Maybe say hello to Superintendent O'Halloran if she could find her, grab her seat among the bigwigs for half an hour, and then take a fake phone call. Something urgent, but not too urgent.

Triona had offered to come with her for moral support

when she saw how nervous Esther was, but her folks had booked a table at a fancy restaurant and Esther could see they were looking forward to having their daughter to themselves. Even Áine seemed to have softened a tad over the last twenty-four hours. It was weird how tense and anxious Triona got around her mum. There were moments when Esther hardly recognised her; angry and silent one moment, and then apparently trying to win her mother over the next. And Áine might be warming, but, Christ, she was warming slowly – an ice queen if ever there was one. Esther thought about her own mum, reflected on the stormy relationship she'd had with Hannah, and wondered if all mother-daughter relationships were as fucked up. Probably not.

Tee's dad had insisted on cooking his specialty for all four of them tomorrow night, an O'Neill family recipe he claimed was the best Irish stew in the west. In truth, Esther wasn't sure she was looking forward to an evening with Triona's frosty mother any more than she'd been looking forward to this event, but at least Cormac would be on hand, ready to chatter any awkward silences into submission.

It was times like these that Esther craved a drink the most. Something to do, something to hold. Something to take the edge off. She longed for that satisfying sting in her throat, the heat in her belly. The promise things would become more bearable shortly…

She gave herself a shake and pushed aside thoughts of alcohol as she squeezed between two knots of cologne-drenched old men – men she was sure could have moved a half-step out of her way when they saw her coming, but clearly preferred to have her brush against them – and spotted her place among the opulently set round tables.

She scanned the place cards to either side. She was seated between the chief superintendent in charge of their constabulary's detective training centre and an assistant chief constable from Devon and Cornwall Police. Esther's own card, which simply read *D.S. Esther Penman, Belfield CID*, looked paltry and out of place by comparison. The table was situated directly in front of the stage where the various speakers would make speeches – hopefully short ones – between courses.

Esther was the first to arrive at her table. Almost immediately, a young man in a smart, waistcoated uniform materialized at her shoulder and asked if she would like a glass of red or white wine.

"Water's fine, thanks," she replied quickly, reaching for the jug of iced water.

The waiter intervened smoothly and poured it for her, and Esther took the opportunity to scan the room. She was the only one at her own table, but several others had started taking their seats elsewhere. Most of the crowd still stood, mingling and chatting; top police and high-rolling civil servants, peppered with a few vaguely familiar political faces. Everyone seemed to know someone else. Everyone except Esther. There was still no sign of Superintendent O'Halloran. Not that Esther was close with the super, not really, but in this context, she would definitely count as a friendly face. The evening hadn't yet properly begun, and Esther was already starting to feel way out of her depth.

Her heart sank further when she recognised Detective Chief Inspector Warren Porter standing near the bar. Porter had been her DCI last year. She'd challenged him over a case he'd closed as suicide, a suicide that had reeked of murder. Persevering against his orders, she had soon unravelled a major drug-smuggling operation. Porter had never forgiven her for it; it had cost him dearly, as far as his career went, and Porter was nothing if not a career man; he'd been languishing in some backroom records branch for six months now.

Before she had a chance to look away, he noticed her staring. His eyes narrowed fractionally for a moment, then he turned aside without acknowledging her.

Esther let out a shaky breath as two men arrived at her table, one of whom looked familiar. Both were in their late fifties or early sixties, deep in discussion about some new initiative to improve police recruitment within black and ethnic minority communities. Esther glanced at their place cards as they sat, and saw that the slightly younger-looking one was a chief superintendent from a neighbouring town, a man called Callow Euston, and the one who looked familiar was *Sir Payton Widgery, MP for Greater Norwick, Justice Select Committee*. The MP glanced at her a couple of times as the two of them conversed, his attention obviously drifting from the topic. At the first opportunity, he cut off the discussion and smiled broadly at her, displaying a set of perfect, shining white teeth. He made a show of squinting at the name on her place card.

"Ah! A frontline detective!" he declared, causing the chief superintendent to glance over. "Payton Widgery, pleased to meet you." He leaned across the table to shake her hand. "What field do you specialize in, DS Penman?" he asked, as he settled himself again, posture adjusted so that he was facing her now instead of Euston.

"Serious and organised crime, sir."

"Fascinating," Widgery replied, nodding at her. "I

recently chaired a committee hearing that discussed new initiatives designed to engage partner agencies and stakeholders to greater relieve the burden from detectives and specialized units. We talk a lot about working with partners in neighbourhood policing, but rarely discuss the opportunities for cross-departmental work – and indeed community input – into more serious criminal matters. I would submit that there's plenty of scope for community stakeholders to get involved with police at a strategic level when it comes to serious and organised crime. That's my humble opinion anyway." Another megawatt smile. "What do you think?"

What the fuck? That sounded like a whole pile of puffed-up political nonsense to Esther, but she could hardly say so straight out.

"I… I guess I'm old-fashioned, sir," she replied. "I just hope people cooperate with us on an individual basis. I don't know much about opportunities for strategic input. Just a lowly DS."

"Oh, don't put yourself down, Esther," Widgery said with another toothy grin. He was deploying the full charm offensive now. "I have no doubt you'll have Callow's job soon enough. He already spends every day on the golf course as it is!"

"Excuse me" Euston piped in, feigning offence with a small smile. "Only every other day, Payton. Only every other day."

They both chuckled as if it were a far wittier riposte than it actually was. Esther felt like she was dying. Euston swirled his highball glass and she could smell the smoky scotch from where she sat. She needed to get out of here, but Widgery wasn't done with her yet.

"Do you have any big cases on at the moment, Esther?" he asked.

She really didn't want to talk about Katie Wilde and Mila Rose. Not now, sitting here in a hotel ballroom with the teenager still missing. She'd spoken with the night duty inspector and run over her investigation plan a dozen times before coming out here tonight, and she knew she wasn't expected to live in the station until the girl was found, but still...

"We have a few big trials coming up over the next few months," she told him. "Hopefully, we'll get some good convictions."

As she spoke, Widgery was squinting at her card again, a slight frown on his brow.

"Wait," he said, "you're the officer who saved that young woman, isn't that right? A few months back. The incident at the old boarding school. Big news at the time."

"That was a team effort, sir," Esther replied. "Police officers rarely get wins like that all by themselves."

"Suspect was killed in the incident," Euston put in, "was he not? As I understand it, the Police Complaints Commission were looking into the matter. Has anything come of that?"

Esther was growing more uncomfortable by the minute. It was all she could do to keep her eyes off their whiskies.

"I believe they've sent a file to the CPS recommending no prosecution, sir."

"But there're still some conduct matters to look at, internally," Euston replied, eyeing her shrewdly as he took a sip of his whisky. Maybe this guy was one of DCI Porter's golf buddies. Had DCI Porter been into golf? She couldn't remember, but she was definitely getting some negative vibes off Chief Superintendent Callow Euston now.

"That's still with Internal Affairs and Disciplinary, sir, so I couldn't say." As the waiter reappeared to offer the two men wine, she took the opportunity to escape with a murmured, "If you'll excuse me for a moment, gentlemen."

She stood and hurried away through the assemblage. She was sweating again. God, this was the most desperate for a drink she'd felt in months. Where were the blasted restrooms?

Her hunt for the toilets brought her closer to the bar. Colourfully labelled liquor bottles lined the shelves behind the smartly dressed bartenders. Was it just her imagination or was there more of her favourite vodka than any other brand? Her mind must be playing tricks on her. She wrenched her gaze from the neat rows of bottles and veered from the bar, bumping into someone as she turned.

The apology died on her lips when she saw who it was.

DCI Warren Porter looked her up and down, his eyes cold.

"You trying to shimmy your way up the ranks now, Penman?" he asked with a sneer.

"Sir," she replied noncommittally. Despite having spotted him earlier, she was not prepared for this encounter. She forced out as amicable a "How are you?" as she could muster, trying not to glance at the bar and the vodka bottles that seemed somehow to be growing closer as she stood there.

Porter didn't reply. He just eyed her up and down again, slowly this time.

"I see you've made an effort tonight," he said. "Pity you could never apply that kind of effort to your work outfits."

"Don't think this would be practical for work, sir."

Porter grimaced. "Still a smart-ass, Penman."

"Sir."

He scowled and was about to respond when he heard his name mentioned among the group of people he'd been speaking with before Esther had bumped into him. He turned to them again, showing his back to her without another word.

And then suddenly, as if the world was conspiring against her, a subtle parting in the crowd left her staring across a short, empty stretch of carpet towards an opening at the bar. A bartender, unengaged by any customers, stood, polishing a glass. He looked up at her, a questioning smile on his face...

Esther found herself rushing from the room, not caring now who she jostled in her bid for the exit. The damn heels were slowing her down. She paused in the hotel lobby to pull them off, leaning on the back of an empty armchair to keep her balance, before making a beeline for the front doors, her clutch bag in one hand and the shoes dangling from their straps in the other.

She was in such a hurry as she rushed through the main doors that she almost collided with Superintendent O'Halloran, who was on her way in.

"Esther!" she said, startled.

"Ma'am!" Esther replied breathlessly.

There was a short, awkward moment as they both stared at one another, then Esther shook her head.

"I'm sorry, ma'am, I can't... I-I have to go."

With that, Esther hurried away into the night, leaving the superintendent staring after her in bewilderment.

15

ESTHER WENT TO Belfield Grammar School first thing the next morning, avoiding the police station and trying hard not to dwell on the disaster that had been her brief appearance at the dinner the night before. She focused instead on the school secretary sitting across from her at a table near the back of the empty cafeteria.

It was good to see Dorothy Long again; it had been a couple of months since Esther had last spoken to her. Dorothy and her son Edwin had been involved in a case Esther had worked just before Christmas. It was the case Chief Superintendent Euston had been referring to – Esther crushed the rising memory of last night again – and it had been a difficult one for everyone involved. She was happy to hear that Edwin was doing better now. According to Dorothy, he was seeing a counsellor and getting his life back on track.

After a brief catch-up, Esther steered the conversation onto the subject of her visit: Mila Rose. Dorothy had pulled

Mila's file and printed a copy for her, and Esther was leafing through the pages as Dorothy spoke. It was a stroke of good fortune that Ms Fredericks, the principal, was at a meeting in Manchester today, giving Dorothy a chance to sit down with Esther over a cuppa and catch up. Fredericks was an exacting manager and Dorothy seemed far more relaxed without her around.

"The Roses managed to get her a place at this school when they adopted her," Dorothy was saying. "A bit of string-pulling, I don't doubt – Pastor Rose is a member of the Board of Governors."

They sat next to the cafeteria doors. Even though the hall itself was empty, there was plenty of clattering and chatter issuing from the kitchens at the far end, where the cooks were preparing for the lunchtime rush.

"What's he like?" Esther asked. "The pastor, I mean."

"Very straightlaced fellow," Dorothy replied. "Very conservative. Likes to take charge at the meetings. Yes, Pastor Rose does like to impress his views pretty firmly. Doesn't seem to appreciate dissenting voices all that much."

"Do you know Vera Rose at all?"

"A little. She sometimes helps out at PTA committee meetings and the like. Chalk and cheese the pair of them. Vera wouldn't say boo to a goose, but I think she'd lie down in front of traffic for Mila. That girl might as well be her flesh and blood, the way Vera dotes on her." Dorothy frowned. "And the pastor is strict," she went on, "but I think he cares for the girl just as much as Vera."

"There's not a whole lot on her file, is there?" Esther mused.

"No," Dorothy replied. "Mila is a good, quiet girl. Keeps herself to herself."

"And no Anitas at Belfield Grammar."

"No Anitas," the secretary confirmed.

"Has Mila been having trouble with any other students? Any fallouts or schoolyard scraps? Any bullying?"

"None that I know of," Dorothy replied. "She's always seemed content here. I don't think she's ever come to anyone's attention, really. A bit of a wallflower, if anything." She fixed Esther with a concerned look. "We're all worried about her, Esther," she said. "Miss Fredericks is convening a special assembly about it. Have you any... leads or anything? Any idea where she might be?"

"Teenagers run away all the time, Dorothy," Esther replied carefully. "Ninety-nine percent of the time they're found safe and sound."

Ninety-nine percent of the time there were no weird Latin messages and cabins in the woods, but Esther kept that to herself, and Dorothy seemed to take the reassurance at face value.

At length, they finished their coffees, and Esther thanked Dorothy for her help. They said goodbye with promises to keep in touch.

Next, she headed to the Roses' house, telling herself along the way that it was important to keep in regular face-to-face contact with the misper's family, and it wasn't just because she wanted to avoid the police station for as long as possible.

The sun was out, and it was growing warmer, the weather hinting at the summer to come. As Esther pulled up to the kerb, she found Vera in her front garden, wearing a wide-brimmed hat and a pair of gardening gloves. The woman was standing stock-still, staring vacantly at the few patchy clouds drifting high overhead, the pruning shears in one hand apparently forgotten. She didn't seem to notice Esther getting out of the car or approaching her. It was only when Esther called her name that she gave a start and turned.

"Detective Penman," she said, clearly surprised to find her standing there. "I'm so sorry, I was just... I was..."

She trailed off, evidently unsure what it was she'd been doing. She looked down at the shears in her hand, and when she spoke again, her voice was distant.

"I started making her lunch this morning," she said. "For school." She tossed her head as she pulled the gloves from her hands. "I had the sandwich half-wrapped in tinfoil before I realised what I was doing."

She stared at the gloves for a moment. Then she suddenly burst into tears.

Esther didn't hesitate. She wrapped her arms around the older woman and held her as she sobbed. They must have stood there for a good two minutes before Esther gently broke from the embrace and, with one arm around Vera's shoulders, steered her towards the house.

"Let's go inside," she said. "I'll make us some tea."

In the kitchen, Esther sat Vera at the table and put the kettle on. "Is your husband home?" she asked, as she went about locating tea-bags and cups.

Vera shook her head. "He's at the church." She fished a tissue from her sleeve and began dabbing her eyes.

"Did you come to a decision on the media appeal?" Esther asked. "It would be better if both of you agree to it."

Vera nodded. "Yes. Yes, of course. We'll do whatever it takes. Tim and I will both do whatever it takes."

The kettle came to the boil. Esther finished making the

tea and took the cups to the table, where she sat across from Vera.

"He's worried too, you know," Vera said, regarding Esther through teary eyes. "Tim," she explained. "I know he doesn't seem it, but Tim has a soft heart. He tries to appear stern – and he does get animated about the Scriptures – but he's a good, caring father."

Esther nodded, but said nothing.

"I just don't want you thinking he was too hard on her," Vera continued, her expression making Esther wonder if the woman intuited a lot more than she seemed to, "or that they didn't get on. There were arguments recently, but Mila loved him too. Their debates about the Scriptures... I don't want you thinking it was something more than it was. And I don't think those arguments would have made Mila run away." Her brow furrowed. "Just run away and leave us. It doesn't make sense."

She closed her eyes and took a deep breath, fighting back more tears.

"I feel so useless," she went on. "You and your colleagues out searching. Tim organising his congregation for prayers and social media appeals and leaflet drops. I just... I don't know what to do with myself. I can't sleep, and most of the time I'm so worried I feel sick."

Esther reached out and squeezed her hand. "Don't be so hard on yourself. You're living through every parent's worst nightmare. Sometimes there's nothing to do but wait. There are police working around the clock to find Mila, and almost all missing teens come back safe and sound at the end of the day. Try to focus on that fact."

That didn't have quite the same reassuring effect on Vera as it had had on Dorothy Long.

"She used to talk to me," she said. "She used to be so open, used to share all her thoughts and feelings. Recently, she's just... changed. Been so *shut off*. I don't understand what happened." The woman looked gaunt and drawn as she heaved another shaky sigh. "Tim and I never could have children of our own. Tim knew how much that upset me. It was his idea, to adopt. And when we met Mila, she just made my heart lift. Such a lovely girl. Such a tragic background. My friends told me we should get a younger child, but... it just seemed *right*, with Mila."

"Teenagers can be difficult," Esther told her softly.

Vera looked at her. "Do you have children?"

Esther shook her head. "No, but I've dealt with enough of them in my job. And I was one. I was the worst type of teenager. Moody and combative. No one finds dealing with teenagers easy. Most teenagers are just angry with the world and don't know why."

Vera gave her a small, tight smile. She was welling up again. Esther pulled a fresh tissue from a box on the counter behind her and handed it to her. As she did so, a photograph in a colourful frame next to the tissue box caught her eye.

"Is that Alton Towers?" she asked.

The photograph showed the three Roses – Timothy, Vera and Mila – along with a handful of other adults and teenagers, all standing in front of a swooping roller coaster. The sky was blue, and everyone was in shorts and T-shirts, beaming for the camera.

Vera smiled through her tears. "Oh yes, that was a lovely day out. We take the children from the Sunday school on trips like that a couple of times a year. It's always good fun. And we usually have plenty of volunteers among the parents. I think some of the adults enjoy the roller coasters more than the kids!"

Esther smiled. "Not me. I've only ever been on one, and I felt like I'd left my guts behind me for most of the day after. Not managed to brave one since."

Vera's smile became wistful. "Mila's like that too. She wouldn't go on the big ones. She was happy to do the boat rides and the tamer stuff with me." She appeared to be losing herself in the memory as she stared at the snapshot. "Yes, that was a good day."

There was a moment of silence as they both studied the photo. When Vera spoke again, the breathiness of her voice made Esther turn.

"Tell me she's alive, Esther."

She was staring at Esther with a fervent plea in her eyes, her lips trembling.

Esther reached out and took both of Vera's hands in hers.

"I believe that she is," she replied, only realising as she said it that she did, in fact, remain hopeful; despite the discovery of Katie Wilde's body, Esther was still working towards finding Mila Rose alive. Even if the idea that the girl had run away in a fit of pique and would come traipsing home, chagrined and shamefaced, was starting to look less and less likely, Esther wasn't looking for another body. Not yet.

Vera seemed to accept that this was all she was going to get. She nodded, gave Esther a half-smile and took her hands back to clutch at her teacup again.

"We have dozens of searchers out combing the woods from dawn to dusk," Esther went on. "My team of detectives are running every lead. We'll find something soon. I'm sure of it."

It was a deflection of sorts, but it was all Esther was able to offer the woman right then.

"People think that when you adopt a child it's not the same," Vera said. "Not the same as having your own. That there isn't the same bond. But it's not true. Not for me. Not for Tim. She's our daughter, Esther." Fresh tears welled as she met Esther's eyes again. "She's our daughter."

Esther nodded. "And I'll find her for you," she said solemnly.

"Do that," Vera replied, her voice almost a whisper.

And with that, Esther knew that she had to. It was like a promise now.

They sat in silence for a few minutes, sipping their tea, before Esther eventually realised she couldn't put off going back to the station forever. She apologised and explained that she needed to return to the office, and asked Vera if she was going to be okay.

Vera nodded. "I'll be fine. Really. I don't know what I was thinking, going out to do the garden. I thought, maybe, if I could distract myself for a bit... but there's no distracting myself from this. No, I'll go down to the church instead. Pray with Tim and our friends, organise more leaflets and posters."

"I can give you a lift, if you'd like?" Esther offered.

Vera smiled and shook her head.

"Thank you, but no. The walk will do me some good."

"Okay," Esther replied. "Well, I'll be in touch. About the media appeal."

With that, Esther took her leave.

Sitting into her little Fiat, she glanced back at the house. She believed Vera about Tim. There was something in the woman's look as she'd spoken about him that told Esther Vera Rose was shrewder than she let on. She'd known what Esther had been suspecting. And she didn't strike Esther as a woman who would have allowed that.

With a sigh, Esther started the car. She wasn't looking forward to running into Superintendent O'Halloran after last night's disaster, but she had work to do. No messages or calls to her work phone didn't bode well for the prospect of progress on the search, but her conversation with Vera made her want to get stuck in at the coalface in her hunt for the girl. She had a sudden need to do something physical, even if that meant plodding through the forest with the search teams for a while. First, though, she would get reports from her team and re-examine every line of enquiry so far. It wasn't that she didn't trust her detectives – they were some of the best on the force – but now and again a fresh eye found something that tired eyes missed…

With renewed determination, Esther pulled out and headed for the police station.

16

THE ENQUIRY OFFICE was busy. As Esther crossed the room, two men broke away from the crowd and moved towards her. The first was in his mid-thirties and dressed all in black denim – shirt, trousers, jacket – and he carried an old-fashioned brown leather satchel slung over one arm. The other was taller, about ten years younger, and wore a small backpack the wrong way round, like a parent might carry a baby in a carrier. As they moved to intercept her, getting between her and the inner door, the man with the backpack unzipped it and pulled out a large Canon camera; the other one pushed his mobile phone into her face as if it were a microphone.

"It's Detective Sergeant Esther Penman, isn't it?" denim-man asked, while the guy with the camera started snapping photos. Without waiting for an answer, denim-man continued, "Bob Chase, *Belfield Star*. What can you tell us about the murdered girl in the woods? Are you following any particular leads?"

Esther was forced to stop short or walk into him. The rest of the enquiry office had fallen silent to watch.

"Is it true the murder was a ritual killing? Are there Satanic cults operating in Belfield?"

One of the onlookers gasped. Esther was caught so off-guard by the questions that she couldn't speak; her mouth worked, but no sounds were coming out. Meanwhile, the photographer moved right up into her face, snapping away. Esther pushed him back.

Undeterred by Esther's lack of response, Chase pressed on. "Is witchcraft involved?"

Thankfully, Pat, the station enquiry assistant, was already bustling out from behind the counter. She rushed through the staff-only door that separated the waiting room from the rest of the station and began shooing the two newspapermen out of the enquiry office.

"Get out, both of you!" she shouted. "You can't take photos in here! Go through the press office like you're supposed to, you rotters!"

The photographer, possibly worried about his camera getting confiscated, slipped out quickly and disappeared. Chase was less timid. He backed away from Pat's waving arms, letting her usher him outside while he continued to shout questions.

"Can you confirm that you've employed a witch as part of the investigation team?" he called out to Esther. "Is it true the police are using séance sessions to track the killer? What have police found in the hills above Belf—"

The rest of his question was cut off as Pat gave him a firm shove and closed the sliding doors using the manual override switch. She heaved a sigh as she marched back across the enquiry office.

124

"I'm sorry, Esther," she said. "They said they were here to speak to you. They didn't tell me they were journalists."

Everyone in the enquiry office was staring at Esther as she turned and followed Pat through the staff door, a tide of murmurs rising in her wake.

"That's okay, Pat," Esther replied. The heavy glass windows were muffling the gossip and muttering in the waiting room. As the enquiry assistant resumed her post at the desk and the shock of the incident began to wear off, Esther's blood was starting to boil. "Besides, I know exactly who's behind that little stunt." *Calvin fucking Brett.* "Thank you for your help with those two."

"No problem, Esther. I'm just sorry I didn't recognise them. Won't make that mistake again, I can tell you!"

Esther was fuming as she mounted the stairs two steps at a time. She had half a mind to go straight to Brett's office, but thought better of it and went instead to Jared's. He was studying a sheaf of documents as she stomped in and shut the door behind her.

"You won't believe what that slimy bastard Calvin Brett has done!" she snarled. "He's gone and set a journo from that rag the *Star* on me! I've just been ambushed in the enquiry office by some asshole going on about cults and rituals in the woods, and whether we've hired a witch to track down the fucking killer!"

Jared hesitated. "We haven't, have we?"

Esther stared at him in disbelief.

"Hired a witch? *No!* Of *course* not!" She paused. "I did… speak to a local personality. Just to find out more about the symbols in the cabin, from someone who understood that stuff. But that's not the same as 'hiring a witch'. Or doing séances to track down a killer, for fuck's sake!'"

Jared put his documents down and sat back in his chair to regard her for a moment.

"Maybe this journalist got their information from your 'local personality,'" he said, "but you're probably right. It probably was Calvin. Only problem is, he's told everyone in the office about your witch visitor. Could have been anyone."

"That little fucking…" She couldn't finish the sentence – it became a growl as she dropped into the chair facing Jared's desk.

He leaned forward. "Listen," he said in a conciliatory tone, "this is manageable. We'll contact the press office and tell them to let the *Star*'s editor know that no witches have been hired, no séances have been conducted, and that anything they print to the contrary will be met with legal action. Can you speak to your witch friend and ask her not to talk to anyone from the press?"

Esther nodded. She suddenly felt deflated.

"Maybe I'm not cut out for this shit, Jared," she said. "The politics. The… *machinations*. It's not for me."

"Nonsense!" he replied firmly. "That's exactly *why* we need people like you in the higher ranks, Esther. Precisely *because* you're not into the scheming and the politics. This kind of shit-flinging has Calvin's name all over it. We don't need more of his like. You're sharp, and you'll get the hang of dealing with crap like this. Speaking of which, how did the dinner go last night?"

Esther shook her head, not quite able to meet his eyes.

"I had to leave early," she told him. "Something came up." *An unexpected freak-out at the bar*, she thought, but didn't say it. Instead, she asked, "Have you spoken to Ma'am

O'Halloran this morning?"

"Haven't seen or heard from her," he replied "Everything okay?"

Esther was wiping her hands anxiously on the front of her jeans. She realised what she was doing and made herself stop. "Yeah, I just… I just need to chat to her at some point. Explain about last night."

"First things first," Jared said. "You contact the witch and I'll send a line to the press office. I have a reliable person there. Barbara. I'll CC you in, so you can go straight to her in the future."

Esther nodded. "I want to catch up with the team this morning too. See where we're at with both enquiries. The Roses have agreed to a full national media appeal."

"Press conference?" Jared asked.

"Might be the best way to get attention," Esther replied. "Can you add a line to your email and attach Mila's picture? Ask your contact to push the outlets to highlight her case a bit more in the meantime?"

Jared nodded. "Will do."

"I want to get back out into Norwick Forest later as well," Esther went on. "See how Sergeant Taylor is getting on with his search."

"No updates?"

Esther grimaced and shook her head.

"That's okay," Jared said. "No updates means no more dead bodies."

"Thanks, Jared. That's cheerful."

He shrugged. "It's something."

Esther stood.

"Chin up, Esther," he said before she got to the door. "Calvin's just trying to distract you. Don't let him. Focus on the job at hand."

Esther sighed and nodded, then crossed the workroom to the sergeants' office. Was it just her imagination, or did a hush fall over the place? Nobody looked up from their computers, but she felt like she was being observed.

Caroline and Spencer were both at their desks in the DS office. They watched her go to her own desk, giving Esther that sense of being scrutinised all over again. As she tugged off her jacket, she glanced first at Spencer and then at Caroline.

"What?" she snapped.

Spencer just ducked behind his computer screen without saying anything.

"Nothing," Caroline said. "You okay?" There was a touch of sympathy in her expression, which just made Esther angrier.

"Fine," she replied tersely.

Caroline seemed to accept the answer. She returned to her work, with one more quick glance in Esther's direction before she went back to her typing.

Esther stifled another growl. She wanted to throttle Calvin Brett. As soon as she retrieved Thelma Faye's contact number, she grabbed her mobile phone and headed for the door again. She knew without looking at them that Spencer and Caroline were watching her as she left, but she wasn't about to ring Faye with those two listening in. This was a phone call she needed to make out in the car park, away from prying ears…

* * *

The shopping basket was already half full, even though she hadn't chosen much.

The veggie garden would be wonderful when it was finished. She would be able to pick things and put them straight on everyone's plates.

No shop-bought vegetables.

No plastic wrapping.

So bad for the environment.

Until then, Anita was determined to budget their money. After all, none of them were working now, and their goal of complete self-sufficiency was still a ways off.

Although she was on a tight budget, Anita was choosing healthy options for the family – organic, when she could find it.

She smiled. That's how she thought of them. A little family.

Her man at home.

Mila, like a sister.

Mayonnaise or mayo light? Mayo light. Calories.

She turned to the fridges. Olive spread? No. It had palm oil in it. Butter. They would just have to be careful not to use too much.

She set the jar of mayo and the block of butter into her basket and moved down the aisle to the pasta.

The shop was cramped and oddly laid-out, an ancient little place with an ancient little shopkeeper doing crossword puzzles behind the counter. And the cash register… God! Anita had wanted to take a picture when she'd seen it – it was like an antique! But with what? She had no phone now. Jason was right about that; they were better off without phones. Better to cut themselves off from the toxic internet and the corruption of the world altogether.

Why did pasta come in so many different shapes? Tubes and strings, flat ribbons and little dickie-bows. She read the names. Tagliatelle, Penne, Fusilli, Farfalle, Conchiglie. For a tiny store out in the middle of nowhere, they sure had a lot of pasta.

But pasta was good.

Pasta kept.

She chose Conchiglie. She liked the shape of them the most. Like little conches. She guessed that's where the name came from.

The old lino floor was gleaming. The tiles themselves were ugly – dull green and off-red – but they were so well-waxed that the lights on the ceiling above were almost perfectly reflected under Anita's feet. She wondered who did the cleaning and the waxing. Not the wizened old woman behind the counter, surely? Perhaps she had someone come in to do it. Or a strong young grandson. Anita wondered if the woman had much family. Maybe she had an equally wizened husband. Anita imagined the two of them, mates for life, shuffling about the shop down through the years, keeping the place clean and stocked up. The thought brought another smile to her face.

But then she heard something that made her smile fade.

"The victim has been named as twenty-year-old Katie Wilde, and police have confirmed they've launched a murder enquiry..."

Anita moved slowly to the end of the aisle. The shopkeeper was still doing her crossword, paying no attention to the dusty, fat television with the grainy picture mounted in the corner behind her. As the newscaster spoke, Katie's face stared out at Anita from the screen. She looked a lot younger in the photo they were showing, but it made Anita flinch and take a step back; not so far that she couldn't still see the TV above a row of sugary cereal packs, though – packs showing frosted flakes, chocolate mini-biscuit things and multicoloured little fantasy-creature shapes, all sparkling with sugar as they tumbled into bowls of milk.

So many things had too much sugar in them.

So bad for children.

Rotting young teeth.

Diabetes.

"Police haven't confirmed whether they are linking the death to the recent disappearance of a local teenager, Mila Rose, but they have released this photo of the girl and asked anyone with information to get in touch."

A photo of Mila on the TV now. The image of her in her school uniform made Anita's breath catch.

She needed to get home.

She needed to get home to Mila.

The shock of seeing her on the television made Anita realise how thoughtless she'd been. Too many rituals, too many drugs. She hadn't been using her head at all.

It wasn't too late though.

She hurried back along the aisles and found the tiny toiletries section. Luckily, there were a handful of boxes of what she was looking for scattered about on a near-empty bottom shelf. Among the blondes, coppers and blacks were a couple of hair bleaching kits. Anita grabbed two of the bleaching kits and several boxes of blonde dye. It would eat into their meagre budget, but Mila's hair was quite dark...

She waited until the newscaster had moved on to another story – a train crash near Exeter – before scuttling out from between the aisles and stepping up to the counter.

The cash register was less amusing this time around.

The old woman took an age to tot up the bill. As soon as she did, Anita paid quickly, stuffed the groceries into her canvas sack and hurried out. By the time she sat into the car, she was shaking. She dropped her keys into the footwell twice before she finally managed to get them in the ignition.

A touch of panic set in when the rusty old Ford's engine coughed and wheezed and failed to turn over on her first two attempts.

She stopped and closed her eyes, took three calming breaths and focused on centring herself.

Harmonising with the universe.

She opened her eyes and turned the key.

The car started.

Calmly and carefully, Anita reversed and put the car into first. She drove slowly to the entrance of the gravelly carpark, refusing to let anxiety get the better of her. But as she pulled out onto the winding country road, she couldn't dispel the image of hunters closing in on their sanctuary.

The cabin was miles from their little cottage. Miles. But still...

She had to get back to Mila.

She was not about to lose another sister.

17

After speaking with Barbara at the press office and working out some preliminary details for the media appeal, Esther spent the rest of her day studying reports from every detective on the team. Some were working the Wilde murder, others were dedicated to Mila's disappearance, but many lines of enquiry were potentially relevant to both cases.

A couple of fingerprints and forensics reports had come back early. There were no prints on the candles from the cabin – they'd melted too much – but Wilde's toxicology report made Esther's eyebrows rise. The woman had had enough LSD and ketamine in her system to kill a small animal. No wonder she'd been able to run so far with those injuries to her feet – she must have been completely out of it! Perhaps that had been a blessing in the end.

When it came to her own team's work, Esther didn't just read the notes they'd logged on the system; she brought her detectives into CID's small conference room one by one, spoke about their discoveries and discussed next steps.

Liz Fellowes and Jennifer Phiri had been sent to every tattoo parlour in Belfield, as well as all the neighbouring towns and cities, bringing photos of Katie Wilde's pentacle tattoo, along with pictures of the woman herself and Mila Rose. Their enquiries hadn't led to much, which explained their downbeat expressions as they'd trudged into the conference room; nobody they'd spoken to had recognised Katie or Mila, and no one would lay claim to having done any of Katie's tattoos, especially the pentacle. It was clearly a DIY job, they'd been told in no uncertain terms, and not a very good one. Esther let the women explain why all the tattooists called it a 'stick and poke' tattoo, talking about things that were alien to her, like colouration and keloids. Although they hadn't had any breakthroughs, Esther tried to buoy them up by pointing out that the information was, in fact, very useful; they'd learned that the tattoo was relatively new, and they'd already identified their next task, contacting suppliers around the borough to find out if they'd sold tattoo needles or inks to anyone in the area recently. It would be another tough slog, but it was a significant line of enquiry. Wilde was more likely than not to have had help, and whoever had helped her might be key to catching her killer, or may even be the killer themselves.

Both women left the conference room with a stronger appreciation of the tattoo enquiry.

Next was Craig Browne. He was working on Mila's background. Esther knew the basics from her initial briefings. Mila had been orphaned at a young age after she and her mother had fled Lithuania in the wake of a particularly nasty domestic situation. Her mother had been a junkie – no family, no associates – but seemed to have turned over something of a new leaf when she got to the UK. Unfortunately, her lifestyle had caught up with her, and when she'd died suddenly as a result of heart failure, Mila had been thrust into the arms of the British social services. With no kin to speak of back in Lithuania – certainly none the authorities could trace – and with no relations in the UK, Mila had wound up at Hodderston Road Children's Home.

Esther had given Craig a list of Mila's teachers, a list she'd received from Dorothy Long that morning, but not all of them had responded yet, and the responses so far were all blandly positive: a good student, no trouble, et cetera, et cetera.

Hodderston Road was a harder nut to crack. Craig had managed to confirm that Katie Wilde had no links to the place – that was a simple task of checking records – but finding someone who had known Mila was another story. It had been almost five years since she'd been a resident of Hodderston Road, and the staff turnover at places like that was horrendous, so Craig had had to do a lot of digging to find someone who'd worked there when Mila was in care. The social services' notes were fairly dry, but he'd managed to track down a retired social worker, a woman called Tabitha Renshaw, who'd agreed to meet him tomorrow.

Craig puffed up a little when Esther told him he'd done good work; Craig was a rookie member of the team, and as yet still a touch insecure in his new detective role. Esther told him she'd like to come along to the meeting with Tabitha Renshaw. She wanted a fresh perspective on Mila, one that didn't come from the adoptive parents.

"Skipper?"

Esther and Craig looked up as Derek Grant appeared in

the doorway to the conference room. He had been out doing CCTV trawls of the area from early morning, and Esther had planned to speak to him whenever he returned.

"Derek," she said, "have you found something?"

He nodded and stepped into the room. He was carrying a set of pages. When he set them on the table in front of Esther, she could see that they were printed stills from a CCTV camera, with the date and time stamp in the top corner. The images were grainy and had a staticky grey line running through the middle of them, but Esther recognised her misper straight away.

"It's her," she breathed.

"It is," Derek replied. "The images are clearer on the footage itself, although even that's not great. But I'd bet my house on it. It's our misper."

There was no doubt, as far as Esther was concerned – it was Mila, dressed in jeans and a dark hoody with the hood thrown back.

Proof of life.

Esther looked at the timestamp.

"Is the date and time correct?" she asked.

"Pretty close," Derek told her. "About five minutes slow."

Esther felt her heart swell. Mila Rose was alive two days ago at 16:24 hours. And judging by the security footage, she'd been with two other people. A man and a woman. None of the print-outs had a good angle of either's face – just side profiles and the backs of heads – but Esther could tell they were young. In their twenties, maybe. The woman was blonde, her hair hanging loose and messy, halfway to her waist. She wore a knee-length woollen cardigan over an ankle-length skirt. The man wore what looked like a dun-coloured poncho and baggy trousers.

"Do we have any better footage of these two she's with?"

Derek shook his head. "Unfortunately not. Their backs are to the camera the whole time."

"They look like hippies," Craig muttered.

He was right. The man wore his hair in dreadlocks and his trousers were oddly colourful.

More print-outs further down the pile showed the three of them getting into a car, but these images were at a greater distance and much blurrier; Esther could just about make out that the vehicle was an old-style blue hatchback.

"What about the car?" she asked.

"Haven't been able to ID it," Derek replied. "Not yet, anyway. I'm doing a trawl for blue hatchbacks in the area at the time, but it's kind of like looking for a needle in a haystack."

"Do we have this footage?" Esther asked. She squinted at the printed stills, as if staring hard enough might make the details clearer. Even Craig had risen out of his chair and cocked his head to get a better look.

"That's a bit of an issue, Skipper," Derek said. "The system is almost as ancient as the owner. It's VHS. I haven't seen a video machine in the station in quite a few years, so I've sent it over to the cyber unit to try and get it transferred to digital. Hopefully we'll have the footage by end of play today. I took these shots from the screen with my phone. They're the best I could get – pausing it made it jump like hell – but we've doubled-down on that area. Jackie and Kyle are going door to door everywhere along that route into town."

"Where is this place?"

"It's a small convenience store, out beyond the city limits on Cumberwell Road. Pretty isolated."

Mark Taylor's search teams had been in full swing at 16:24 on Saturday, but in a completely different part of the Norwick Hills.

"They only have the one camera, unfortunately," Derek added, "so there's no footage of them inside."

Esther savoured the moment. This was as close to a breakthrough as they'd come so far. Seeing these blurry images, seeing Mila alive two days ago, apparently walking about freely, gave her a burst of fresh hope. Her promise to Vera suddenly seemed more achievable.

"Print out a few more of these, Derek, would you?" Esther said. "I need to take them to the Roses to see if they can help us identify these other two people."

"Will do, Skip."

"And get the support department to print out a giant satellite map of Norwick Forest, one that covers right up over the other side of the mountain," Esther directed. "Clear a wall in the main office. Our misper is somewhere that side of town, probably somewhere in the forest. Let's get the helicopter up and have them check wherever they can for moveable structures. RVs, tents, newly built cabins. Anything like that."

"It'll be tough with all that tree coverage," Derek mused.

"I know," Esther replied, "but it needs done. See if you can get a hold of the Borough Council's land registry maps for the area too. Maybe there are old houses out there. If they're hippies, they're more likely to be out there than somewhere in the city."

"On it," Derek replied.

As he and Craig left the room, Esther peered down at

the print-outs again. Her heart was lighter, staring at an image of Mila, alive and well. Even if the picture was two days old, it was something. Something she could bring to Vera, to give the woman a bit of hope.

The fact that Mila Rose now firmly qualified as a suspect in a murder investigation was something Esther would keep to herself…

18

MILA SAT IN front of the cloudy mirror, watching Anita run her fingers through her hair to gauge the length. She stood directly behind her, with a pair of long-bladed scissors in her left hand and a thoughtful frown on her face.

"I think, maybe... to about here?" she suggested, pinching a lock of Mila's freshly dyed hair and holding it in front of her shoulder, just below the jaw.

Mila wasn't sure. She'd never worn her hair that short before. But then, she'd never gone blonde either. She was trying to decide whether she liked it or not.

Anita smiled at Mila's expression in the mirror. "Maybe a touch longer," she conceded, adding another inch.

Mila still wasn't sure, but she smiled anyway. Her friend had been so excited about cutting her hair that Mila didn't want to disappoint her.

As Anita brought the scissors in and began snip, snip, snipping, Mila closed her eyes and let herself drift, relaxing to the feel of Anita's fingers in her hair.

Bumping into her old friend on the way home from

school last month had literally seemed like fate. Anita had that same magnetism, that aura of possibility and freedom about her as she'd had back at Hodderston Road. She seemed to understand Mila like no one else did. More than Vera. Certainly more than Tim. With Tim, there were no grey areas, no room for doubt. It was either Christian purity or heathen hellfire. There was no in-between. It was as if he was stuck in the nineteenth century or something. Mila had had more than enough of his Bible-bashing. Talking about the Word Of God like it was emailed down from Heaven, instead of the scribblings of a few zealots, cobbled together centuries after they'd died by some Roman politicians who wanted to stop an empire falling apart. She'd read *The Da Vinci Code*. She knew *all* about it.

There had been arguments. 'Debates', Vera tried to call them. But debates didn't involve that amount of yelling. Not school debates, anyway.

That had been the start of it. The start of Mila realising she was literally just an ornament. Something to be seen and not heard. Independent thinking was outlawed in that house, where ornamental daughters were expected to diligently and dutifully do as they were told, and no more. Demurely. Was that a word? Yeah. Demure. She was expected to be demure. Might as well dress up in a frilly bonnet and ankle-length dress with petticoats and clutch her Bible to her breast *demurely*.

One day she'd been so pissed off that she'd tossed her Bible into the fireplace. Tim had exploded. Grounded her for a week. Total overreaction. It had been a statement, for frig's sake! The fire hadn't even been lit!

And then, the very next day, Anita had walked back into Mila's life, still blazing like the sun. Like a sign from God –

ha! – talking about how she'd missed Mila, missed her little sister. Telling her all about her new boyfriend and how they were going to purify themselves and become One With Nature. How they'd got themselves a little house. If Mila was so unhappy, she'd suggested, why didn't she come and live with them? No rules. No church. No bullshit. Only truth.

And freedom.

Mila had felt the suffocation of the Roses' house more than ever after she'd hooked up with Anita again. Realised how stifling and oppressive it was. No freedom of conscience or thought. Just Tim's crappy religious talks.

With school becoming almost as bad – Mila had somehow managed to get the shittiest teachers assigned to her for the year – she'd decided she'd had enough. Fate or God or whatever had given her an escape route, and she took it.

Five days. Five days of freedom.

And already she was having her doubts.

She did her best to hide them. She didn't want Anita to know. Anita would think she was being a baby. Mila was not a baby. She *could* take care of herself.

But then there was that other night in the woods – Jason's big 'ritual' – the night Katie had ditched them. Mila hadn't been expecting that; she'd quite liked Katie. She'd seemed chill. She thought Katie had liked her too. They'd talked about how they were both looking forward to having more people as part of their community, with everyone taking care of each other. That was Anita and Jason's grand plan, to build a commune of free-thinkers. People who didn't want to put up with the Authoritarian State of Things. A haven where anyone who wanted to be truly free could live, away from the drones of society, away from the manipulators feeding everyone plastic and fake vaccines to control them, hammering their brains with 5G radiation, all so a bunch of fat cats in ivory towers could make more profits.

Anita talked a lot about The Fat Cats in their Ivory Towers – so much so that Mila now imagined them as actual fat cats in actual ivory towers. She shook her head slightly to clear the image.

"Hey, careful," Anita laughed, "no sudden movements. You'll end up like Vincent Van Gogh."

Mila giggled. She opened her eyes and grinned at Anita, who smiled back. Mila watched through the mirror as her friend set to work again, lifting her hair, measuring and snipping. Lift, measure, snip.

"Did Katie say anything to you?" she asked. "About leaving?"

Anita's hesitation was barely perceptible. Mila only noticed because she was watching her. Anita didn't meet her gaze. She continued her task – lift, measure, snip – as she shook her head and made a face. Even pulling a face, Anita was pretty. She still had that piercing in her nose, the one she'd got when they'd skipped school one day; a little blue stone sparkled in it now, so small you hardly noticed the thing until it caught the light.

"Katie was always a bit flaky," she replied. "A bit... I don't know... *temperamental.* I wasn't sure she was completely committed to our community, to be honest. Not like you and me." She winked at Mila. "It takes commitment, changing course like this. Pulling off the shackles of today's society. It can be hard." She shrugged. "Maybe Katie wasn't ready for it."

"But to just leave like that? Out in the forest? If I wasn't so wasted, I'd have tried to stop her."

Anita shook her head. "She might've had a bad trip."

She left off her trimming for a moment and rested her chin on Mila's head, their faces atop one another as she regarded her in the mirror.

"And you weren't *wasted*," she said. "You were experiencing other planes of existence. Seeing them, even if only briefly."

Mila nodded obediently, but the truth was she'd just felt wasted.

Anita straightened again and continued her trimming.

"Katie might come back," she said. "Once she realises her mistake. If she apologises, I might even let her stay with us again."

The scissors flashed around Mila's shoulders as Anita kept cutting, and a minute or two later she stepped aside.

"Done!" she said. She lifted a hand-mirror from the bed behind her and used it to show Mila the back, like a real hairdresser would.

Mila turned her head slowly one way, and then the other, examining the finished product. Anita had taken a good couple of inches off, her hair falling to a little above the shoulder, and she'd given her bangs that ended a shade above her eyebrows too; the result was a tad uneven, but Mila kept that to herself.

"What do you think?" Anita asked.

Mila nodded, smiling. "It's good. I like it."

Anita beamed at her.

"Hey, sexy new look, Mila," came a male voice from the hall.

Mila shifted her gaze in the mirror as Anita turned. Jason

stood lounging against the door frame, grinning that lopsided grin of his. Mila thought about their last conversation in the woods outside the cabin. She didn't have many conversations with Jason – it was as if Anita ran some kind of carefully orchestrated interference – but recalling that last time made her cheeks burn; she could see them going bright red in the mirror.

Jason was good-looking, even with the dreadlocks, and Mila would admit she'd been quite taken with Anita's new boyfriend when they'd first been introduced, but there was something about Jason that made her uncomfortable. Especially when they were on their own together. He'd never done anything, but it was as if the energy in the room shifted subtly each time they were alone. And he looked at her a certain way sometimes. More often these last few days since Katie had left and it was just the three of them.

He was looking at her that way now.

Mila realised the towel Anita had draped around her shoulders had slipped on one side and that she was only wearing a bra underneath. She quickly tugged the towel up to cover both shoulders, conscious as she did so that she accidentally allowed it to fall open at the front. She hastily pulled it together again. Jason's smile widened. Anita stood stiffly, smile gone, scissors held in a tight fist by her left side. She was glaring at him.

"Go and chop some vegetables for dinner, love," she said, her voice as stiff as her posture.

"Sure thing, babe," he replied and, with a wink for Mila, he sauntered off.

Anita didn't look at Mila as she began brushing hair off herself with a small hand towel.

Mila felt awkward. She tried to break the tension.

"You still want to show me how you mix that natural homemade eye shadow you use?"

Anita glanced at her in the mirror. There was no smile now.

"Sorry, Mila, not tonight. I want to get the dinner started. Can you tidy up the rest?"

Without waiting for an answer, she turned and left the room.

Mila sat, staring at her reflection for a long moment, before her eyes drifted to her new bedroom in the background. It was bare, and smelled a little musty. That hadn't bothered her at first, not when the adventure was new and the future full of strange promise. But now, sitting here alone, she realised that she missed her old bedroom. And she was starting to miss Vera too – although every time she found herself weakening on that front, she reminded herself that Vera had never once stood up to Tim, even when Mila could see in her eyes that the woman knew she was right about something, she just stayed quiet or tried to quell the argument by diverting the conversation. Mila might have been pissed with Tim, but with Vera she was just... disappointed.

A tear escaped and ran down her cheek.

She had only been gone a few days, but she was already starting to miss her old life. Her cuddly toys, for frig's sake. How could she miss cuddly toys?

She scrubbed the tears from her eyes with the heel of her palm. She wasn't a child. She deserved to be listened to and treated like an adult. Right at that moment, though, Mila felt every inch a child.

Standing and letting the hair-covered towel fall to the floor, she snatched up a baggy sweater from the bed –

natural sheep's wool, of course, at Anita's insistence; she was systematically weeding every artificial material from the house, bit by bit – and pulled it on over her head. She grabbed the small dustpan and brush and got down on her hands and knees and began sweeping up the hair trimmings.

She was stronger than this. She wasn't about to embarrass herself by behaving like a baby, crawling back to her fake parents. No. She needed to grow up.

Once she'd finished sweeping up, she headed downstairs to the kitchen to see if Anita needed any help with the dinner.

19

THE BREAKTHROUGH WITH the CCTV had fuelled Esther through the afternoon, even if it hadn't led to any more discoveries.

Neither Vera nor Tim had recognised the pair in the security footage printouts, but Vera had been so relieved to see Mila alive that the trip out to the Roses had been worth it just for that. She'd clutched the picture to her chest, closed her eyes and wept. Tim had seemed to be doing his best to hold back tears of his own. Esther had left the print-out with them; it wasn't really best practice, but it would be sent to all the media outlets soon anyway.

It had been growing late, the light already starting to fade, when Esther had driven up into the Norwick Hills to see how Mark Taylor was getting on with his search. The command tent was busy, with all the searchers returning for the night, but there had been nothing more to report; Taylor assured her he would phone as soon as anything came up. He had been curious about the CCTV sighting though, and was going to spend the night working on plans to expand the search in that direction.

Now Esther sat at the kitchen table next to Triona, her work mobile on the table beside her plate; she'd apologised to Cormac and Áine, explaining that her missing person enquiry ran twenty-four-seven, and she needed to be contactable overnight. Even when it was too dark for searchers to comb the forests, even when all the premises the detectives could visit and the specialist departments they liaised with were shut, the uniform crews would remain on the lookout for Mila through the small hours. Cormac had waved away her apology, insisting her work was very important and of course he understood. Áine hadn't said anything, but Esther had grown used to not expecting much of a response from her. Perhaps she considered Cormac's reply an answer on behalf of both of them. Or perhaps she just didn't care for Esther's work.

On her arrival home, Esther had tried to help Triona's dad in the kitchen, but he'd laughed and chivvied her out, saying it was well under control – 'clean as you go' was how he liked to do things – and that she'd been out working hard all day and should go and sit and have a drink. Triona had already confided that she'd not actually told her parents yet that Esther was an alcoholic; Esther had been surprised by how stung she'd felt, thinking Triona might be embarrassed by the fact, but now that she'd met Áine, she was starting to understand Tee's reticence.

Cormac ladled stew into the deep bowl-plates Triona had picked up at a flea market a few months back for fifty pence apiece; she insisted they were her favourite set now, despite the price, or maybe because of it. A bottle of red stood open in the centre of the table. Cormac poured a glass for Triona and himself, but when he came to Esther's glass, she quickly placed her hand over it and muttered that she was on-call and so technically still on duty.

Once Cormac had taken his seat, Áine closed her eyes and clasped her hands together and began to pray aloud. Triona grimaced and glanced apologetically at Esther. Esther, for her part, waited politely.

"Bless us, O Lord," Áine recited, "and these, Thy gifts, which we are about to receive from Thy bounty, through Christ, our Lord. Amen."

Never raised in any kind of religious setting, Esther knew enough to know that 'Amen' was like 'The End', but she waited patiently for Áine to unfold her napkin, drape it over her knees and lift her spoon before picking up her own cutlery. Triona had no such compunctions and tucked in as soon as the Amen was out of her mother's mouth.

"Oh wow!" Esther exclaimed, as she took her first mouthful. "Cormac, this is delicious! You have a gift."

Cormac blushed a bright red, endearing him to her even more.

"Well, thank you, Esther, that's very kind," he replied. "But I'm a bit of a one-trick-pony in the kitchen, I'm afraid. It's a family recipe, and I have to confess that I think Áine actually does a better job of it when she gives it a go. I can make a mean fry for those mornings-after too, but my skills don't go much beyond that!"

"Now, Da, that's not true," Triona chastised him fondly. "No one mans a barbecue quite as well as you do." She turned to Esther. "If you want properly cooked burgers, my da's your man. Everyone else turns them black. Everyone back home, anyway."

"Sounds like you're a keeper, Cormac," Esther said with

a grin. "You caught a good one, Áine."

Áine just sniffed.

"So, how's the investigation going?" Cormac asked Esther. "I don't mean to be nosey. I'm sure you can't tell us the nitty-gritty or anything, but is it going well?"

Esther gave a noncommittal head bob. "It's progressing. Slower than I'd like, if I'm honest. I'm kind of torn between hoping the phone stays silent and hoping it rings. You never really know what the news is going to be."

"It must be a difficult way to live," Áine put in. "Always on duty."

"Oh, I'm not always on duty," Esther replied. "It's just because it's a misper – sorry, a missing person case – and it's live, I have to be ready to go back in at any time."

But Áine went on as if Esther hadn't spoken. "Then again, I suppose you girls both do live unusual lives, don't you?"

Esther glanced at Triona and saw that her girlfriend had grown rigid, her spoonful of stew hovering motionless halfway to her mouth.

"But that's society, these days," Áine went on, appearing to grow in confidence now that she'd finally found her voice. "People just do what they want. No sense of propriety."

"Ma," Triona said, a warning in her tone.

Cormac opened his mouth, but Áine didn't give either of them a chance to intercede.

"No, Catríona," her mother said, "the truth is you do live unusually. You might as well admit it. I actually blame myself. I was too lenient. Too indulgent." She shot Cormac a look. "We both were." The way she said that left no doubt as to who it was Áine believed deserved the better part of the blame.

"Ma, can you not, please?" Triona said sharply. "Not tonight."

Áine fixed her daughter with a stern glare. "You want me to hold my tongue, dear?" The softness of her voice belied the sting in her words. "You want me to keep my peace? When I've been keeping my peace for years?"

"Christ, you have not!"

"Mind your tongue!" Áine snapped. "Don't you dare use the Lord's name in vain! Not in my presence!"

"Now, girls, come on," Cormac said, but he sounded defeated, as though he recognised that his usual smooth intervention wasn't going to cut it this time.

"You've chosen a sinner's life, Catríona," Áine said, ignoring her husband. Her voice was firmer now as she glared at Triona, and Triona glared right back. "I *have* kept my peace long enough. You live in sin. You have no respect for God or the Church or its teachings. Teachings that are there for a *good reason*, Catríona. The wisdom of centuries. Societies and civilizations have fallen into ruin because of their sins and their decadence. It always ends in tragedy. If you read the Bible now and again, you would know it. How can I keep silent when I see you making the very mistakes the Church warns us about over and over. Living in sin. Day-in and day-out."

Both Cormac and Triona appeared to be on the verge of responding – Triona gathering her breath to possibly start shouting – when Esther spoke. All three pairs of eyes switched to her suddenly, as if they had forgotten she was there.

"I don't think it is living in sin," she said simply. She reached out and took Triona's hand. "I love your daughter,

Áine. She's kind and strong and generous. She's the most wonderful person I've met in my life. And if loving someone like that is a sin in your world, then I think it must be a very cold and lonely world to live in."

Áine blinked, clearly not having expected such a rebuke from Esther, and Cormac was studying her with a surprised look on his face too.

After a long moment of tense silence in which nobody moved or spoke, Áine lifted her napkin, dabbed at her lips and then set it carefully down next to her plate.

"If you'll excuse me, all of you," she said as she pushed her chair back and stood. "I have a headache. I think I need to lie down for a bit."

She walked out, her back stiff. When she left, there was a collective exhalation, as though both Triona and her father had been holding their breaths along with Esther. Then Cormac gathered up his napkin and set it down.

"I should go and check she's alright," he said.

"No, Da, just leave her," Triona muttered. She was still clutching Esther's hand on the tabletop. "She's just doing her martyr act again. I'm sick of it."

"I'll be back down in a minute, love," Cormac replied, tapping their entwined fingers affectionately as he rose. "I'll just see if she needs anything first."

Esther suddenly felt inexplicably guilty, almost as if Áine hadn't been insulting them to their faces moments before. She felt as if she was the one in the wrong, the one who had ruined the evening. She shook her head.

"Shit, Tee, I'm so sorry. I—"

She was cut off mid-sentence as Triona leaned over and kissed her hard on the lips. The kiss lasted a long time, and when they parted Esther could see Triona's eyes were glimmering with unshed tears. She was smiling, though, and still clutching Esther's hand.

"I love you too," she whispered.

20

A HUSH FOLLOWED Esther as she crossed the detectives' workroom. Many of the desks were empty, with most of her own team out conducting enquiries into the Mila Rose and Katie Wilde cases. Those who remained had their heads down, although Esther thought she caught a faint tittering from the far end of the room as she wove between the desks.

When she got to the detective sergeants' office, she stopped short and stared.

An old-fashioned broomstick was resting against her desk, a witch's hat perched on her keyboard.

Spencer was the first to laugh, and although Caroline tried to keep it in, Esther could see her shoulders shaking.

"Your face, Esther!" was all Spencer could say.

"He told us you'd find it funny," Caroline said, a little defensively. "It is a bit, you have to admit."

Esther didn't have to ask who 'he' was. Inside, she was mortified, but she schooled her features.

"Haha," she said dryly. She glanced over her shoulder at the workroom and made herself plaster a smirk on her lips. Made herself look unruffled. "Very funny, assholes."

Heads appeared over computer screens, the laughter growing now that they could see she had taken the joke well.

Esther walked to her desk and picked up the hat and broom. She saw that no expense had been spared on the things: the broomstick was an artfully crafted item, bundled twigs tied to the end of a knobbly wooden staff, and the hat was hardly less impressive, cut from thick felt with a wide, floppy brim. Unwilling to let anyone think Calvin Brett had got to her, she gamely set the hat on her head and carried the broom to the door.

"Get back to work," she told the detectives' room at large, "or I'll turn you all into toads."

More laughter. She stepped back into the sergeants' office.

"This was Calvin, wasn't it?" she asked, looking from Spencer to Caroline.

"Ah-ah, DS Penman!" Spencer replied, nudging his spectacles up on his nose, an annoying habit of his. "Snitches get stitches, you know that."

Esther rolled her eyes and glanced at Caroline, who seemed about to answer when she caught sight of someone in the doorway.

"Ma'am" was what she said instead.

Esther turned. Superintendent O'Halloran was standing at the door to the DS office, lips pursed, frowning as she took in the scene. Jared was hovering behind her. When he looked at Esther, he frowned too. Quickly, Esther pulled the witch's hat from her head and set the broomstick down in a corner.

"Will you two excuse us for a few minutes, please?" O'Halloran said to Caroline and Spencer.

It wasn't really a request, coming from a superintendent, and both DS's quickly complied with mumbled "yes, ma'am"s as they got up and hurried out.

"Close that door, Jared, will you?" O'Halloran said after they'd left.

Jared did as he was told, and then it was just the three of them. Jared had a newspaper folded under one arm; the superintendent must have interrupted his morning review of the day's horse races.

"Ma'am, I wanted to apologise," Esther began, "about the other night, the dinner—"

The superintendent waved the apology away. "Forget about that, Esther. Family before work." *Family?* Esther glanced at Jared, whose face was suspiciously blank. "I hoped it might help," O'Halloran went on, not noticing the look, "but your strength lies more in the fact that you are a practical copper. A doer, not a bullshitter. Our upper ranks are full of bullshitters. Myself included."

Esther must have looked surprised by the remark, because the superintendent gave her a wry smile as she took one of the visitor seats by the wall.

"I'm good at bullshit," she explained. "Doesn't mean I have to like it. Or start believing it, the way too many do." She flapped her hands. "Oh, do sit down, the pair of you, you're making me nervous. And relax. We have a problem, but all problems come with solutions." She gave a dry chuckle. "If I was doing a promotion board, I might say all problems come with an opportunity to find solutions and, in the process, grow and develop an understanding of our own resources and capabilities, as well as discover useful ways we can liaise with partner agencies and key community stakeholders." She looked at Esther. "Fifty words where half a dozen would do, but that's the kind of thing they like to hear at boards. We'll do some one-on-one, if you want, Esther. I'll give you a few pointers. Might give you an edge. You'll need to inject a little bit of bullshit to score."

"Yes, ma'am," Esther replied as she found her seat. Jared took one of the other visitor's chairs. Much as Esther hated that crap, a few mentoring sessions from Superintendent O'Halloran definitely sounded more manageable than an evening with a bunch of stuffy old egos in dinner jackets.

"I want to see you get this promotion, Esther," the superintendent said, a touch more sternly. "The top team needs people like you. Not the windbags and self-serving preeners we seem to be getting more and more of lately. And we need more women. I make no apologies about saying that. We need more women and more diversity. I want you to succeed."

"Yes, ma'am," Esther said in a small voice. She suddenly felt like a schoolgirl who'd been dragged into the headmistress's office.

"Which is why I want to help you deal with this little mess," she said, indicating the witch's hat and broomstick.

Esther frowned. "Ma'am?"

O'Halloran hesitated. "You've not seen the papers?" She turned to Jared.

With a grimace, Jared passed the tabloid he was holding to Esther.

It was today's copy of the *Belfield Star*. Unfolding it, Esther saw that most of the front page was taken up by a kind of Blair Witch poster mock-up. The headline emblazoned across the bottom read:

SATANIC MURDER!
BELFIELD POLICE INVESTIGATE
WITCHCRAFT LINKS TO NORWICK
FOREST SLAYING

Heart sinking, Esther scanned the first couple of paragraphs, unsurprised to see Bob Chase's name on the byline, with his smarmy mug next to it.

> *Cops investigating the slaying of a woman whose body was found in the Norwick Forest on Saturday are looking into the possibility it was a ritual Satanic murder, the* Belfield Star *has learned. Detectives are trying to stay one step ahead of the cult... by recruiting a witch of their own!* Cont'd on page 5.

The newspaper rustled noisily as Esther turned to page five. She was shocked to see an image of herself scowling back at her. It was a small photograph, an inset among a half-page that was full of very few *actual* column inches and a hell of a lot of graphics stolen from a variety of famous horror movies. Scanning the article, Esther decided against protesting that she'd not given any comment. It was abundantly clear that she hadn't – the article repeatedly stating that police had refused to comment, twisting it to make it sound like they were hiding something. Esther felt her cheeks growing warm as she read the piece.

"That fucker Chase ambushed me," she exclaimed. "Didn't tell the enquiry office assistant he was press."

O'Halloran shook her head. "It doesn't matter. Chase

likes to stir things up. You're never going to get someone like him onside. It's just unfortunate that he has this little morsel to work with. I got you that invitation for the event at the weekend in the hope that people would get to know you, to recognise your name. What we don't need is them recognising your name for the wrong reasons. It's not the end of the world, though. We can fix this. First of all, I need to know about this witch. I'm not suggesting you've recruited a witch, but Chase is working off something. What is it?"

Esther took a deep breath and told the superintendent about Thelma Faye. While she was at it, she briefed her up on both the murder investigation and the misper enquiry. When she was finished, O'Halloran seemed satisfied.

"Okay," she said. "Our next step will be to get some of the media on our side. The press office has already had a few outlets looking for a comment on this piece"—she indicated the newspaper in Esther's hands—"but I've managed to put them off for the moment. It wasn't too difficult, it being the *Star* – thankfully, there are not very many people who take that rag seriously – but we'll need to get something out to turn this around. Here." She plucked a worn business card from her pocket and passed it to Esther.

DAMIEN WESTMAN
Crime Editor
Belfield Examiner

"Damien and I go back a long way," O'Halloran said. "He's pro-police, unlike most of them, and he's already asked for a comment. I've put him off, told him I'd get back to him later. I want you to contact him. Tell him I gave you his name. But keep this contact close. Keep it quiet. Feed him information before the press office tells the other papers – above-board, shareable information, obviously." She said that in a tone that suggested this qualification was subjective. "But he'll be a sympathetic ear. Or at least, more sympathetic than most. Certainly more sympathetic than the *Star*."

Esther frowned, fingering the frayed edges of the card as she studied the name. This definitely felt like activity above her pay grade.

O'Halloran seemed to sense what she was thinking. "You are the right woman for the next DI spot, Esther. I'm quite convinced of that. Not just because we need more women in the ranks, not just because we need more diversity"—there was no inflection in that statement, but it didn't stop Esther wondering whether Calvin Brett's accusations were doing the rounds, and wondering what O'Halloran had heard—"but because you're *you*. You're sharp, you're dedicated, and you're straight down the line. We need that. This is the kind of thing you need to get a handle on now. The press, the media, the politicians. It all creeps in quite quickly at inspector rank. You need to be able to convince people you can handle it. So. What's the plan going forward?"

"We'll hold a press conference with Mila's parents this afternoon," Esther replied. "Get her face out into the public arena, a spot on the evening news. I think five days missing warrants a full national appeal. Apart from that, we continue to work the lines of enquiry. We're expanding the search in the Norwick Hills, alerts are out to all forces, and I have my team working every lead on the Wilde girl, as well as Mila Rose. We're regularly cross-referencing the findings." Esther leaned forward. "These cases are linked, ma'am. I'm sure of it. A break in one, and we'll have a break in both."

O'Halloran nodded and stood. Esther and Jared followed suit.

"Okay then," she said. "Work your leads. Speak with Barbara in the press office – she'll manage the press conference for you." She turned to Jared. "Esther should take the lead with that."

Jared nodded. "Yes, ma'am. I'll leave the TV cameras to you ladies. No one needs to see my ugly mug on the telly while they're having their tea."

O'Halloran turned to Esther. "Do you think the girl is still alive?"

"I do," Esther replied without hesitating.

The superintendent studied her for a moment, then nodded. She glanced once more at the hat and broomstick. "Just keep your head in the game, Esther. Ring Damien. Get him on your side to start with."

Esther nodded. "Ma'am."

With that, O'Halloran opened the door and left. The murmur outside abated as the superintendent swept through the room. Esther caught more than one pair of eyes glancing towards her and Jared.

"Well, that went better than expected," Jared mumbled, as he crossed to her desk and lifted the witch's hat. He rubbed the felt brim between thumb and forefinger, as if admiring the quality. "Brett?" he asked.

Esther shrugged. "I assume so."

"He's a cheeky little git."

"It is actually kind of funny," Esther conceded. "And

here's me thinking Calvin had no sense of humour."

Jared set the hat down again.

"You really think she's alive?" he asked quietly. Too quietly to be heard by anyone in the detectives' workroom.

Esther nodded. Since seeing the CCTV pictures Derek Grant had found, it was more than wishful thinking.

"I do," she said.

And she *did*. What she didn't know was whether Mila was a suspect or another potential victim. And if she was the latter, how much time the girl had left…

21

Tabitha Renshaw lived in a modest bungalow on the western edge of Belfield, out beyond the industrial estates and a stone's throw from the city limits.

"Excuse the mess, officers," she said, as she bustled into the living room with a tray. She was short and skinny, with hair dyed midnight black and wide, pink-rimmed glasses hanging from a gold chain around her neck.

Esther glanced about at the spotless living room. Nothing was out of place. It was clear that the carpet had been freshly vacuumed, and a hint of lemon polish hung in the air.

Their hostess set the tray down on a gleaming glass coffee table and poured three cups of tea, asking whether anyone wanted milk or sugar.

"One sugar for me," said Craig, and added "ta" as he reached out and took the proffered cup.

"Just a small drop of milk," Esther replied.

"There's some biscuits, too," Tabitha added, nudging

the plate of assorted cookies towards the two detectives as she sat back in her armchair across from where Craig and Esther shared the sofa. "Help yourselves."

Esther smiled her thanks, but left the biscuits alone. Craig reached forward and plucked three shortbread fingers from the plate.

"So," Esther said, "Mila Rose. You worked at the children's home when she was a resident there?"

Tabitha nodded. "Rimkus, she was called back then. Mila Rimkus. Little dote. Lovely and polite. But very quiet. Oh yes. Quiet as a lamb when she first arrived. I knew, straight away, that Hodderston Road wasn't the place for her." Her lips compressed in a tight line, and she frowned. "There are plenty of children's homes about the county, and most are like Hodderston Road. More bad kids in 'em than good. Which means the good kids have very little chance. Turn to the dark side themselves, or get picked on mercilessly. Not much of a choice. I felt a... I don't know... an *instinct* to protect Mila, as soon as she arrived. There was something about her. She'd been through so much already. You're aware of her background?"

Esther and Craig both nodded.

"Well, she'd had it tough up to then, that's for sure," Tabitha went on, "and I was pretty certain being at Hodderston Road wasn't going to make things any better for her. I'd been working there, on and off, for over ten years, so I knew the place, and I knew the kids. Believe me. The names and faces might change, but the personalities and attitudes don't."

"How long was Mila at the home?" Esther asked.

"Not all that long, in the end, thankfully," Tabitha replied. "I made sure of that."

"Can you tell us what you remember about her?" Esther asked. "Or anyone she was particularly close with while she stayed there?"

Craig, having devoured his biscuits and drunk half his tea, had his notebook and pen at the ready now. Esther would have preferred him to be a bit more circumspect in getting it out, but Tabitha seemed hardly to notice; her eyes were already misting over with memory, and she was more than willing to talk.

She spoke again about how quiet a girl Mila was when she first arrived. Well-behaved and well-mannered, Tabitha had grown concerned about bullying. The kids in that place were a tough bunch from bad backgrounds, angry and vicious for the most part. Foreign children were usually the most vulnerable in that environment, and Tabitha had taken a special interest in Mila from the start. Despite the turbulence of her early years, Mila had presented as calm and stable, applying herself at school and staying out of trouble. She quickly became fluent in English, eventually losing the slight American twang she'd adopted from watching U.S. TV shows and American YouTube channels. Yes, she'd been picked on, as most foreign kids were, but Tabitha had done her best to protect her from the worst of it.

And then a new girl had arrived at Hodderston Road – an older girl, a teenager called Anita Jess.

"Anita?" Esther asked, sitting forward as a memory flashed into her head. *Anita! 44 D.*

"Anita Jess," Tabitha repeated. "A very troubled girl with a string of convictions for drug possession and larceny. Slight and skinny she was, but alley cats are slight and skinny too, and Anita was as wild and vicious as any alley cat."

Anita Jess seemed to have no interest in following the rules or going to school, according to Tabitha. She did her own thing. And with laws and policies being what they were, the social workers weren't much able to intervene.

And when Anita took a shine to Mila, two things happened. The first was that Mila stopped getting bullied; the other children at the home either left her alone or gave her a wide berth. The second was that she started to get into trouble...

"What sort of trouble?" Craig asked.

"Nothing serious. Playing hooky. Smoking a bit of weed. That sort of thing. Nothing that involved the police, thankfully. It was all dealt with in-house. The most serious thing was the disappearances."

"Disappearances?" Esther asked.

"Mila and Anita started going missing all the time. Sometimes just the two of them, sometimes with other kids. Sometimes overnight. That's not something that would normally cause any alarm for us – the staff, I mean – but it alarmed me, because I could see what was happening to Mila. She was turning into one of them. One of the bad ones. It broke my heart."

"Where did they go when they went missing?" Esther asked. "Mila and this Anita girl?"

"Took a while for us to figure that out," Tabitha replied, "but once we did, we found them at that same spot every time afterwards. They used to take themselves off up the hills, to a spot overlooking a part of the old quarry. Sometimes it was a whole group of them. Sometimes it was just Anita and Mila. Drinking alcopops and smoking."

"Drugs?" Craig asked, unnecessarily. The rookie detective would eventually learn which questions were important and which ones weren't, but Esther let it slide.

Tabitha nodded. "Now and again. Just cannabis, as far as I know. But it wasn't that so much as the general behaviour that had me worried for Mila. It was a blessing when Anita got caught shoplifting – without Mila in tow for once, thank God – and that was her. Fifteen years old or not, with her criminal record, she was off to a youth detention centre for three months to get through about half a dozen suspended sentences.

"But I knew that was only one problem solved, and maybe not for long. Sooner or later, Anita would come back. And if not her, then there would be others. Other Anitas. Mila didn't stand a chance in that system. That polite, sweet little girl was going to be corrupted by the worst our local authority kids' homes had to offer." She looked at Craig and gave him a grim half-smile. "You're surprised to hear me say that?" A glance at Esther. "He's not long in, is he?"

Esther shook her head.

"Spend enough time working in these places and you'll soon realise hope is in pretty short supply," Tabitha told Craig with a sigh. "But I still had hope. Back then. For Mila.

"So I did something I'd never done before in my thirty years as a social worker. I let myself get personally involved."

Tabitha went on to explain how she'd grown to know Pastor Timothy Rose and his wife Vera, having met Timothy through all his work with struggling teens.

"The pastor seemed to have no end of patience with those kids, always organising things with the local authority through his church, trying to get them off the road to ruin, as he saw it. Five-a-side footie tournaments, go-karting, hiking. You name it."

And as Tabitha grew closer to Vera, she learned about their struggle to have children, and she became convinced that she could persuade them to consider Mila. Timothy had a good heart, someone who always wanted to do something when he saw suffering in others, and Vera, although she was thinking about a baby or a younger child, might come around too.

She pitched the idea of adopting Mila to them. She didn't hold back either. The couple had known Tabitha for a few years by that time. They were aware of how long she'd worked with the social services. When Tabitha predicted what would happen to this polite and dutiful young Lithuanian orphan without intervention, they understood she wasn't exaggerating.

At first, Timothy and his church workers simply invited Mila and a few of the better-behaved children to take part in extra events, sports days and family events for the congregation. They were exactly the kinds of things Anita would have sneered at. But with Anita's bad influence removed, Mila was already beginning to revert to her old self. Tabitha sensed she had this window of opportunity, a brief chance for Mila, before Anita returned or some other wayward teen took her under their wing.

It worked. With Anita out of the picture, Mila really hit it off with the Roses and many of the church-going kids her own age. She began taking more of a role in the pastor's church activities too. It didn't take long for Tim and Vera to fall in love with her.

On her twelfth birthday, the pastor and his wife threw a birthday party for her in the church hall. That evening, they sat her down and asked her if she would like to become part of their family. Mila had been so happy she'd cried. They all had.

With Tabitha working on the inside, and Mila effectively parentless, things had fallen into place more quickly than usual, even with all the bureaucracy.

"I remember the smile on her little face when she packed her bag that last day at Hodderston Road," Tabitha said wistfully, eyes moist. "We threw her a small party. Just the staff really. There weren't too many of the kids who could be bothered to come down to the kitchen for it. But I was delighted for her." She wiped her eyes, apologising as she fished a tissue from her pocket and blew her nose loudly. "I do hope she's okay."

"We're doing all we can to find her," Esther replied automatically. "The vast majority of missing teens show up safe and well."

Tabitha laughed a mirthless laugh. "I know, but this is different, isn't it, Officer? The statistics might say so, but most missing teens are just out gallivanting for a night or two. Out drinking or partying."

"Maybe Mila is too," Craig offered helpfully.

Tabitha looked at him for a long moment. "Maybe," she said quietly, but she didn't sound as if she meant it.

"It would be really helpful if you could give us some more details about this Anita Jess girl," Esther said.

Tabitha sighed. "She'd be, what, twenty or so, now?" She shook her head. "I can't add much more to what I've said. The department will have a record of her date of birth and, I don't know, you might be able to track her down on your own systems then. I have no doubt she'll have had dealings with police many times over the last five years. But

I don't think she ever made contact with Mila after that stint at Hodderston Road. Though, to be honest, I retired shortly after that and haven't stayed in touch."

"Do you think you could show me where that spot overlooking the quarry was?" Esther asked, as she pulled her phone from her pocket. "The place they disappeared to together? On a map of the area?"

"I think so," Tabitha replied, unfolding her pink eyeglasses.

Esther brought up a map of northern Belfield and the Norwick Hills, then went over and knelt next to Tabitha, who studied the area, using her fingertips to zoom in here and there until she pointed to a spot on the edge of the disused quarry complex.

"Here," she said. "There's a clearing on the clifftop there. It was hard to get to in a car, if I remember rightly, but not impossible. There's an overgrown track goes all the way up. A long uphill walk on foot, and once we knew they were heading up there all the time, it fell out of favour with a lot of the kids. It's quite a hike out of town." She frowned. "Not Anita and Mila, though. They were found there every time."

Esther looked at the satellite image. The spot Tabitha had pointed out wasn't anywhere near either the CCTV sighting or the place where Mila's phone had pinged on Friday night. And it was miles from Taylor's search operation. It might turn out to be nothing – a link to an old haunt Mila hadn't been to in five years or more – but Esther felt a surge of excitement at having a fresh lead.

Craig took a few more details about Anita, along with whatever rough dates and times Tabitha could remember in relation to Mila's disappearances with the girl, and then

Esther thanked the woman for her time.

"Please find her," Tabitha said, as she saw them to the door. "That girl was one of the good ones."

Esther nodded. "We'll find her."

She was saying that a lot to people, she realised.

22

MILA RAN HER thumb across the pentacle tattoo on her wrist. She'd had to hide it from Tim and Vera in the days before she'd left, in those days when the call to adventure was still a bright hope, a possibility, an opportunity she'd been savouring. She found it odd that this tattoo reminded her of the only other tattoo she'd ever worn. It hadn't been a real tattoo, just one of those coloured stamps that came in children's party bags along with a bunch of other gimmicky toys and sweets. She'd picked it up at one of Tim's church fetes, so the bag had been largely Jesus-themed. By pressing the stamp onto the inkpad that came with it and then onto the back of her hand, she'd donned an image of a heart with a crucifix in the centre and the words 'Jesus Loves Me' in curly script beneath. She'd worn it proudly for a day and a half before it had washed off completely. Then she'd forgotten about it, lost it somewhere among the bric-a-brac in her room.

When she'd first started hanging out with the Roses, Tim

had seemed so cool. Well, maybe not *cool*. Entertaining was probably a better word. All the church functions. All his games and activity days. He'd been so interesting. He'd made Mila feel special. At some point along the way, he'd changed. Or was it her who'd changed?

Everything had seemed so clear and obvious when she'd left.

It didn't seem so clear and obvious anymore.

She was beginning to realise just how different Anita had become since their time together at Hodderston Road. It had been a horrible place, that kid's home. At the start, the other children had mocked her accent and made fun of her struggle to string proper sentences together in English. Most of the boys had been okay, but some of the girls had been really nasty; Mila had survived more than one physical attack, often lucky to get away with only a few claw marks and some missing strands of hair. She'd hated it there. She remembered how lost she'd been, clinging to tiny life raft, like her teacher at school — Mrs Waltham at Hodderston Road Primary had been so sweet to her — and the social workers, especially Tabitha.

But when Anita Jess arrived at Hodderston Road, everything had changed. She was unlike anyone Mila had ever met before. Or since. It was as if they had a connection straight away. Anita had said she sensed it too, like they were estranged sisters or something. They'd laughed at that — they looked so different — but Mila had clung to the idea. She'd never had a sibling, and Anita was like an older sister from a fairy tale, more than happy to beat the shit out of anyone who tried to hassle either of them. The bullying stopped, and Mila found her first real friend in years.

The adults hadn't been as happy about their friendship at the time. Sure, Anita was a few years older than her, and it was true that she didn't like school all that much – they'd skipped out on class together a few times – but Mila's days playing hooky with Anita had been so much fun. Different and exciting. Anita had a way of making walls dissolve, of coming up with fantastical futures that made the grey place where they lived seem a little less shitty. She used to talk about the two of them flying away somewhere. *Let's fly away, Mila,* she used to say. *Fly away together, like birds.* And that's what Mila had wanted to do, back when she'd lived in the kids' home, and again over the last few months.

Anita might still be electrifying and full of energy just like Mila remembered, but there was a sadness that ran through her friend's sunny demeanour like a fracture now. Even when Anita was in a good mood – which wasn't always, and her dark moods were *stormy* – there was something a little broken in her smile. She'd always been a bit temperamental – quick to explode at anyone who pissed her off – but these days she literally snapped at any little thing.

Like the other day, when she'd flown off the handle after Mila stumbled across that photograph. She'd found it in the bedroom that was always closed, the one Anita said was out of bounds because it hadn't had a ritual 'cleansing' yet. Anita was as obsessed with ridding the commune of bad energy as Jason was with clearing the air of electromagnetic waves; there were sticks of incense and odd-smelling candles burning in most rooms morning, noon and night. So, when Mila spotted the bedroom door ajar, yeah, she'd been a little curious…

Her old friend was so evasive when it came to talking

about her great-uncle, or her family generally. At first, Mila had simply ignored this. Families were messed up; she understood that more than most kids her age, and she thought maybe Anita felt the same. Mila knew Anita had spent her childhood moving from one care home to another – not to mention her trips to juvie – and this guy here hadn't reached out to help. Perhaps she still resented him, even though he'd left her a house. A *literal house!*

The room itself had smelled stuffy, the heavy netting on the windows giving the place a retro gloom. It was clearly an old man's bedroom, untouched in his absence, with hints of the longer-departed wife still about the place. Mila wouldn't have stayed – she would have left straight away and pulled the door closed behind her – if it wasn't for the box of framed photographs sitting on the old four-poster bed. She'd picked some out. A lot of them were of the same auburn-bearded man – she guessed it must be Anita's great-uncle – but many more were family photos, taken in the scrubby yard at the front of the cottage. The bearded man was in all of them, changing only a little – the photos seemed to span his middle years – and in most of them he was standing next to a kind-faced woman with grey curls stacked on her head. But what struck Mila as odd were the kids, usually five or six at a time in each picture; they were always different. Well, not always. A few of them popped up in multiple photos, looking sometimes a little older, sometimes younger. But mostly they were different children.

Mila had cut herself on one of the frames. She'd pulled the thing out, glass tinkling to the bottom of the box as she'd done so, and that was when she'd realised that the picture – another group of kids with the smiling couple out in the front yard – contained someone she knew. It was Anita, standing at the end of the row, scowling at the camera. She looked young – years younger than she'd been when Mila had first met her at Hodderston Road. The frame's glass was completely smashed, spiderwebbing out from the centre of the photograph so that most of the rest of the faces were obscured. Mila had decided then and there that she would ask Anita about her uncle and all the kids whenever her friend was in a receptive mood, but at that very moment Anita had appeared, and she'd totally *freaked*. Literally *screamed* at Mila to get out. Mila had been scared. Bigtime. Anita hadn't hurt her, or even touched her, but the way she'd reacted… Mila had run from the cottage and into the forest to get over the shock of Anita's reaction.

It had taken her half an hour to muster the courage to go back. She'd been expecting some kind of lecture when she'd eventually returned, but Anita acted as if nothing had happened. And Mila hadn't been able to make herself bring it up since.

She was trying to remember Anita as she'd been during their Hodderston Road days, recalling their blood pact, when they'd cut the tips of their pinkie fingers with Anita's penknife and pressed them together, swearing allegiance. They'd done it one night at sunset out at their favourite spot, under the huge oak tree overlooking the old quarry. They'd carved their initials into that tree with the same penknife; Anita had insisted they do it properly, spending an hour or more digging *AJ + MR 4EVER* so deep into the bark it would be visible for generations.

Anita really had been like a real-life big sister back then – or how Mila imagined a real-life big sister ought to be – protecting Mila and making her feel good about herself for the first time in she didn't know how long. Maybe ever.

These past few months, Mila had wanted that again, that sense of being special, of feeling good about herself.

Instead, she was starting to feel isolated. Being held captive in the House of Pastor Holier-Than-Thou might have been driving her crazy, but this brand of freedom was just as stifling. They'd dumped the radio and television and burned all their mobiles, destroying everything with a signal. The outside world had vanished from Mila's life, and it felt weird. Not good-weird, like Jason said it would. But he kept insisting it was essential. They needed to keep their new community safe from interference. Mobile phones and television sets, AI and the internet: they were all part of a multinational governmental plot to control humanity around the globe. The Chinese and the Americans, they pretended to be against each other, but really, they were in cahoots. Part of a conspiracy that went back decades, back to some American president called Nixon who'd brought the Chinese Communist Party into it all. That's what Jason said.

Jason's ramblings about Satanism had seemed interesting at the start. About how it wasn't devil-worshipping but rather an attitude, an ability to say no to authority and hierarchy and all the rules that powerful people made, rules designed to keep everyone else in the dirt. It had contradicted everything Tim had been shoving down her throat for so long, and promised something she'd been craving. Freedom. Independence.

But the more she heard Jason talk, the more he reminded her of Tim. Full of self-righteousness. It was simply a different type of dogma. His lectures about global plots and government control were as bad as the pastor's fixation on

Scriptures and the Psalms. And to be honest, a lot of it was starting to sound a little daft.

Mila couldn't help get the sense that all she'd done was move from one cage to another, an endless swamp of bullshit, only the foul aromas changing, the sucking mud as clingy in one as the next.

Maybe Katie had realised the same thing.

Mila shivered as she recalled the night at the cabin in the woods. Her first ritual. She glanced down at the gauze around her left hand. She'd barely cut herself that night – just enough to add some blood – but it had stung, especially afterwards when Anita had applied her poultice of honey and herbs.

The whole thing would have been pretty surreal even without the stuff Jason had put in the tea – stuff that had made Mila's head swim and eventually caused her to pass out. He'd got her to burn her uniform and mobile phone as part of the ritual. They were 'bonds of slavery', apparently, and ridding herself of them would help liberate her from the shackles of modern life. A step on the path to real freedom.

He'd told her to strip naked too, like the rest of them. Sure, they'd draped some wool robes around themselves, but Jason hadn't been too worried about keeping his robe closed. She thought about him trying to engage her in conversation after they'd set fire to everything. She could hardly remember the words, she'd been so focused on not looking at the thing hanging inches from her face.

It wasn't like she'd never seen a man's dick before. She'd seen porn on the internet. But it was very different when it was there, in front of you, in the literal friggin' flesh. She could tell that Jason was proud of his dick, or wanted her to look at it anyway, the way he'd stood there, pretending to be all chill, talking crap. It was a big dick, in fairness. But Mila had not wanted to look at it directly. She kept glancing at Katie, who was pirouetting and gyrating around the fire, her own robe cast aside like it wasn't zero friggin' degrees or something. And Anita, who was staring over at Jason and Mila with a stony look on her face. Mila had felt really, *really* uncomfortable right at that moment. If it hadn't been for the fact that Katie was off her face and clearly trying to get some attention – Jason's attention – the situation would have been totally unbearable.

Mila had actually been relieved when Anita told them it was time to start the ritual. By then, she could feel the tea working. Soon the trees were swirling and dancing like Katie, adding their own rhythm and hum to Jason's weird incantations. It hadn't been English, whatever gibberish he'd been mumbling.

Try as she might, Mila couldn't recall very much from that night. The stuff in Jason's tea had knocked her clean out after an hour, and she'd woken up in her bed at the cottage the next morning, with the sun well above the horizon and a headache strong enough to bring tears to her eyes. She figured Anita must have wrapped her in the blanket – this house had no central heating or electricity, those being more shackles of modernity – at least, she hoped it had been Anita. The thought of Jason carrying her around naked brought back that image of him standing next to the campfire, swinging about in front of her face. She shook her head to clear the picture from her mind.

But some thoughts wouldn't go away with a shake of the head. Like the thought that maybe Anita and Jason were even more controlling than the Roses. Like how it was weird that Anita always seemed to know where Mila was, how she always seemed to just *be there*, watching her at unexpected moments. And destroying all their phones and shit? Mila wasn't sure about that at all. It had seemed like a good idea when she'd been hammered, freeing her brain from the slavery of the internet. But now that she was sober, Mila simply felt more isolated still.

And yet, where could she go now? Run away again? Slink home to Tim and Vera? No. Tim would believe he'd scored a point on her. Jesus: One; Mila: Nil. No thanks!

She reminded herself that if she wanted to, she could just walk away. Literally just walk down the lane to the main road and hitch a lift or something. They were isolated out here, sure, especially with no phones or internet, but it wasn't like she was chained to a wall or anything.

She was free to leave whenever she wanted.

She realised she was rubbing at the pentacle on her wrist quite hard now and stopped. Crude and homemade it might have been, but it was real. It would take more than a bit of rubbing, more than soap and water, to get rid of this one.

No, this tattoo wouldn't come off as easily as a coloured stamp.

23

ESTHER RECOGNISED DAMIEN Westman from the tiny portraits that sat next to his bylines in the *Belfield Examiner*. He was sitting exactly where he'd said he would be, at the back of the coffeehouse in a nook lined with old books and pictures of Belfield in the early 1900s. He had a laptop open in front of him and was typing rapidly as Esther approached. When she sat down across from him, he glanced up and closed the laptop.

Westman was a good-looking guy, with sharp features, a mop of curly brown hair that hung over his forehead on one side, and striking brown eyes that peered out at her from behind thin-rimmed glasses. Mid-thirties, Esther guessed.

"DS Penman," he said. "Welcome to my office."

Esther quirked an eyebrow and looked around.

"Well, my *other* office," he said with a small smile. "I get more done here than in the *Examiner*'s noisy journalist pen. So. What have you got for me?"

"You want to do a story about the body in Norwick

Forest, and the missing teenager?"

Westman leaned in. "They *are* linked, then?"

Esther had to struggle against her better instincts to keep talking, but Superintendent O'Halloran trusted this man, so she would give him the benefit of the doubt; the superintendent had always struck Esther as a fairly prudent operator.

"The link between the cases isn't confirmed," she told Westman, "but the evidence points that way. We have telecoms geolocation that puts Mila Rose's phone in the area where Katie Wilde's body was found, in and around the time she was killed."

Westman was old school. Despite the laptop, he had produced a reporter's notebook and was jotting quickly as Esther spoke. She glanced uneasily at the notepad but forced herself to continue.

"We also found a cabin. There were... symbols daubed on the walls and chalked on the floor. Pentacles."

Westman stopped and looked at her over the tops of his glasses.

"Are you saying there *is* an occult aspect to this story?"

"We might have occult symbols," Esther replied, "but what we do *not* have is witches working on the case, or any confirmation there's a serial killer – Satanic or otherwise – on the loose. One dead body. One missing teenager, seen alive and apparently well three days ago. That's what we have."

"But we have symbols and pentacles," Westman insisted.

Esther took a deep breath and began working through their discoveries, though she did her best not to stray too far from the line of information they'd be releasing at the press conference later. She talked him through what they'd found at the cabin, the broken and burned mobile phones, the state of Katie Wilde's body, the stab wounds. She even sketched some of the symbols into his notebook for him. She provided the basics from the autopsy, although she left out the details of the toxicology report. Westman was a little disappointed that she hadn't brought any photographs along – just to give him an idea, he added hastily, not to print or anything – but providing him with physical pieces of evidence would have been a step too far for Esther, whatever O'Halloran thought of the man.

When she finished speaking, Westman seemed satisfied. He sat for a long moment, considering his notes.

"It's a good story, this," he mumbled.

"This is real, Mister Westman," Esther replied coldly. "It's not a story. There's a missing girl, and a murder victim. These are real people. The Roses are beside themselves with worry. It's a serious situation, and what your colleagues have done is make a joke out of it."

Westman grimaced.

"Ben Chase is a rival, not a colleague, Esther," he replied. "If I can bring him down a peg or two it will be my great pleasure to do so. But I'm not about point-scoring," he added hastily, and had the decency to look a touch embarrassed as he said, "I'll give it a serious tone."

Esther nodded, trying to hide her uncertainty. This manoeuvring and media management was way out of her comfort zone, but something she was going to have to get used to if she got the DI post.

"The press conference with the Roses will be at three p.m.," she told Westman as she stood to leave. She gestured towards his notebook. "You have more there than we'll be revealing later. Please use the information responsibly."

Westman sat back and studied her for a moment. At length, he nodded.

"I appreciate it, Esther." He gave her a lopsided smile. "The *Examiner* is not the *Star*. We try to do at least a little bit of proper journalism."

Esther gave him a quick nod in response, still not entirely comfortable with the whole situation, then turned and left. The die was cast, she thought, as she stepped out of the coffeehouse, and there was no point in her worrying about it now.

* * *

Mila knocked timidly on the bedroom door. It was already ajar, and when she pushed it wider, she found Jason lying on the bed, one arm behind his head, holding a battered paperback open in front of him. He was always reading the same book these days – Nietzsche's *Beyond Good and Evil* – but he didn't seem to be making much progress on it.

"Sorry," Mila said, about to turn away, but Jason sat up quickly and scooted to the end of the bed, the wooden beads he wore on his wrists clicking as he moved.

"No, Mila, don't go," he said. "I was just thinking about you. Come here, sit down. Chat with me for a minute."

Like Anita, he was big into natural stuff, but his pale linen shirt and trousers were creased and overworn. He had a pair of old leather sandals that he wore outside sometimes, but he usually went barefoot.

"Anita was looking for me," Mila replied in a quiet voice.

She wished she sounded more confident. More like Anita. Her quiet voice made her sound like a little girl.

"Anita can hang on for a minute," Jason insisted with a smile, setting his book down and patting the bed next to him. Mila felt drawn, like his blue eyes had some kind of magnetic pull. She found herself sitting next to him on the bed without quite knowing how she'd got there. She forced herself to sit calmly and not flinch as he reached out and touched her hair, tugging a lock of it between forefinger and thumb. "I like what Anita did with your hair. Makes you look older."

Mila felt the blood rush to her cheeks. She couldn't think of anything to say. She hoped Jason didn't notice her trembling.

"You're not too lonely here, are you?" he asked. "I know our little commune has shrunk a bit since you joined, but there'll be others. You'll have more sisters again soon."

She glanced sideways at him. He was smiling through his patchy beard. For some reason, she found herself staring fixedly at his gleaming canines. She could see how some women might find that smile kind of sexy.

"You know it's the witches in a coven who are in charge, right?" he said, still smiling wolfishly. "Not the guys. It's a Mother Nature thing. Women in charge. I'm just your slave. And Anita's. And any other sisters who want to join. If they do the ritual, obviously." He had leaned in slowly, pushing her hair away from her neck. Mila thought he was breathing her in. His voice became low, intimate. "If you're lonely you can tell me. You don't always need to go to Anita. And you'll have more sisters soon."

Mila could feel his breath on her neck. Glancing down, she could see a bulge rising inside his left thigh, could literally see his huge erection pushing against the loose linen. She tried to slide away, but he had his arm around her waist now and she couldn't move.

"This is an open community," he was murmuring. "You're as much in charge as Anita is. This community is yours equally. We're all equal here."

"I don't think Anita would like this," Mila heard herself squeak, angry at herself for sounding stupid, but too alarmed to get more of a grip. Sure, she'd considered what screwing Jason might be like, but the fantasy had never really taken off. She'd had crushes, thought about other boys, but with Jason it just felt... *off*. Around him, she felt even less ready to lose her virginity than usual, and she knew she didn't want this now.

Jason seemed oblivious to her rising distress. He chuckled.

"Anita's cool," he said. "She understands. This commune was her idea as well. She gets it. We all share our love here. We love each other. It's all open. We do what we feel, what our bodies tell us we want. We listen to that inner instinct, the power in all of us. You have a power in you, Mila, I can sense it. You just need to tap into it. You'll be a powerful woman. I can help you tap into that power. Help you open up, let go, get in touch with your inner—"

The sound of a creaking floorboard cut him off. Anita was standing in the doorway. Jason's arm was suddenly gone from Mila's waist, and he seemed to have magically put a couple of inches between them in an instant.

"Hey, babe," he said, smiling at her. He reached back and picked up his Nietzsche again. "I was just telling Mila about how she'll have more sisters again soon. This is going to be a revolutionary group, am I right?"

Anita's smile was brittle, and as she glanced from Jason to Mila and back, Mila could see that the smile never touched her eyes.

"Of course," she replied woodenly. "We're just the start." She turned to Mila. "I called for you."

Mila, her cheeks burning like they were on fire, stood shakily. She could hardly meet Anita's eyes. "Yeah, I was just… I…"

Anita thrust a small canvas tote bag towards her. "Those mushrooms I showed you the other day. You remember? I need you to go into the forest and collect more for tonight's dinner. You think you'll recognise them by yourself?"

Mila, eager to please, nodded quickly. "Yeah. Definitely. How many do you want me to collect?"

Anita seemed to consider this for a moment. She glanced at Jason again. "Try and fill the bag, if you can."

Mila took the bag hesitantly. It suddenly looked a lot bigger. It would take her hours to find enough mushrooms to fill it. But she didn't argue, just gave Anita another nod and hurried out of the room.

24

PC IMELDA FISHER pulled over and checked the address again, just to be sure she had it right. *44 Denton Lane.* Something about it tickled her memory, but she couldn't quite figure out what.

She stared across the road at the entrance to the little track as a string of cars came around the bend at speed, every one of them braking hard when they caught sight of her marked patrol car. Denton Lane itself was exactly that: a lane. There were no road signs or markings on the tarmac. Wide enough for only one car at a time, it curled away among wild hedgerows, a tuft of grass running along its centre. According to her maps, the plot for 44 would be about a mile down that track.

Another couple of cars came racing around the bend, the SUV in front braking so hard at the sight of her that the Mini behind almost collided with it. She sighed. She was going to cause an accident if she sat here any longer. She put the patrol car into gear, flicked the indicator switch and turned onto Denton Lane, hoping as she did so that she didn't meet a tractor coming the other way.

The road was pitted and potholed, and getting above fifteen miles an hour was difficult. There were gravelly laybys at intervals to allow traffic to pass safely, but she didn't meet any tractors. In fact, she didn't meet any other vehicles at all, or see anyone. Every now and again, the overgrown hedges on either side parted to reveal fields or the odd boarded-up bungalow. If the derelict houses were anything to go by, the population of Denton Lane had abandoned it some time ago.

A quarter of a mile in, the cattle gates overlooking the long fields of churned-up mud were replaced by trees. This trail was on the very edge of Belfield's policing district, well beyond the suburbs, and the verges of the Norwick Forest crept right up to the roadside here.

Imelda was on her own today. Her probationer had called in sick. She didn't figure she was on the force long enough to be thinking the job was fucked, but she remembered that when she was a rookie everyone from her squad had been too scared to take a sick day in case they got canned before they got out of their probation. Covid had changed that. Everyone went sick at the hint of a cough these days. And, Christ, Brendan was a nice enough boy when she managed to coax a few words out of him – funny too; surprisingly so – but he was bloody lazy. She'd been a Field Training Officer less than two years, but even in that time Imelda figured the quality of recruit was sliding bigtime. That's why she was studying so hard to pass her Trainee Investigator exam and get detective status. She wanted to get into a department where everyone was experienced and competent.

She glanced at the two *Blackstone's* policing and law manuals lying on the passenger seat. She'd figured that if she got a bit of downtime on her shift, she'd hit another couple of topics – although it didn't look like that was going to happen at the moment, with the list of outstanding calls on the screen growing by the hour. She had been thinking of doing the exams for a while now; she was sick to the back teeth of the crap she found herself doing as part of Uniform Response these days. She'd joined the job to catch proper criminals, not babysit twits and scumbags in the hospital emergency department because custody sergeants were too nervous to let them sleep off the drink in their cells. Coaxing Jimmy the Perv or Toothless Maggie off the motorway bridge for the third time in a week. Breaking up domestics between pisshead one and pisshead two and knowing neither would make a statement or go to court in the end. Or the constant missing person reports, like the one she was attending now. Most of them weren't real mispers, not like that teenage girl CID had taken on. The Lithuanian one. Mila. That was the thing about uniform: any proper investigations got taken off you. Another reason why Imelda wanted to be a detective. If she got her exam, she'd apply to join Esther Penman's team. There was something about the DS, something Imelda had found inspiring; she couldn't quite put her finger on it, but the woman had reignited Imelda's interest in being a detective.

Hitting a pothole that jarred her teeth, she forced herself to focus on the task at hand. She'd had a sinking feeling when she got this particular misper call – old guy not seen in a while – that it was going to turn out to be a sudden death. A slip in the bathtub, or just a peaceful death in bed – neither one would be pleasant if he'd been rotting for a few days.

She found number 44. It was an early twentieth century two-storey cottage on an isolated stretch of the track, the woods marching right up on either side of the property. The building itself wasn't in the greatest state of repair, but someone had recently had a go at clearing the garden; a lot of it was still thick with weeds, but the part that stretched around towards the back had been dug up, with squares of dark earth divided by planks suggesting some kind of vegetable patch was being planted. A set of olive-green garden furniture was stacked as if put aside for dumping and there was a rusting car in the drive, a blue Ford hatchback that was at least twenty-five years old, if not more.

She ran the licence plate.

As expected, it came back insured and registered to George Haribald, her sixty-eight-year-old misper. He'd been phoned in as missing earlier that morning by some concerned local shopkeeper who hadn't seen him in a while.

Imelda climbed out of the car and set her hat on her head, relieved to see that there were no bluebottles in any of the front windows. Maybe she'd be spared the sudden death after all...

She picked her way up the weed-riddled drive.

As she approached the house, she heard arguing. A woman's voice raised in anger, shrieking almost, and a male voice shouting back. The words were muffled, like they were coming from upstairs or a back room. Christ, a domestic! She stepped quickly up to the door and hammered it with her fist.

The house fell silent.

She hammered again.

Footsteps. A young woman snatched open the front

door. She was early twenties, but something in her eyes and the set of her jaw spoke of several decades' more worth of experience. She also had the makings of a real beauty, with blue almond-shaped eyes, naturally full lips and high cheekbones, but her blond hair was straggly and straw-like, and there was something frayed and haggard about her that reneged her to merely pretty. A small blue stone, a piercing, twinkled on the left side of her nose. She was breathing a touch heavily, but as soon as she saw the uniform, she gave a start; in a flash, she was giving Imelda her biggest, friendliest smile.

"Hello, Officer, is everything alright?"

If anything, the woman's reaction made Imelda even more suspicious. Who the hell *smiled* when a police officer appeared at their door?

"I'm looking for Mister George Haribald," she told the woman. "People down the local shop haven't seen him in a couple of weeks. They were getting worried."

The woman shook her head, her expression turning apologetic. "Of course. I'm so sorry. George is my grandfather. He's taken poorly and gone to stay with my mother for a bit. She thought the sea air might help."

Imelda pulled out her notebook. "You're Mister Haribald's granddaughter?"

The woman nodded, her big smile back. "That's right, Officer. Lucy Templeton."

Imelda jotted the name down. "What's your mum's name?"

"Karen Templeton." Imelda felt Templeton's eyes on her as she wrote down the names. "Her maiden name is Haribald, obviously." Imelda jotted that too.

"Where does your mum live?" she asked.

"Hornsea. She has a caravan out there. Sorry. A mobile home. She hates it when I call it a caravan." Templeton gave a little laugh. "Took an age to convince Gramps that it would be good for him, but we managed eventually. Part of the deal was that I would stay here and keep an eye on the house while he's away."

"Does your mum have an address up there?"

Templeton nodded. "It's Hornsea Bay Caravan park. That's why I always call it a caravan. It's in the name, isn't it?"

"She have a number I can contact her on?"

The woman's smile became apologetic again, her brow creasing. "No, I'm sorry. I lost my phone the other day. And who remembers phone numbers these days? Lost all my contacts."

Imelda hesitated, pen hovering. Templeton glanced at the pen and notebook briefly, and then fixed Imelda with a steady blue gaze.

"I heard shouting just now," Imelda said. "Is everything okay here?"

"Oh, that was only me and my boyfriend. It's fine. It was just an argument about dinner. We're okay."

"If it's a domestic matter, I'm obliged to come in and speak with both parties. You guys have any kids?"

Templeton laughed, then stopped abruptly, still looking amused as she cleared her throat and shook her head. "Um, no. No kids, Officer."

"Mind if I come in?"

The woman seemed to consider the request for the briefest moment, then stepped aside and held the door open. "Of course. If you're 'obliged to', then I suppose you must."

Was that a touch of sarcasm there? Imelda gave Templeton a tight smile as she slipped past her, tucking her notebook and pen away as she moved down the hall.

The faint aroma of cannabis smoke hung in the air. A small table stood just inside the door, the kind that might once have been home to a telephone and an address book, perhaps a framed photo or two, but the polished surface was bare now. Old-fashioned wallpaper covered the walls, and a smattering of dark, square patches suggested pictures had been removed recently.

"Redecorating?" Imelda asked conversationally, as she pushed open the nearest door to reveal the living room.

"Just cleaning up while Gramps is away," Templeton replied. "Place was a state. Not sure he's fit to live on his own anymore, if I'm honest."

Imelda glanced at her. She was watching Imelda warily now as she scanned the sitting room. The smell of cannabis was stronger here. Several large weavings in some kind of Celtic style, with lots of swirls and loops, hung from the walls, one blocking most of the light from the front window. On the mantelpiece was an ornate dagger in a carved wooden stand. The blade appeared to be silver, or plated in silver – it was about eight inches long and flared oddly, wide at the base but with a sharp point, and the handle was designed to look like bone. Next to the fireplace stood a wicker chair with several sets of woollen robes tossed across the back of it and a weird headpiece lying sideways on the seat; the thing looked like it should have been mounted on a wall, but Imelda could see it was hollow inside and, realistic though it might have looked, it wasn't any creature she recognised, like a cross between a bull and a deer. Beside the weird costume piece lay a canvas bag full of black candles.

The woman must have noticed Imelda's frown.

"The candles are vanilla scented," she said. "Comforting. Some say it's an aphrodisiac."

Imelda made no reply. To her, it looked as if Lucy Templeton was making herself right at home in her grandfather's house.

"You think you'll be here long?" she asked.

"I have no idea," the woman replied. "Might be a while."

Imelda stepped from the living room and moved towards the kitchen at the back. Templeton followed her. She'd left the front door open, a sign she wanted to keep this visit as brief as possible.

"Your grandfather probably won't appreciate you smoking weed in his house," Imelda said, glancing over her shoulder to catch the woman's reaction.

Templeton's face was a mask. She said nothing, returning Imelda's look without expression and folding her arms tightly beneath her breasts as she followed her into the kitchen.

* * *

Anita's heart was pounding hard as she followed the cop to the kitchen. She had to cross her arms to hide her shaking. What did this woman want? Was she really here because some local shopkeeper complained they hadn't seen George in a while? Or did she know something? She was looking around the kitchen, snooping the way cops do.

"Where's your boyfriend?" she asked.

Anita clenched her jaw. *Hiding, the prick!* What name to use? No. She couldn't choose a name now. He was too stupid. He wouldn't play along, and she needed him to be normal.

Anita was trying to be normal.

But, really, had she ever been normal?

Her cheek spasmed as she suppressed a laugh at that last thought and quickly turned it into a shout.

"Jason!"

She got some small satisfaction from seeing the cop jump at her sudden yell, so she did it again.

"Jason! Get downstairs!"

The cop didn't flinch this time. Her jaw was clenched as she gave Anita a hard stare.

"There's no need to shout," she said stiffly. "That can often lead to arguments."

Anita gave the woman a tight, unfriendly smile. She wanted this prim, sanctimonious bitch out of her house. She'd had enough of coppers to last her a lifetime already. Some of them pretended to be nice, but they were all assholes out to screw you over in the end. She'd learned that the hard way.

Jason padded softly into the kitchen, tossing a few of his thick dreads over his shoulder as he favoured the police officer with that breathtaking blue gaze of his. Anita felt a twinge of jealousy. She hated it when he looked at other women like that. Even without the smile, it was like he was saying 'I want to fuck you' without opening his mouth. She felt herself grow tense. Felt that familiar fiery ball of heat form in her belly.

If the cop noticed his smouldering gaze, she did her best

to hide it, pen and notebook poised once more.

"What's your name, sir?"

"Jason."

"Jason…?"

"Tanner. Jason Tanner. You want my number?" And there it was, that white-toothed smile of his. How was it she found his *incisors* sexy?

"And your address, please, Mister Tanner?"

Jason laughed, leaning back against a countertop. "I'm here at the moment. With my girlfriend." He winked at Anita.

In his thin linen trousers, both women could clearly see the soft, curving ridge of his manhood. Jason was proud of his big cock, Anita knew. The cop had noticed now too. She was blushing and trying to avoid looking. As much as Anita wanted Jason to play his part and get this bitch out of their house, watching this to-and-fro stirred the boiling rage inside her. The air felt warm, even though Anita knew it wasn't – it had never been warm in this house. Why did she put up with this?

A shaft of sunlight caught a drop of water hanging from the branch of a tree in the garden outside. It glimmered brightly. It looked like a star, twinkling at the end of the branch. A fallen star. So bright. No one else seemed to have spotted it. It must be a sign.

A sign just for her.

A sign from Mother Nature.

Fly away.

"Your girlfriend?" the cop asked.

Anita felt a sudden moment of panic, but Jason answered smoothly, unprompted.

"Lucy," he said with a laugh. The fucker had been

listening the whole time, letting her deal with this bitch cop by herself.

Anita found her voice.

"I'm sorry, Officer, but I'm not sure there's any need for you to be here," she said, as much to get the cop moving and out of the house as to get her out of range of Jason's leering stare. The woman might be a snooty bitch, but she was a young and good-looking snooty bitch. Besides, she'd suddenly remembered Jason teasing her once by saying he liked women in uniform. It was too much. She was going to explode. "You can see there's nothing going on," she said, her voice hardening, "so I'd like you to leave now."

The cop turned and regarded her for a long moment. Anita felt her own cheeks starting to warm. Jason pushed himself away from the countertop. Fucking right, he could stop showing off his dick to this woman. Basically inviting her. Bastard.

"I'd like to just make sure there are no kids," the cop replied.

Anita opened her mouth to refuse, but Jason cut in before she had a chance to speak.

"No kids, Officer, promise." That cheeky, flirty fucking grin again. "I'll give you a quick tour if you'd like?"

He gestured towards the kitchen door in an 'after you' motion. The copper's gaze darted from Jason to Anita and back, and then she nodded.

He did these things on purpose.

To make her jealous.

Or was he losing interest?

He watched the copper closely as she put her notebook away, his stare clearly grazing her ass as she turned and went back into the hall. What the fuck was with her trousers?

Pockets on the legs like in the military, and tight around her bum like she wanted everyone to look!

Jason could bloody well stop looking.

He could stop looking right fucking now!

But he was staring. Staring as she walked away towards the stairs.

"No kids at all?" the woman asked, glancing over her shoulder. Was she flirting too? *FUCKSAKE!* "From other relationships or anything?"

Jason laughed again. An infuriatingly inviting laugh. He had moved out ahead of Anita so that he could follow the bitch upstairs, practically shoving her out of the way to get a better view of the woman's ass in those trousers.

FUCKING BASTARD!

Anita felt her cheeks burning.

Anger. Hurt. Fury. Pain.

She trailed her treacherous, womanizing prick of a boyfriend and the bitch cop down the hall, but stopped at the door to the living room as they reached the stairs. Something caught her attention, a glimmer at the corner of her eye. She turned to see that the afternoon sun had found its way into the living room and was shining off the silvered blade of the athamé.

Another sign.

She stopped there while Jason and the cop climbed the stairs. Waited until she could hear their heavy treads on the floorboards overhead.

* * *

Imelda wasn't comfortable with Tanner standing behind her. She stepped to one side on the lower landing of the stairs and nodded for him to proceed.

He gave her another sleazy smile and obliged.

"How long have you two been staying here?" she asked, as he climbed the steps in front of her.

"Oh, not long," he replied. "It's Lucy's house and all."

"Lucy's house? I thought it belonged to her grandfather?"

"Oh yeah, well, sorry, her family, I mean. I'm just a blow-in. Helping out, you know?"

Tanner pushed open the first door on the left. An old man's room, the air musty and stale. Whatever cleaning they'd been doing hadn't reached this room yet. A pair of tartan slippers sat next to a bedside table, on which lay a set of reading glasses and a couple of dusty books. Old Westerns. The bedcovers were tucked in neatly around the edges of the four-poster bed. A wardrobe in the far corner stood half-open, the sleeves of some old-fashioned checked shirts visible within.

"As you can see, Officer," Tanner was saying, already moving down the hall and pushing open the other doors to offer her a view, "no kids."

"Lucy's grandad not need his glasses while he's in Hornsea?" Imelda asked, lingering in the doorway of the first room.

"Uh, yeah, I guess he has other pairs, maybe?" Tanner replied uncertainly.

Imelda went to the next door, the nearest room across the hall. It was decorated in drapes and tapestries, with throw-rugs on the floor and a much stronger smell of cannabis. A bunch of dreamcatchers turned in the wind

201

from an open window. Two single beds had been pushed together to make a double, the woollen blankets strewn messily across them. Lucy and Jason's room, she guessed.

The door at the end on the right revealed an empty bathroom. It didn't bear any trace of children. No step stools or bath toys.

The only room with any sign there had ever been youngsters in this house was the third bedroom, where cartoon characters marched across torn and faded wallpaper that was still festooned with greasy spots from old sticky tack. A set of ancient bunkbeds stood against one wall, the bedframe devoid of mattresses. A single bed on the other side with a sheet, pillow, and one thin blanket had been left unmade. Apart from the beds the only other furnishings were a dresser sitting between the beds, and a wardrobe. A canvas bag lay against one wall, some female clothes spilling out. Something lying on the dressing table caught Imelda's eye – a grey stone keyring.

"Who's staying with you?" she asked, nodding towards the unmade bed.

Tanner shrugged. "Friends, sometimes."

"What about the stuff in the bag there?" Imelda stepped forward and rifled through the clothes. Women's undergarments and some homemade skirts.

"Lucy's stuff. Haven't moved all the way in. Don't know how long we're staying, you know? But as you can see, there are no children here."

Imelda nodded. Tanner was still leering at her. Templeton hadn't followed them upstairs, and the two of them were alone. Imelda suddenly felt uncomfortable.

"Thank you for your cooperation, Jason," she said, moving past him and back down the stairs.

* * *

Anita was standing by the fireplace now. She didn't remember moving, or picking up the athamé. The bone handle was warm in her grip. From the sunlight. The sun was angled through the window just the right way, cutting past the Celtic drapes, bringing warmth.

Nature's warmth.

Mother Nature nudging her.

"We're both here most of the time," Jason was saying as he came back downstairs with the cop, charm still turned up to full. "If you have any more questions, just call by."

Anita moved to the doorway between the living room and hall. Jason and the cop were at the front door now.

Anita clutched the athamé in her left hand, behind her, unseen. Sometimes it was better for things to be unseen. For people to be unseen.

She had spent her life being seen only when she least wanted to be.

Seen by those she hated, those she feared. Unseen by everyone else.

Unseen.

The police officer bid them good day and set off down the short driveway to her car. Even with his back to her, Anita could tell that Jason was watching the woman's ass again.

She watched him watching her.

Forgotten.

Unseen.

* * *

Jason Tanner gave Imelda another white-toothed smile and a wave as she sat into her patrol car.

There was something odd about that pair. Drugs, for a start. But without a warrant or a clear domestic offence, Imelda wasn't really in a position to go rummaging around the house for cannabis. She'd feed the intel into the system when she wrote up the domestic.

She ran both names through her patrol car's onboard computer as she started the engine.

Another glance back at the house. Tanner still standing in the doorway. He waved again. *Creep.*

Imelda's radio began to chirp. It was the control desk looking for a free callsign to assist with a detained female shoplifter in town. She sighed, picked up the handset and pressed the transmit button.

"Bravo Charlie One-O-Five, I'm about to come clear, I'll take that shoplifter. And I have an update for the concern for safety call on Denton Lane if you're ready for it. Over."

Tanner was gone now, the front door closed.

"Yes, go ahead, One-O-Five. Over."

"Spoke to George Haribald's granddaughter, a Lucy Templeton. Says the subject is with her mother in Hornsea at the moment. One Karen Templeton. I'll write it up when I get back to base and make a couple more enquiries, but you can close that one for now. Put me on the shoplifter call. Over."

"Roger, One-O-Five. Out."

There were no hits from her person checks on Tanner or Templeton, but Imelda decided she would run a few variations when she got back to the station – do a bit more digging into Mister Haribald, his granddaughter and her creepy boyfriend.

* * *

Anita watched from the living room window as the cop car turned in the weed-choked drive and trundled back down Denton Lane towards the main road. The fire inside her was stoked, raging. She continued to stare out the window as the car disappeared, watching the wind gently move the tops of the trees that crowded right in on the narrow lane here. The Haribald house was the last house on the road. There was nobody within a solid mile of them here. That had fed her fear of the place when she was young. The isolation. Cut off from anyone who might help, who might listen.

But nobody listened.

Nobody ever listened.

She didn't know if the other kids she'd lived with had suffered as she had. There were no girls her age when she was here. But there were others – she knew that now – girls she didn't recognise. She wondered where they were and how they felt about it all, after they'd got away. As for Anita, the fear and hate had lingered in her. It was why she'd come back.

You had to face what you feared.

You had to kill what you feared.

She turned as Jason appeared in the living room doorway. He was grinning, leering, exactly like he'd been leering at that cop.

"Worked, I think," he said.

"It was working *before* you decided to come on to her," she replied softly.

Jason guffawed. "Oh come *on*, Annie."

She hated when he called her Annie.

"Don't call me that," she replied, almost a whisper.

Come on, Annie. That's what he used to say. She shuddered. Nothing had happened here. Mostly the bedroom. She hadn't been able to make herself get a proper start on that room yet. Couldn't make herself stay in there long enough. It was still just as he'd left it. *Little Annie. You look sweet in that outfit.*

Come here, Little Annie.

Jason didn't hear her last remark. At least, he gave no indication that he'd heard. He just threw his head back and let out a sharp, mirthless laugh.

"You know what?" he said. "Fuck you and your jealousy. This is *not* what being a Satanist is about. You just don't get it, do you? You can't be so fucking jealous and controlling and be a Satanist. Maybe you should try something else instead, huh? Like a convent!"

He turned his back on her, turned to leave, and that's when she snapped.

Snap.

Crack.

Like something breaking.

It was her.

Little Annie.

Broken at last.

She launched herself, snarling, biting, swinging and punching.

She'd forgotten about the knife. At least, she wasn't thinking of it when she attacked. That's what she told herself afterwards, that she didn't do it on purpose.

It was the sight of the blood that shocked her back to reality. When she landed on Jason's back and began clawing and biting, flailing and swinging, they both stumbled clumsily through the door and into the hallway.

She couldn't tell how long it lasted. Seconds. Minutes. As clarity returned, she took in the blood – rich and red – spattered across the white of the kitchen door and the walls of the hall.

The blade fell from her hand.

Jason was crouched, wincing, staring in amazement at the bright crimson coating his hands. The red on his shirt was much darker, like claret. It was leaking with frightening speed down his trousers and onto the floor, where it was soaking into the carpet and spreading.

He looked up at her then, his terrified eyes full of disbelief.

Anita gasped and brought her hands to her mouth. What had she done?

As Jason collapsed to the floor, she darted forward and tried to gather him up, to hold him together.

"Oh my God, Jason!" she cried. "Oh God, oh God! Where did I get you, baby? Where did I get you?"

But she could already see, as she cradled his head in her arms and frantically tried to pull the linen shirt away from his skin, that she had got him everywhere.

25

THE MURMUR OF the gathered press corps subsided as Superintendent O'Halloran led the way to the dais. She, Esther and the Roses took their seats behind a long table facing the reporters. It was clothed in pristine white, like a wedding table, but that was where any similarity to such an occasion ended. Lined with microphones, it stood in front of a backdrop emblazoned with a repeating pattern of the constabulary logo. On a stand to one side was a blown-up photograph of Mila Rose, smiling for the camera in her school blazer.

"Thank you all for coming here this afternoon," the superintendent announced, once everyone was settled. "As you know, we are here today to ask for the public's help in locating a missing teenager. Mila Rose is sixteen years old..."

Esther sat next to the superintendent and tried not to fidget. Tim and Vera were on her other side, the pastor sitting tall and straight, no stranger to attention, Vera, by contrast, hunched in on herself. There were about twenty people in the chairs facing the dais, along with half a dozen cameramen at the back of the room. Tripod-mounted cameras were trained on all four of them as they sat under the glare of the lamps.

"...Detective Sergeant Penman will give you an update in relation to that matter."

Esther blinked at the mention of her name. She'd missed some of O'Halloran's opener. Luckily, they had done a run-through with Barbara Yeovil from the press office earlier, so Esther was able to launch smoothly into her speech.

"Katie Wilde was found by search and rescue teams looking for Mila in the Norwick Hills three days ago," she told the assembled journalists. "Forensic experts put her time of death at around midnight on Friday. Miss Wilde was the victim of a particularly vicious attack, stabbed repeatedly and left to die." Vera made a small noise, a stifled sob. "Miss Wilde's lifestyle was transient in nature," Esther continued. "As such, we are asking for the public's help not only in reporting any sightings of Mila, but also in helping us piece together Katie Wilde's last few days here in Belfield. If anyone saw Katie between the fourth and eleventh of April, we would urge them to contact police at our dedicated incident room."

Barbara had prepared a page with all the contact details printed in a big bold font, and the numbers had been shared with the press already, so Esther hadn't been required to memorize those, thankfully. As she read them out for the cameras, she was aware of Vera crying quietly. Tim reached out and put his arm around her.

"And we have Mila's parents here," the superintendent

said, picking up seamlessly as Esther finished reading out the incident room contact details. "They would like to make a direct plea to the public."

Not entirely true. Pastor Rose had been keen, but poor Vera had been getting cold feet. Only Superintendent O'Halloran's gentle coaxing had convinced her that it would be better if they both appeared here together. She'd urged Vera to imagine that Mila was watching somewhere and was able to return. This was an opportunity to not only ask the public for help but also let Mila know they were thinking of her, and that they were worried sick about her. Because the possibility she'd run away and was free to come home was still a very real hope.

It had been a delicate balancing act, explaining to the Roses that Katie Wilde's murder and Mila's disappearance were potentially linked on the one hand, and on the other was the possibility that Mila was sitting in a bus depot or train station somewhere, confused and angry, but entirely free and safe – and that she might just see this news conference and be persuaded to return home. Esther understood how difficult that must be to take in, and how frustrated they must feel – even if they did hide it well – at how few real answers she could give them.

"Mila, if you are out there, know that we are thinking of you, and praying for you to come home safe to us," Timothy Rose began. He addressed the gathering with the confidence of a preacher, one arm around his wife, rubbing her shoulder soothingly as she sobbed silently next to him. He spoke about how much they missed her, and how much her friends missed her. Even without his wife crying next to him, the heartache in his words was clear. There were tears in his eyes too.

"Mila, if you are listening, please come home," he finished, and only now did his voice finally threaten to break, "and if there's anyone out there who knows where Mila is, please bring her back to us."

O'Halloran let a moment's silence punctuate Pastor Rose's words before she addressed the gathering again.

"Ladies and gentlemen," she said, "DS Penman and I will take one or two questions."

"Is there any indication that Mila has left the country?" a blonde female journalist cut in over the rising clamour. She sat near the front, and Esther recognised her from one of the bigger television stations. "Is she being treated as anything other than a missing person at the moment?"

Cleverly coded, Esther thought. The woman clearly didn't want to say it straight out in front of the parents, but what she was really asking was whether they were treating Mila as a suspect. It made Esther wonder whether Superintendent O'Halloran had wanted the Roses at this news conference for another purpose: a way to keep the press in line.

The superintendent made a tiny gesture, unseen by the reporters: a gentle pat of the table with her left hand, the hand closest to Esther. That was the signal, a way to ensure they didn't interrupt each other. The question was Esther's.

"We have no information to suggest Mila has left Britain," Esther replied. "She is being treated as a high-risk missing person at this time. She is a juvenile, and she is vulnerable. We want anyone with any knowledge at all about her whereabouts, or anyone who thinks they may have seen her over the past week, to come forward and let us know. Even the smallest bit of information might help us find her."

"Are there any more details on the murder?" another journalist shouted from the back, half a second after Esther stopped speaking, quelling another rising tide of questions. "Any details about a potential suspect or suspects?"

Superintendent O'Halloran shook her head. "The information we've given you here today is all we can share at the moment."

"Is it true that the team investigating the murder of Katie Wilde have engaged the services of a witch to help track down her killers?"

There he was. Bob Chase. Sitting at the far end of the second row, his legs out to one side, crossed jauntily at the knee, a snide little smirk on his lips. His words brought total silence to the room. Heads turned towards him.

Now that he had the floor, he went on quickly. "I have sources telling me that a local Wiccan witch has been assisting with enquiries here at Belfield Central Police Station. Is she part of the task force?"

The assembled journalists turned to the dais for a response. It seemed to Esther that every pair of eyes in the room bar the superintendent's were focused on her. She even saw the Roses turn and look at her.

The super gave the table another barely perceptible tap with her left hand.

"There are no witches or wizards on our task force, Mister Chase," Esther replied, going for as amenable a tone as she could muster. "We interview a lot of members of the community when we investigate a murder. You should know this. I think you've been reading too much Harry Potter."

A faint chuckle rose from the other journalists. If Bob Chase took any offence at the reply, he gave no indication.

In fact, he smiled as he jotted something in his notepad.

O'Halloran pointed to another rising hand, and Esther found herself answering a question on the timelines. After two more relatively innocuous questions, one of which the superintendent fielded herself, O'Halloran pushed back her chair to indicate that the conference was at an end.

"Thank you, everyone, for coming," she said to the room at large as she stood.

A murmur rose amidst the gathering as O'Halloran and Barbara Yeovil ushered Timothy and Vera out of the room. They returned to the adjoining lounge area, where they'd been offered tea and coffee before the news conference began. Esther followed, closing the door on the chattering reporters in her wake.

"Thank you both," O'Halloran said to the Roses. "Pastor, you were very succinct, and I think people will respond to your words. If Mila is watching, I think you've done a very good job at convincing her to come home, or pick up the phone at least."

Vera sniffed and wiped her eyes. "I'm sorry, I couldn't... I just..."

"Not at all, Vera," O'Halloran said. She reached out and gave Vera's arm a reassuring rub. "Your tears might speak more loudly to Mila and anyone else watching than your husband's words."

Anyone else watching. More code. *Captors.* Or killers. But it didn't appear as though either Vera or her husband had picked up on it. Vera just nodded mutely, blowing her nose into a tissue. The pastor still had one arm protectively around her shoulders. For his part, he seemed to be mulling something as he looked at Esther.

"What was that journalist saying about witches?" he

asked.

Esther shared a quick look with the superintendent. Clearly neither the Roses nor their friends were readers of the *Belfield Star*. Esther had anticipated the question, just as she had anticipated it being raised in the news conference itself.

"There were some occult symbols found near the body of Katie Wilde," she told him. "We keep an open mind about everything during a murder investigation. These symbols were painted on the walls of a cabin in the woods near her body. They might have something to do with her death, or they might not. We simply don't know. But we have to investigate every line of enquiry. A local woman who knows about these things was interviewed. That's all. Bob Chase is a journalist who likes to create sensationalist stories. He's been trying to twist it into something it is not."

"Occult symbols?" the pastor replied. "What kind of occult symbols?"

"Pentacles, chaos symbols, that kind of thing. But they might have been painted by kids who had nothing to do with Miss Wilde's death."

Timothy frowned. He looked on the verge of saying something else, but a glance at his wife made him hesitate. Superintendent O'Halloran spoke into the momentary silence, deftly bringing the post-conference discussion to a conclusion.

"Pastor Rose, Missus Rose, thank you both so much for agreeing to do this. I know these things can be nerve-wracking, but I think you both did very well today. If Mila is out there watching, hopefully your appearance in the media will take us one step closer to getting her back safely. If you'll excuse DS Penman and I, we have a briefing to go to, but Barbara will be here until you feel ready to leave. Esther will be in touch with you soon to give you any news and updates from the press conference. If you want any tea or coffee before you go, Barbara will see to it."

After Esther said her own goodbyes, the super steered her towards the door on the other side of the small room, away from the one that led into the conference chamber, where there was always a risk of a lingering journalist or two.

"I think that went rather well, all things considered," O'Halloran said. She said it with a sigh in her voice, as though she had been holding herself tightly for the last hour and was only now allowing herself to relax.

Esther's phone began to ring. Carl Etebo's name appeared on the screen.

"Sorry, ma'am, I need to take this. It's CSI."

"Go ahead," O'Halloran replied.

"Carl?" Esther said as she put the phone to her ear.

"Esther, my dear, I have some results for you. We've got some identifications from the blood swabs taken at the cabin."

"Go on."

"It was a bit of a muddle, but forensics managed to get some clear samples from the batch we took. They come back to two people on our system... and one other."

"One other?"

"It's Mila," Carl said. "Some of the blood is a match for Mila Rose. It matches the DNA sample we got from a hairbrush her parents gave us."

Esther's heart seemed to stop in her chest. She closed her eyes, but Carl continued on in her ear.

"One of the others is Katie Wilde," he said.

Esther sat heavily onto a soft bench that stood against

the wall. O'Halloran was watching her now, brow creased.

"What about the third one?" Esther asked.

"Flagged up on the police system as wanted," Carl replied. "Jason Laird. That name mean anything to you?"

Esther shook her head, realised Carl couldn't see that, and said, "No." Her mouth was suddenly dry.

"Well, his profile is clear in the semen samples taken at Wilde's autopsy, but the blood's a mixed bag, so some samples are pretty difficult to break down. There may be others in there."

"Okay, thank you, Carl," Esther replied. "Carl, you wouldn't do me a favour and send those results through in an email? I'll need to get a BOLO alert out to all forces."

"Already done. Sent them to you twenty minutes ago. When I didn't get a response, I guessed you were out of the office, so I thought I'd better give you a call."

"Thanks, Carl."

"Okey-doke."

Esther hung up and looked at the superintendent. She was very conscious that the Roses were possibly still in the next room with Barbara Yeovil. This was something they would have to be told. Maybe not yet, but soon.

"What is it?" O'Halloran asked, clearly disconcerted by Esther's sudden brooding silence.

"It's the blood we took at the cabin in the woods, near to Katie Wilde's body," Esther replied. "The forensic lab have extracted three different profiles. One of them is Katie Wilde, and another is Mila Rose."

The superintendent seemed to deflate a little with the last words. Perhaps it was seeing this reaction in a colleague that helped stiffen Esther's resolve.

"But they've got another profile," she went on, "and

given the amount of blood in that cabin, we're not talking life-threatening amounts here. This could be a positive development. It's something to go on. Search and rescue teams have crisscrossed that forest for the last three days. If Mila's body was there, they would have found it by now. Like they found Katie's."

O'Halloran gave a brief nod, although she didn't look convinced.

"The Roses will need to be told," she said solemnly.

Esther nodded, but hesitantly. "I'll let them know, after I've done a bit of digging into this other profile – this Jason Laird – and get an alert sent out to all constabularies."

When the superintendent agreed, Esther left and headed for her office. Not quite running, but moving a good deal more briskly through the corridors than anyone else.

"How'd the press conference go?" Caroline asked, as Esther hurried into the DS office. She was pouring hot water from a kettle on the sideboard – their little makeshift tea-station. Spencer was nowhere to be seen.

"Good, yeah," Esther replied distractedly.

"You get any shit from Bob Chase?"

"Nothing I couldn't handle."

"Cuppa?"

"No, thanks."

Logging into her computer, Esther read Carl's email, then pulled up *Jason Laird* on PNC.

Caroline tossed her tea-bag into the bin and regarded Esther for a moment, but seeing that she wasn't going to get any more out of her, she went back to her own desk.

There wasn't a lot on Laird, and only two mugshots. The first photo was taken when he was arrested in his teens for shoplifting and cannabis possession, but the most recent came after an arrest in Cardiff for possession of class A drugs with intent to supply. Cocaine and LSD. He'd skipped on police bail and the Welsh police had flagged him as wanted. There were almost ten years between the arrests, and he'd grown his hair long in the interim, fashioned it into dreadlocks. This was the man Mila had been with in the security footage, Esther was sure. Could the woman be Anita Jess? Esther had asked Craig Browne to put together a bulletin on Mila's old acquaintance after their conversation with Tabitha Renshaw. He'd sent it through to her a short time ago for approval. Esther opened it and studied the photo of Jess. It was another mugshot. Jess was blonde and skinny, just like the woman in the footage with Laird and Mila. How many skinny blondes were there in Belfield? Far too many for the link to be conclusive, but it was too much of a coincidence – the note, the footage. Esther pulled up Jess's full profile on PNC. It contained quite a few custody photos. She was a pretty-looking teen in most of them, although the effects of drugs and a boozy lifestyle were already evident in the progression of photos, right from her pre- to late teens. Jess still had a striking face, with big almond-shaped eyes, high cheekbones and full lips, but her blonde hair was dishevelled and ratty in her most recent photos and there was a gaunt, starved look about her that seemed to grow more pronounced as she grew older.

With Jason's lifestyle obviously a rootless one – his last address was preceded by four others within the prior year, from Leeds to Manchester and as far south as Bournemouth – Esther didn't hold out much hope that they would locate him at his last known addresses. Still, the enquiries had to be done.

She threw together a request for South Wales Police.

The address check would come back negative – she'd put any money on it – but something useful might be discovered. Some new lead.

Next, she put together a BOLO application – a Be-On-the-Lookout alert – for both Jason Laird and Anita Jess and emailed it to Jared. Once Jared authorised the applications, the alerts would go live to every force in the UK.

She attracted another curious look from Caroline as she hopped from her desk and hurried from the room. The other sergeant was clearly bursting with questions, but she'd have to wait.

Jared was already reading her email when Esther tapped at his open door and stepped into the office.

"Can you send that one out straight away?" she asked.

His eyes flicked from the screen to Esther.

"These are suspects for the Wilde woman?" he queried.

"And I think we can be relatively certain that Jason Laird is the man with Mila in the security footage from Saturday," she explained. She relayed what Carl had told her over the phone. "Jess is a longer shot, but she's definitely a person of interest in the misper enquiry."

"Is Jason Laird our prime suspect? Or all three?"

Esther hesitated. She didn't know. She said as much. "But Laird is the key to both cases," she added. "Finding him will be the break we need. If there was any doubt Katie's murder is linked to Mila's disappearance, I think it's pretty much blown out of the water now."

Jared grimaced and nodded. "I'll send this out now. Let's hope Mila's still alive."

"Let's hope they all are," Esther said softly.

26

THE FIRST THING Mila noticed as she stepped through the back door was the smell. It struck a primeval chord in her, something instinctive that made the little hairs stand up on the nape of her neck.

The tote bag was barely a quarter full, but her mushroom-picking chore had become tedious and she'd decided to cut it short. It had been Anita who'd seemed to have a knack for finding the clusters of wide-capped St George's mushrooms the last time. Her friend had been in one of her positive moods that day, and Mila had enjoyed foraging in the forest with her. Why did Mila remember Anita as always being so positive during their time at Hodderston Road? Had she really been like that, or had Mila somehow filtered out memories of the mood swings in the intervening years?

Either way, she'd come to a decision. Cutting short her mushroom hunt, she'd marched back to the house, determined to say her piece before her courage failed her.

She wanted to go home.

Anita wouldn't be happy. But there it was. Mila had been thinking more and more about it over the last couple of days, and her dreary trudge through the woods just now had helped her finally decide. Despite all their flaws – in spite of all the recent arguments – Tim and Vera had been good to her. They had taken her in, pulled her from that horrible care home. And it was a comfortable life, whereas this experience – living with Anita and Jason, tasting freedom, getting a sense of adulthood and what it might be like not to have your whole life dictated – hadn't panned out quite the way Mila had expected. What it *had* done was give her a new appreciation for what she'd left behind.

Maybe she wasn't ready for complete independence yet. Maybe, when she was, she'd be better prepared.

She'd worked out a little speech. A way to thank Anita for everything and let her down easily.

What she was going to say to Tim and Vera, on the other hand… that was something she'd work out later.

But when she stepped through the back door and into the kitchen, the smell hit her. And a noise, like a faint whining, broken by heavy, panicked breathing. The door to the hall lay open in such a way that Mila couldn't see into the corridor.

Despite a real sense of unease – an instinctive knowledge that something very, *very* bad had happened – Mila found herself taking a tentative step forward, and then another, moving across the room until the hallway came into view.

It was like a scene from a horror movie. There was blood everywhere – pooled thickly on the hall's old carpet, seeping across the kitchen lino, spattered up the walls and across the door. Jason lay, his eyes open, expression frozen in shock. It looked as if his clothes had literally been dunked in blood. Crouching over him like an animal was Anita, sobbing quietly. Her hands were red, her hair matted and linen shirt damp with the stuff.

Jason was dead. Dead, and staring right at Mila.

How could there be so much blood in one person? Mila's breathing grew rapid and panicked.

How could there be so much blood?

Finally, she managed to gather enough air into her lungs, and she screamed.

The piercing note cracked the air. Anita's head snapped up. Her face was pale and drawn, stark against the red of the hideous tableau all around her, like some creature from another world.

As Mila's scream faded into rapid, gasping breaths, she finally wrenched her gaze from Jason and met Anita's eyes.

At first, her friend seemed not to recognise her. Cheeks wet with tears and mouth agape, she looked confused, like a lost child. But as Mila gathered her breath for another scream, Anita rose quickly to her feet. She almost slipped in the blood when she stepped over her boyfriend's body into the kitchen, but managed to catch her balance at the last moment.

"Shh-shh," she said, one trembling hand stretched out in a plea. Her other hand clutched at her linen skirts, holding them up out of the red puddles as if she wasn't already covered from head to toe. "Shush, Mila. It's okay. It's okay. It was an accident."

"He's dead!" Mila shrieked.

Anita moved closer, both hands outstretched now. Her arms were slick with blood, both of them, all the way to the elbow.

Mila shook her head, a futile denial of what she was seeing. Her breathing grew laboured again.

"It's fine, baby," Anita said. "Mila, it's fine."

"He's *dead!*"

Anita smiled tremulously, almost like she wasn't hearing Mila's words. A tear escaped and rolled down her cheek. Her hands were still reaching, as though she were beckoning a child, but her hushing noises became a little more desperate as she advanced and Mila started to back away.

"It's okay, Mila, honey. It's okay. We can manage this."

Mila stared at her, aghast.

"We need to call the police!"

Anita's expression changed. The beseeching look faded. Her hushing ceased. Her arms, still outstretched, came to resemble less a beckoning gesture and more an instruction to calm down, to hold on a minute.

"We need to think this through, Mila. It was an accident. An accident, yeah? But if we call the police, they'll arrest me. They'll split us up again." Anita's eyelids fluttered, and more tears fell. She swallowed. "They won't believe me, Mila. They won't believe me when I tell them it was just an accident. They'll lock me up. I can't go through that again, Mila. I can't."

Anita licked her lips, tried for a smile, but Mila could tell her friend was scared.

"You believe me, don't you, Mila?" she asked, her voice shaking. "You believe me? You're my sister now. We're bonded. And we can't let them split us up. Not ever again."

A sense of dread stole over Mila as Anita inched closer. This was wrong. They had to tell the police.

"No, Anita," she said firmly. "We have to report this!"

Anita stopped and sighed. The look she gave Mila then

was the one she used to give her when they were younger and Mila had said something particularly naïve or childish, a sort of amused, condescending, indulgent look.

"Oh, Mila…"

The moment hung, like a high-pitched note that fades slowly. As Anita stared at her, Mila's sense of dread quickly became a sizzling panic that spread through her whole body.

It was instinct that drove her to act more than conscious thought. She spun and darted for the kitchen door. In a split second, the amused indulgence vanished from Anita's face. She lunged.

Mila screamed. She swung the bag of mushrooms, catching Anita on the side of the head, but as a makeshift flail it did very little, and the woman's hands were in her hair now, yanking her back.

Mila managed to pull herself away, but Anita circled, putting herself between Mila and the back door. Mila glanced over her shoulder. Jason's body blocked the hallway – the only other escape route – and the thick pool of blood that filled the corridor from wall to wall looked like an uncrossable ocean to Mila at that moment.

Anita was panting now, standing in a half-crouch.

"Wait, Mila!" she said. "Just let's calm down a second and think about this." Her words belied the wild and frantic light in her own eyes.

Mila didn't wait. She made a dash for the front door, crushing her squeamish panic as she headed for the blood-filled corridor and Jason's prone body.

But Anita was too fast. Before Mila even registered what had happened, she was crashing to the floor again, the breath knocked right out of her. She found herself lying nose to nose with Jason, inches from his vacant, staring eyes.

She screamed. She screamed and screamed, and she didn't stop until a sudden pain bloomed at the back of her skull, shattering her grip on consciousness.

* * *

PC John Devon was possibly the most boring police officer in the whole constabulary. On her return to the station, Imelda had been reassigned a city centre foot patrol with him. He was easily the longest-serving officer on the team and, John being John, he'd soon found a way to procrastinate. Apparently, he'd had 'a couple of quick tasks' to clear up before they headed out. Then there'd been a few emails to respond to. And an hour after getting their new detailing by the sergeant, here they still were, sitting at the bank of computers in the constables' workroom, Devon with a fresh cup of steaming tea in his bony hands. God knows what excuse he would find next.

Well, if the sarge wasn't going to do anything about it, Imelda would just catch up on her own bits and pieces too. Problem was, being next to Devon made it hard to concentrate. The man always had something to moan about. Perhaps the guy was right and things *had* been better in the 'good old days', before computers and all the extra admin that went with them, but it didn't stop him from sitting in front of the damn things all day. If she heard him complain about the new domestic report forms one more time, she might very well scream.

She tried to tune out his nasally voice as he launched into

another doleful lament, this time about body-worn cameras and what a curse they were. Instead, she focused on the screen in front of her, trawling PNC to find anything she could on Lucy Templeton or Karen Templeton, or Karen Haribald as she might have been listed. Problem was, Imelda drew a blank with every search.

She dug through archived incidents at 44 Denton Lane. George Haribald was linked to that address going back years, although there were a ton of other names too. More than the usual amount. Some went back decades. It looked like Haribald and his wife, Wendy, had once run a foster home – for quite a lot of children – and there were so many names linked to the address over the years that it took a fair bit of digging to confirm none of them were actually born to Wendy; they were all kids taken in from social services. A lot of them had a bunch of other addresses listed against their names as well, which suggested they'd bounced from foster home to foster home throughout their childhoods.

But she couldn't find any Karen Haribald linked to the address, or a Karen Anything for that matter.

It was puzzling. Imelda was puzzled, and she didn't like being puzzled. She'd decided she was going to have to pay Lucy Templeton another visit, maybe with a warrant this time.

She switched browsers, logging on to the external internet, and did a search for Hornsea Bay Caravan Park. Google threw back a list of holiday parks, but none with the name 'Hornsea Bay'.

"…and what happened to a good, old-fashioned clip around the ear, eh? A ticking off and a kick in the arse to send them on their way?"

Imelda emerged from her research and realised Devon

had turned to her. Usually, he prattled away happily without the need for interruption, but he was looking at her as if he expected a response now. She rewound his last words in her head.

"Nothing, John, except that society frowns on it these days. Police officers kicking kids in the arse. Doesn't look good."

Devon harrumphed and turned back to his screen.

"Kids had a bit of respect back then," he muttered, as he sipped his tea. "No answering back in those days. You got a hiding from a copper, you kept your trap shut. If you told your parents, you'd just get another leathering from them for getting into trouble with the police. People were on our side back then."

"Yeah, well, when you find yourself a time machine, be sure to let me know," Imelda replied distractedly. "I'll be the first to send you off with best wishes."

Devon, about to take a slurp from his mug, hesitated, unsure how to take that.

Just then, their terminals emitted a simultaneous *ping*, and they both turned to see a little alert flash at the bottom of their screens. A force-wide bulletin. Another ping announced the arrival of a second. Imelda frowned. Two alerts in quick succession were rare.

She clicked on the first, and a High Risk MisPer notice popped up, a familiar face smiling back from the screen. It was Mila Rose, the missing teenager Imelda had passed to CID last week. She scanned the notice quickly, but there was nothing in the bulletin to suggest any major developments had been made. The text was pretty standard stuff, but that wasn't unusual; high-risk mispers often got alerted repeatedly until they were found. Or until their cases grew cold.

Opening the second notice, she gasped as a pair of custody mugshots filled the screen.

"Oh, shit!"

Devon turned to her, frowning. "What is it?"

Instead of answering, Imelda quickly scanned the text of the alert.

BOLO: *Jared Laird and Anita Jess are persons of interest in the murder of Katie Wilde and the case of missing person Mila Rose, aka Mila Rimkus. Any sightings should be reported immediately to your main control centre and the duty detective at Belfield CID.*

"Oh shit oh shit oh *shit!*"

Devon looked startled as Imelda suddenly bounced out of her seat and raced from the room.

27

MILA FELT A wave of nausea wash over her as she resurfaced. Blinking in an effort to dispel the gloom, she fixed her eyes on a swirl of dust motes dancing lazily in a beam of pallid light.

She was lying on a cold, hard floor.

She tried to lift her head and pain flared at the back of her neck. Gasping, she waited for it to subside before she made another attempt, relieved to find that she could move. Her hands were sticky with drying blood, which brought another wave of nausea, but at least she wasn't bound.

She sensed that she was alone. She could hear faint sounds, but they came to her as if through thick walls.

She sat up and took in her surroundings.

The only light came from a small window near the ceiling, made murky by the grime that coated the frosted glass. All about her lay boxes and broken furniture. A set of open steps fashioned from rough wooden planks rose from where she lay on the dusty concrete floor to a doorway above. She recognised the door's panelling, having stared at it from the other side often enough. She was in the basement.

There were bloody handprints on the door and the steps were marred by dark red footprints. Looking down at herself, she saw that her jumper was covered in red stains. *Ugh!* She tugged it off quickly and cast it to the floor. There were dark patches on the knees of her jeans too, but she couldn't bring herself to take those off.

An image of Jason's vacant stare flickered involuntarily to her mind and, before she knew it, she was sobbing uncontrollably, pain and nausea forgotten.

Stop it! Get a grip of yourself!

It took her a minute or two, but she managed to stop crying and breathe evenly again.

Okay, so she was in the basement. Anita must have dragged her down here. Jason surely didn't – she stifled another urge to cry. The door to the basement was probably locked; it had always been locked, and now that she was finally on the other side, she had little doubt it still was. Nevertheless, she pushed herself to her feet and climbed the steps, shakily at first, but growing in strength as she went. When she got to the door, she paused. Gingerly, she placed her hand around the dull brass knob and turned it slowly, testing.

Just as she suspected: locked.

She put her ear to the wood. The faint sounds she'd thought she'd heard a moment ago had stopped. Wait, no… There *were* sounds. Up above. Creaking floorboards on the upper floor.

Mila lifted her fist, about to start hammering, but hesitated. Maybe it would be better not to let Anita know she was awake yet. Perhaps the smarter thing to do would be to take a few minutes to figure things out.

She continued to listen. Was that the sound of the shower running? She couldn't be sure.

She crept back down the steps to examine her cluttered prison cell. At little more than three hundred square feet, it had a low ceiling, and walls of unpainted grey cinder blocks. The single, solitary window didn't appear to have any catches or means of opening, and even if it had, the thing would have been far too small for Mila to squeeze through. As it was, it gave just enough light to see by. A switch on a timber pillar near the bottom of the steps was linked by a cable to a light socket that dangled from the ceiling, but the socket was empty, and an experimental flick of the switch confirmed there were no other fixtures.

Stacks of cardboard boxes stood to one side of the chamber. A quick peek into the most accessible ones revealed old plastic toys and kids' clothes, the clothes mouldy from the damp air.

Broken furniture had been stuffed into the gap under the stairs. Mila yanked one of the spokes out from an old spindle-back chair. The wood had rotted and it came away easily, but as she gave it an experimental swing, she realised it was far too small to be effective. If she was going to arm herself with something, it needed to be something heavier.

On the opposite side of the basement, below the window, stood an old chest freezer, and a workbench covered in battered paint cans. A toolbox and a heavy-duty plastic tub were tucked beneath the bench.

Setting down the spindle, she crossed the room, crouched in front of the toolbox and pushed it open. Inside, she found a rusty saw and a few screwdrivers, a wrench and a mixed tub of nails and screws. And a hammer. That was more like it. She lifted the hammer and swung it, testing its weight. It was just a simple nail hammer, but it would do.

Next, she moved to the plastic tub. The lid was fastened by foldable clips. She flicked back the snaps and pushed it open.

Papers and envelopes. A quick shuffle through the uppermost layers suggested they were an archive of utility bills and tax returns. She shoved the top half of the pile to one side, but it looked like more of the same below.

She was about to close the lid again when something caught her eye. A large brown envelope sitting amidst the documents had been disturbed by her rummaging, and a glossy photograph had fallen partway out. The fleshy colour was what grabbed Mila's attention. When she tried to pick up the envelope, it tore, and the contents spilled across the floor. Two dozen photos, some landing face down, but more landing face up. The images made Mila's heart lurch in her chest and her gut twist in revulsion. Nudes. Girls. Younger than Mila. And some younger again.

She bent to scrape them back together, to get them out of her sight, but as she gathered them up and shoved them roughly back into the torn envelope, she froze.

It couldn't be.

But it was.

Anita.

Like the photo from the bedroom, she was years younger than when Mila first met her – eleven or twelve, maybe – but the face was unmistakable, with those big eyes and the baby fat already giving way to high cheekbones.

Unlike the other girls, Anita's expression wasn't frightened. It was angry.

Mila suddenly felt ill. Straightening, she dropped the photo and stepped back, staring at the pile of tumbled prints like they were poisonous snakes that might rear up and strike her at any moment. She gripped the hammer tighter, but felt powerless in the face of what she was seeing.

As she stood there, heart pounding, feeling confused and sick, she became aware of the faint humming. There might not have been any lightbulbs, but in a house with no electricity, here was the unmistakable sound of energy. It was coming from the chest freezer.

The lid wasn't fastened, but it was so sticky from lack of use that Mila had to set her hammer down and use both hands to pry it open. It came away with a sucking sound, releasing a cloud of white vapour.

The body inside was doubled-up, folded into the cramped space atop a few ancient bags of peas and greens. Even with blue skin, and a beard and eyebrows that were fringed with ice, Mila recognised him immediately. Another familiar face in this underground chamber of horrors.

The old man from the photographs.

Anita's great-uncle.

Mila knew, at some level, that this was the moment she needed to be smart – the crucial moment when she ought to take a second to pause and think – but the scream was out of her mouth before she could stop it.

* * *

Esther peered down at the set of aerial photographs, a series of shots that covered both sides of the Norwick Hills. There were no indications of encampments out in the wild. The only signs of human life to be seen were along the road that snaked up and over the hills into the neighbouring county, along with glimpses of the search and rescue volunteers who were combing the area methodically.

"I've gone through them a few times, Skipper," Derek Grant said from where he sat in front of her desk. "I can't see anything that would indicate a group living out in the woods."

"No," Esther murmured. "Nor can I." She sighed and settled back in her seat. "Okay, next steps are to—"

She cut off as a breathless young PC in uniform appeared in the open doorway. Esther recognised the officer as the one who had been dealing with Mila's case before CID took over. *Fletcher?* The girl knocked on the door as she stepped in, despite the fact that both Esther and Derek had turned at the sound of her appearance. She'd also attracted the attention of Caroline and Spencer, who'd been diverted from their work by the sounds of exertion, sounds that weren't very often heard on the CID floor.

Fisher. Imelda Fisher.

"Imelda, is everything okay?" Esther asked.

"Sarge," Fisher replied, her face flushed, "that BOLO you just sent out – I've seen those two!"

Esther half-stood. "You mean Anita Jess and Jason Laird?"

Fisher nodded quickly. "Both of them. They were at an address up on Denton Lane. I attended another misper call up there, for an old guy. Those two were at his address. They gave me false names."

Esther was already grabbing her coat. "Do you have a car?"

Fisher produced a set of keys from her pocket.

"Let's go." Esther turned to Derek as she left the office. "Tell Jared," she ordered. "Grab a car and follow us up to Denton Lane."

She heard the detective reply "Will do, Skip!" as she and PC Fisher headed for the stairs.

By the time they reached the stairwell, they were running.

28

SHE'D BEEN THINKING about what to do. Working and thinking. Now she was scrubbing. Scrubbing and thinking.

She'd ripped up the carpet and dumped it at the end of the back garden. She would burn it later. After that, it had just been a matter of scrubbing the walls, the skirting boards and the kitchen floor.

And mopping up the blood.

Scrubbing and mopping.

Now she was scrubbing herself.

Scrubbing, scrubbing, scrubbing.

For some reason, it was harder to get the blood off herself than it had been from the walls and floor. Every time she thought she was clean, she would notice a little more redness on her flesh and have to start again.

She couldn't put Jason in the freezer. No room left. And burying him would be too difficult. The ground this high up was hard and rocky. If she'd struggled to dig a vegetable patch, there was no chance she would manage to dig a grave. That's when she'd remembered the quarry, and their special place, her and Mila's.

Two birds. One stone.

She would take Mila to their old spot. She'd make her understand.

The boot of George's car was too small for Jason, so she'd had to drag him across the rear seat and cover him in that tartan blanket, the one that had spent its life draped across the parcel shelf. The blood from the body wasn't nearly so bad as she'd feared. She'd been worried it would leak all over the place, but maybe it had drained out or something; there'd definitely been enough of it in the house. Bucketfuls.

Bucketfuls of Jason's blood.

She retched again. Wet hair hanging in knots, she watched the water from the shower splash and circle the drain. There was nothing left in her stomach to puke up now, but she retched anyway. That's when she noticed how pink her thigh was. More redness. How had it got *there?* She began to scrub.

Scrub, scrub, scrub the blood away.

Yes, she'd been thinking. Thinking about Mila. She would take her to their special place. That would make her remember. Remember their bond. Their bond of sisterhood.

A memory prompt.

Their special place, their special bond.

Once Mila remembered that, she would understand.

Sisters.

Sisters forever.

Abruptly, Anita realised that the pink she was seeing – on her thigh, her arms, her hands – was her flesh rubbed raw from her scrubbing. It wasn't blood. She laughed. Silly! The blood was gone.

She was clean.

Scrubbed clean.

She knocked off the shower.

As she dried herself, she considered what she would say to Mila. The poor girl was probably scared. Maybe hurt too; she'd taken a bit of a tumble at the bottom of those basement steps.

All of a sudden, Anita was blindsided by a powerful rush of love and pity for Mila. Tears welled in her eyes as she thought about her little sister waking up, frightened and alone in that basement.

A distant, muffled scream reached her ears.

The basement.

The freezer.

George!

Anita tugged her clothes on quickly, not bothering to tie the linen belt dangling loose from her hemp culottes. She raced out of the bathroom and down to the basement door.

"Mila?" she called desperately. "Mila?"

She twisted the key in the lock. Without the carpet, the corridor had an odd echo, making this familiar hallway seem suddenly foreign.

"Mila!" Anita called again.

She set her hand on the doorknob, but when she went to twist it, the thing came alive in her hand and spun out of her grip. The door swung open, slamming into her nose and sending her stumbling backwards. She lost her footing and landed hard on the carpetless floor. Her head smacked against the wall, but the dull ache it produced at the back of her skull was eclipsed by the bright, sharp stinging in her nose.

Despite the tears that suddenly blurred her vision, she made out the figure bounding over her towards the back door.

"Mila!" she screamed. She tried to grab her, but the girl was too fast and Anita too stunned and too slow to react.

She blinked away the tears. Wiped her eyes. Bright red blood spilled over her arm and onto the floor. Her mouth was filled with the sour, coppery taste of it.

More blood.

She stared for a brief moment at the red drops falling from her nose, then shook herself. No time. She dragged herself up and into the kitchen.

Mila was racing down the yard, heading for the woods.

"No, no, no, no!" She couldn't let Mila go! She couldn't lose Mila too!

As Mila vanished into the trees, Anita didn't hesitate. She snatched the freshly washed athamé from the draining board and raced out the door after her.

* * *

Mila plunged deeper into the forest, frantic and disorientated. Branches and twigs lashed her face and arms as she ran. The trees seemed to loom up and block her path, while at the same time they didn't seem nearly thick enough to conceal her escape.

A plaintive cry from behind made her glance over her shoulder.

Jesus, she could still see the house! And Anita, running

down the back yard after her! She needed to move faster...

Her toe caught on a bulging root and she fell. Spitting out soil and rotten leaves, she scrambled to her feet, snatched up the hammer and ran on.

She could hear Anita calling her name now, pleading with her to stop. But she couldn't stop. Anita had lost her mind. She'd killed Jason. Killed her great-uncle – if the man even *was* her great-uncle – and probably wanted to kill her too, to shut her up...

Panting, a painful stitch forming in her side, Mila suddenly had to grab hold of a thin spruce trunk and wheel ninety degrees to prevent herself from falling headlong down a steep, fern-covered slope that appeared abruptly in front of her. She leaned over with one hand on the ground in an effort to control her descent as she took the hill at an angle. She lost the hammer in the manoeuvre, but at least she didn't go tumbling down the slope with it.

"Mila!"

The proximity of Anita's voice startled her. The ridge dipped up ahead, and that was where the woman appeared, scarcely twenty yards away, that strange ceremonial knife in her left hand – the one they'd used to cut their palms during the ritual.

The fright of this sudden appearance, so close, made Mila lose her footing. Before she knew it, she was falling – literally rolling down the hill like a barrel. The forest raced by in a blur of spinning trees as she tried in vain to arrest her fall. The bottom ended in a stony stream, and it was there that she came to a stop with a crash, her left elbow smashing painfully into a jagged rock as she hit the cold water.

With a grunt, she rose to her hands and knees, her

peroxide-blonde hair dripping. The pain from the blow to her elbow made her left arm give way almost immediately, and she landed face-first in the stream again. Gasping and spluttering, she pulled herself out of the water with her good arm.

She looked up to find Anita standing over her.

"Oh my God, Mila, are you okay?"

Mila tried to scramble away, but Anita pounced on her.

"No!" Mila cried, trying to wriggle free. She scanned about for the knife and felt a surge of relief when she saw that Anita had dropped it nearby.

"Mila, stop!" Anita wailed, and Mila was shocked to see that Anita was crying. "Please, stop! I need you!"

She had little choice. Anita was stronger anyway, and with Mila unable to use her left arm – her elbow was throbbing with a hot, ugly pain now – she could do nothing but play along as Anita straddled her and pinned her to the ground.

A tremulous smile touched Anita's lips as she reached out tenderly and brushed some dirt from Mila's cheek. Her own nose was slightly swollen, her upper lip smeared with blood, but she seemed oblivious to it.

"I need you," she repeated. "I need my sister."

Anita's eyes had taken on that faraway look that Mila recognised from whenever the woman got high. Even with the knife tossed to one side, the glassy-eyed way Anita was smiling at her told Mila she should tread carefully. Her friend was clearly unhinged. She quickly discarded any notion of mentioning the body in the freezer.

"Sisters," Mila repeated warily.

Anita gave a delighted laugh and clapped her hands.

"You remember!" she chirped. "My little sister." She

reached out and stroked Mila's cheek again with the back of one finger. Then her expression turned grave. "And right now I need your help, little sister. More than ever before."

Mila nodded slowly. "Okay."

"It was an accident," Anita said, eyes filling up again. "Jason. I didn't mean it."

"I know," Mila replied carefully.

Anita nodded, her face pinched as she forced a smile.

"Come on," she said. "You can help me get rid of him. Once we're free of him and it's just the two of us, everything will be better. I promise."

As Anita stood, Mila glanced at the ceremonial dagger lying among the pine needles not five feet away. Almost as if in answer to her thoughts, she felt a spasm in her left elbow and hissed.

Anita frowned, then hunkered down to examine Mila's injury.

"That looks bad, honey," she said, pursing her lips and shaking her head. "Something broken, I think."

No shit, Mila thought. Her elbow was swollen and growing darker. Bending it sent arrows of pain up her shoulder and down her forearm.

Anita looked at her seriously. "We'll have to get that seen to afterwards."

With a decisive nod, she stood again and held out her hand. Gripping Mila's good arm, she hoisted the younger girl to her feet. Any hope that Anita had forgotten about the knife evaporated as she bent and scooped the thing up again.

With Anita clutching the ritual knife in her right hand and supporting Mila with her left, Mila let herself be led. She cradled her injured arm against her stomach at an angle

– it hurt the least in that position – and they set off through the forest, back towards the house, like children in some dark, twisted fairy tale. It was all Mila could do not to glance around as she tried frantically to come up with some way to escape. But Anita had a firm hold of her right arm; in fact, her grip seemed to be growing tighter the closer to the cottage they got. And she still had the knife. For all Mila knew, it was the knife she'd used to—

The notion made her grow clammy and breathless; she buried it quickly and forced her mind to other things. She needed to stay calm. She needed to think. There was a way out of this. There must be.

Mila had expected Anita to lead her back into the cottage, but instead she brought her around to where the car was parked at the top of the drive. Opening the front passenger door, Anita gestured for her to get in.

"Where are we going?" Mila asked.

Anita smiled coyly. "A surprise. You'll see. You'll like it. I promise."

Mila had no option but to comply. The passenger door closed with a heavy *thunk*. As Anita sat in on the driver's side, she clicked the locks shut on all four doors. Mila, unable to quell another surge of panic, glanced around. And that's when she saw the blanket-covered pile on the back seat, and the lifeless hand that was sticking out from under one end.

She couldn't help herself – she let out a shriek and snatched at the door handle with her good hand.

Quick as an adder, Anita leaned over and grabbed her.

"Don't!" she snapped, all tenderness forgotten, her face and voice hard.

Her grip on Mila's right wrist was so fierce that Mila

winced.

"Please, Anita," she gasped. "You're hurting me."

Anita's mouth was a tight line as she let go, and the look she was giving Mila was that of an elder disappointed in a child.

"I shouldn't have to do this," she said crossly, pulling the belt from the hoops of her skirt-pants. Reaching over, she tugged Mila's seatbelt across her body and snapped it into the fastener. Then, more deftly than Mila would have expected of her, she looped the linen belt through the gap in Mila's seat belt and tied it in a secure and messy knot to her own. Mila's eyes slid to the bone handle of the ritual dagger, poking up from the pocket of the driver's door. Within reach, and at the same time so very far away.

Anita started the car.

"We're doing this together," she said firmly, as she nosed out of the driveway, and Mila didn't think she'd ever heard four more sinister words spoken.

29

"IT'S GONE," FISHER blurted, as she hit the brakes and skidded to a stop in front of 44 Denton Lane.

"What's gone?" Esther asked.

"The car," the officer explained. "The blue hatchback – the Ford Fiesta. It was parked here when I left. It's gone."

"You got the reg?"

Fisher nodded.

"Get on to Despatch and get it alerted. I want any live hits radioed through to us straight away."

With that, Esther leapt from the patrol car and hurried towards the cottage. A quick check of the front door confirmed it was locked. She raced around the side of the house, where she found the door to the kitchen standing wide open. She slowed before she got to the threshold. Reaching into her pocket for her pepper spray, she advanced cautiously.

"Hello?" she called. "Hello, it's the police! Is there anyone in?"

Silence. Esther wrinkled her nose as she stepped inside. There was an acrid scent in the air, a tang of citrus and vinegar. She scanned the worktops, but nothing struck her as out of the ordinary.

Stepping lightly across the kitchen – keeping to the edge of the room out of scene-preserving habit – she reached the door to the front hallway. It had a stripped-down look. There was no carpet, just raw floorboards and rows of jagged carpet-grippers along the walls.

A door stood open under the stairs. It was slightly smaller than the kitchen door in every dimension, the broad, wooden steps beyond leading down into a musty-smelling basement.

"Hello?" she called again. "Police! Anyone home?"

She noticed a splatter of red on the planking directly in front of the basement door. As her eyes drifted over the skirting, she saw that some of the wallpaper had been scraped off. But it looked like the job had been left unfinished, with only the bottom half cut away.

Stepping carefully over the small red splatters, Esther crouched and peered into the basement. There was a faint wash of daylight, but it did little to illuminate the underground chamber. She couldn't make out many details. A dusty floor. The lower tiers of a stack of boxes.

"Hello?"

No reply or sound from below. She sensed it was empty.

Peering up through the banister railings to the next level, she could see no further than a halfway landing where the stairs turned.

Movement at the corner of her eye made her spin, but it was only PC Fisher appearing at the back door.

"That's the vehicle alerted," she told Esther, glancing

cautiously around the kitchen.

"Doesn't look like there's anyone home," Esther replied. "Come here, but be careful where you step." She pointed to the small spatters of what looked like blood on the floor of the hallway, which the uniform officer duly avoided.

"The carpet's been pulled up," she told Esther as she stepped into the corridor. "There was carpet when I was here a couple of hours ago."

Esther nodded. That explained the bare carpet-grippers.

"Keep an eye on this basement," she instructed the officer, "while I check the rest of the house."

A second door, a few feet down the hall, opened onto the living room, which was an odd mash of old and new. Outdated wallpaper had been overlaid with fresher, Celtic-style throws and hippy wall-art. The large, front-facing window was half-covered by more Celtic drapes, cutting the room in two – half in sunlight, half in shadow. At the centre of the mantelpiece stood a wooden frame, carved as though it was meant to hold something for display, but whatever usually occupied the space was missing now. A distinct odour of old cannabis smoke hung in the air. Nearby, on a chair, sat a strange costume headpiece, like a life-size bull or something, along with a pile of grey woollen robes. The animal head looked like it should've been mounted on a wall, but it lay on its side, and Esther could see that the inside was hollow, wide enough to slip over someone's head and wear as part of some weird Halloween costume. She didn't examine it too closely. Once she was satisfied that there was no one else in the room, she made her way upstairs.

Pepper spray at the ready, eyes watchful, she approached the blind corner of the landing. Peeking carefully around the corner, she found the second storey corridor empty. The same dark, decades-old carpet covered the stairs and upper floor. Even without Fisher's confirmation, it was obvious that the downstairs carpet had been removed recently: dust matted the edges of the carpeted steps, whereas the wooden planks of the ground-floor hall were clean and dust-free.

Turning her attention back to the upstairs corridor, Esther counted four doors, two on either side. They were staggered so that they didn't face each other directly, with most of the light coming from a small, frosted window at the far end of the hallway.

She edged forward to the first door, which stood ajar. Stepping inside quickly, she placed her back to the wall to maintain a peripheral view of the corridor as she scanned the bedroom.

More outmoded fixtures overlaid with New Age décor. The grim, Seventies-style carpet had been covered by rough woven rugs. A dozen dreamcatchers turned gently by an open window, the feathers on their willow-hooped frames fluttering in the breeze. A pile of books lay scattered against one wall next to a pair of single beds that had been pushed together to serve as a double bed. *The Satanic Bible* and *The Satanic Rituals* by Anton LaVey, several titles by John Pilger, Friedrich Nietzsche's *Beyond Good and Evil* and a tumble of other books about Wiccan witchcraft, spiritualism and healing energy. There was a trace of cannabis smoke in this room too, and an elaborate bong on the far side of the bed looked like it saw plenty of use. On the whole, the room itself was kind of bare, as though it had recently been stripped of furniture and only half-redecorated.

Esther went to the next door, which was closed. Taking

248

hold of the handle, she pushed it open and kicked it wide.

Another bedroom. Also empty. Unlike other parts of the house, this place seemed to have been left frozen in some previous decade. The windows were heavily netted, and the ugly orange-brown wallpaper gave the whole chamber a sepia tint. The wardrobe stood half-open, stuffed with the kind of clothing favoured by an older generation. The four-poster bed was neatly made, and on the bedside locker atop a couple of old paperbacks sat a pair of thick-rimmed glasses. A set of tartan slippers lay below. The place had an unaired smell.

Leaning to one side to make sure there was nobody behind the door, Esther moved on.

Of the two remaining doors at the end of the corridor, the first stood wide open and the second was ajar.

A peek through the first revealed a bathroom – all ugly, olive-coloured tiles and plastic moulding – with a trashcan next to the sink overflowing with boxes of blonde hair dye.

The second was another bedroom, this one sparser and more soulless than the others. There were spots on the walls – lots of greasy little marks from the posters and pictures that had once been tacked there – as well as old biro and crayon scribbles on the peeling wallpaper, which was ancient and faded and had repeating patterns of generic cartoon characters marching across it. A set of bunk beds, devoid of mattresses, stood opposite a single bed, its covers rumpled and undone. A dressing table with a triptych of mirrors lay between both beds and, at the bottom of the single bed, a canvas bag with clothes spilling out of it.

Esther's heart beat a little faster when she spotted a grey stone keyring on the dressing table. It was a knight on horseback, sword raised overhead, and the word *Lietuva* etched below.

Mila's keyring.

She'd been here. But where was she now?

There were wisps of blonde scattered along the bottom of the mirror, as if someone had been cutting hair and done a bad job of cleaning up. More strands covered the floor beneath the dresser.

A narrow wardrobe stood at the back of the room, the empty hangers within rattling as Esther snatched it open. But there was nothing else inside. No school uniform.

The window next to the wardrobe overlooked the back garden, where the Norwick Forest came right up on all sides of the property, adding to the eerie sense of seclusion at 44 Denton Lane. Someone had made an effort to start a flower bed along the northern edge; the earth was freshly dug, wooden planks delineating the space into rough squares. On the other side of the wild lawn was a pile of rubbish: household furniture and a roll of carpet. The carpet from the downstairs hallway. Esther had been so focused on the house that she hadn't noticed it when she'd entered the garden. Its underlayer of rubber was outermost, dark stains seeping through in patches. Esther frowned and stepped closer to the window. They looked almost like—

All of a sudden, there was a loud curse from somewhere downstairs.

Imelda!

Esther raced from the bedroom and hurtled back down the stairs.

"Imelda?" she shouted.

"Down here!" came the woman's reply from the basement.

Esther was forced to slow when she got to the basement

stairs. The rough wooden planks were thick and broad, but there was no handrail.

A small, grime-encrusted window near the ceiling admitted just enough light to see by. It looked like the space had been used for storage for years, with boxes stacked high on one side of the room.

She found PC Fisher standing in front of an open chest freezer, but it was the glossy photographs scattered across the floor that caught Esther's attention. Glimpses of naked flesh gave Esther an immediate sense of what the photos were, and as she grew closer and saw them more clearly, she felt a shiver pass through her.

"Oh God," she breathed.

Sad and frightened faces said the children in these pictures had already been through too much. Their eyes spoke of a lifetime of hurt in just a few short years.

"Yeah," Fisher replied grimly. "Girls. Young girls. And that's not all."

Esther could see that Fisher's cheeks were pale, her jaw clenched. She was wearing a pair of blue nitrile gloves and the red light on her bodycam told Esther it was recording.

"I came down here because I thought I heard faint noises," she explained. "Clicking, or ticking, or something. Turns out it was coming from this old freezer. Someone left it open."

Inside the freezer was the body of a man, curled into a foetal position atop bags of frozen vegetables. His face was blue and contorted as if in pain, his bushy beard and eyebrows flecked with white frost. It was hard to tell his age in that state, but Esther estimated mid-sixties.

"I think I've found George Haribald," Fisher murmured.

"Radio this in," Esther instructed. "Get a couple of

crews down here to seal off the property, and task CSI."

Fisher wasted no time in getting on to Despatch as Esther conducted a quick rummage of the rest of the basement. It was a cursory search, to make sure there was no one else down here – alive *or* dead – but the only thing she found was a crumpled woollen jumper in one corner, stained with blood. It looked like a recent addition, unlike the contents of the boxes, which were full of old toys and mouldering clothes.

"Let's get out of here," Esther said, once she'd confirmed the boxes held nothing of relevance – most were covered in a decade of dust and clearly hadn't been disturbed for many years. "I want to keep this scene preserved for CSI."

Fisher seemed happy to follow her up the stairs.

"There's a crew on its way," she told Esther as they climbed the steps.

Back in the hallway, the officer made as if to close the basement door, but Esther stopped her.

"No," she said. "Leave it as we found it." Then she remembered the roll of carpet she'd seen lying in the garden, the dark stains that had caught her attention before Fisher's cry from the basement had distracted her. "Make sure that front door is secure. We've come in through the back door, so we'll establish that as our entry point. Do you have a crime scene logbook?"

"In the car," Fisher replied.

"Get a scene started. Call in the time."

"Will do, Sarge."

Fisher followed Esther's footsteps as she skirted the edge of the kitchen floor and emerged into the garden again. While Fisher headed off to get her scene log from the patrol car, Esther picked her way across the yard, eyes searching the grass as she went.

The jumble of garbage at the end of the lawn hadn't been there long, judging by the impressions on the grass around it. The carpet had been tossed atop a broken old television set and a variety of other appliances. Esther stared at the brown-red patches on the carpet's underlay. She used the torch on her phone to light up the squashed tunnel of the roll's interior and saw that the carpet was the same dark pattern as the one upstairs. Even with that dark patterning, there was no mistaking the blood. There was a *lot* of it. What was worse was that Esther could smell it. This was fresh – far too fresh for it to have come from her man in the freezer. At least she could see there were no more bodies in there.

The crunching of gravel announced the arrival of a second police callsign. Esther straightened. Two uniform officers climbed out of the car and set their hats on their heads.

As PC Fisher went to brief them, Esther used her phone to look up her current location on the map and estimate the distance to the old cabin where Mark Taylor was running his search. It was a long way from here. Too far for a casual walk. This cottage was right on the edge of the wilderness. Miles of wooded hills lay between where she stood and the cabin. Even with Taylor's military-grade operation, it would have been days before the search parties came anywhere close to Denton Lane.

Esther looked up and stared into the forest, gloomy beneath its evergreen canopy.

Where are you, Mila?

"Sarge!"

Esther turned. Fisher was signalling to her from the front yard.

"Despatch have a hit on the Fiesta!" she shouted.

Esther immediately broke into a run.

"Where?" she asked, as she hurried towards Fisher, whose uniform colleagues were glancing at the house uncertainly.

"On the B-nine-six-three," Fisher replied. "An ANPR camera on one of the mountain roads picked it up. About three miles from here, heading eastbound."

"When?"

"Just now."

"Let's go!" Esther said. "You two"—she gestured to the new arrivals—"hold this scene. Run some tape around the back garden too. There's a roll of carpet covered in blood at the bottom of the yard – don't go near it." Without waiting to answer any of their questions, she raced over to PC Fisher's patrol car. "Imelda, come on! We're going after that car!"

Fisher handed the scene log to the taller of the two uniformed men. Esther snatched up the car's radio mic as Fisher sat in the driver's seat.

"Despatch, this is DS Penman out at Denton Lane. You receiving? Over."

A male voice crackled over the radio. *"Callsign with DS Penman from Despatch, receiving. Send your message. Over."*

"The sighting on the registration sent out just now. The one in the Norwick Hills. Is that hit between our position on Denton Lane and the site of the search operation?"

"I'll just check it on the maps. Wait one."

Fisher started the engine. Without waiting for further instructions, she pulled out and accelerated down the lane as quickly as the rutted track would allow.

The despatcher's voice came back over the car speakers. *"That's a negative. Opposite direction. Sighting was eastwards of your position, eastbound, approximately four minutes ago. Over."*

Esther hesitated and frowned at the map on her phone. And then a thought occurred to her.

"What about the old quarry? Over."

Esther gritted her teeth as the patrol car bounced over one pothole after another.

"That's a roger on that. Vehicle was clocked about half a mile from the old quarry. Over."

"Despatch from Penman," Esther replied, "we've got a potential murder scene here on Denton Lane, and the suspects may be in that vehicle. There might also be a vulnerable high risk misper onboard too. One Mila Rose. Send out a message to all units to be on alert for that car and for three persons: Mila Rose, Anita Jess and Jason Laird. Photos are on the bulletin sent out within the past hour."

"Wilco. All units, that's all units, be on the lookout for a blue Ford Fiesta, registration…" The despatcher began reciting the details of the car, followed by those of the three persons from Esther's earlier bulletin.

Esther set the radio back down as Fisher slowed momentarily at the junction with the main road. Checking that the way was clear, she gunned the car out onto the smooth, wide tarmac and headed east.

"The old quarry, I'm assuming?" she said, as she reached down to press the button that activated her blue lights.

Esther was studying the map on her phone again. Several smaller roads made a sparse web across the hills around the quarry site, but Esther was mulling over what Tabitha Renshaw had told her about Mila and Anita sneaking off there regularly when they were young. That spot at the quarry was a good bet. If not, their current course would take them out onto the motorway, and if they got as far as there, they'd be pinging cameras every few minutes, whether they went north or south.

"The old quarry," she confirmed. "If they get to the motorway, traffic branch will soon get them stopped."

"Roger that," Fisher replied, flicking on her blues-and-twos and shifting the car up into sixth gear.

30

ANITA WAS RAVING. That was the only word for it. Everything revolved around sisterhood, apparently, and their blood pact all those years ago. That was the important thing, the only thing in the *world* that mattered.

"Jason is just a guy," she said again, for about the hundredth millionth time. "Just a guy."

Hunched forward over the steering wheel, she made constant rapid movements: sniffing and wiping her nose with her wrist; brushing the tears from her eyes with the back of her hand.

They were going way too fast. Their speed had crept up gradually while Anita had rabbited on about sisterhood and guys and disloyalty and blood pacts. Drivers blasted their horns as she overtook on blind bends, shooting forward whenever the road opened up in front of her.

"I would never have let Jason come between us," she said. "You know that, right? Mila? You believe me?"

Anita turned to look at her then. She stared at Mila for

such a long time that Mila became alarmed and gave a quick, mute nod, just so Anita would look back at the road again.

They were going to crash and be mangled. That's what was going to happen. If Anita didn't slow down, they were both going to die.

But it wasn't only the thought of crashing that had Mila wishing Anita would focus more on the road. Every now and again, she ran her fingers gingerly over the cloth belt Anita had used to tie their seatbelts together. The knot was on Anita's side, and she would have to undo it to get free; unfastening either seatbelt would only pull it all tighter, alerting Anita and keeping Mila pinned to her seat. She needed to get her fingers on the knot. If she could just slide it around so that it was closer to her…

Another car horn wailed as Anita swerved back onto her side of the road after a particularly ill-considered overtake. It was a blessing that the traffic was so light.

"Guys are trouble," Anita muttered. "They're all bastards. Every last one of them. You hear me, Mila?"

Mila pulled her hand away from the belt as Anita spun to fix her with another maniacal stare. It was like Anita was in a different world, both seeing Mila and not seeing her, with eyes that were slightly unfocused and red from crying. Mila was beginning to wonder if she was actually high. On meth or something.

"Please watch the road, Anita." Her words were thick with fear. "I don't want to die."

Anita's expression changed so dramatically that it sent a chill up Mila's spine. It went from intense frown to horrified shock and sympathy in a fraction of a second.

"Oh, I'm so sorry, sweetie!" she cried, turning her gaze back on the road and braking hard. A moment later, they were doing just over forty again. And then another sudden shift, to bright smiles and a cheery voice. "Here we are!" she announced.

She spun the wheel, too fast, and the car dipped wildly as they turned, taking a half-hidden exit onto a track that led uphill between the trees. The manoeuvre brought a soft thump from the backseat. Heart lurching, as much from the abrupt change in direction as the awful sound, Mila risked a glance over her shoulder.

Jason's body had shifted under the force of the turn and the blanket had fallen partially away. His lifeless, glassy eyes stared accusingly at her. Mila whimpered, but Anita paid no notice. She was talking in rapid-fire speech again, the steering wheel clamped in her white-knuckled fists as she navigated the dirt track, higher and higher, until the trees began to thin and a stretch of sky opened up ahead of them.

"I think it's the best place for him," she was saying, "and kind of right, you know? Like coming full circle and shit. This is our place, Mila. It's ours! It's exactly the right place to say goodbye to him. Then we can start fresh. You and me. New town, new start. Maybe London. What do you think about London? Or Edinburgh! Oh my God, Mila, you should see Edinburgh! It's, like, one of the most beautiful cities in the world!"

Mila knew now where Anita was taking them. It had been years, but she remembered this track, knew where it led, and right now, she absolutely did *not* want to be in a car with Anita up here.

Trying hard to ignore Jason's body in the back, she reached down until her fingers found the cloth belt once more. It was taut against the seat belts. She began tugging at it gently, trying to get that knot around to her side. She hardly dared breathe for fear of attracting Anita's attention. Anita was nattering on about Edinburgh now, and all the sightseeing they could do when they got there.

This was a nightmare. Mila needed to get free before Anita reached the top of the hill. If she got to that clearing, the way she was driving this rust-bucket, neither of them would live long enough to see Edinburgh, or London, or even Belfield ever again.

31

ESTHER HELD HER mobile phone to her ear with one hand, using the other to brace herself against the dashboard as Fisher executed another overtake at well over the posted limit. There wasn't much traffic on these mountain roads, not with the motorway so close, but people drove like Sunday drivers up here. They were high among the Norwick Hills now, and beautiful views of Belfield in the valley below appeared between the trees every few hundred yards.

"I don't know about the old man," Esther was telling Jared, "but there were pictures, Jared."

"Pictures?" Jared had her on speakerphone, so Derek Grant in the driver's seat could hear her too.

"Photographs," she replied. "Naked pictures. The girls were young, Jared."

"Oh."

"Yeah."

"Was Mila…?"

"I don't think so. I didn't take a good look at them, but they were prints, and I got the impression they were pretty old."

"So how does Mila fit into this?"

"No idea, but we need to get this car stopped."

"Where are you now?"

"We're north of Belfield, heading towards the old quarry."

"Why there?"

"Something Mila's old social worker said. Anita Jess was with Jason Laird at the cottage earlier. Mila and Anita used to run away up to a spot overlooking the quarry when they were young. Happened so often that the carers knew where to go looking every time they disappeared. It's a long shot, but it's something. Until the car pings on the motorway, or somewhere else, it's as good a place to check as any."

"You think Mila's in that car?"

Esther stared up the mountain to her left, where evergreens marched in steep, dark ranks towards the sky.

"I'm not sure." She thought about the blood on the rolled-up carpet in the yard. "I think she might be. But I'm not so certain that she's still alive anymore."

There was a moment of silence on the other end, and then he said: "We don't know until we find the car. We'll meet you at the quarry and keep an ear on the motorway channel."

"Okay."

As she hung up and put her phone away, something flashed past and caught her eye – a steel pole with a camera affixed to the top.

"Wait, slow down!" she said to Fisher. "That was an ANPR camera we just passed."

She snatched up the radio mic as Fisher slowed the car to a crawl and pulled in.

"Despatch from DS Penman. Over."

"Send. Over."

"Any more hits from the traffic cameras on our blue Ford?"

"Negative."

"Received." She set down the radio and turned to Fisher. "We've come too far," she said. "That camera would have picked them up if they'd come this way. Spin around. We must have missed a turn-off."

As Fisher turned the car, Esther brought up the satellite map on her phone again. There was forest on either side, but the quarry was just to the north of them here. There were two main access roads – neither of them much more than overgrown tracks nowadays – but they were further to the west.

"What about this?" Fisher asked, as she pulled in and knocked off her blue lights. She'd stopped across the road from a track that was barely more than a pair of tyre-wide ruts leading away up the slope between the trees.

Esther looked down at her phone and zoomed in on their location. The track was so small and well hidden that it wasn't visible on the satellite image. But she could see that if it kept on in roughly the same direction, it would bring them to a clearing overlooking a flooded section of the old quarry. Esther recognised it as the spot Tabitha Renshaw had shown her that morning. She looked from her phone to the little track, then up and down the main road. The Ford had either had its licence plates switched, or it had turned off the road somewhere along this stretch.

"The quarry is up that general direction," she told Fisher.

"And I didn't see any other exits. Did you?"

Fisher shook her head. "Didn't even see *that* one."

"Take it," Esther decided. "Let's find out how close to the quarry it brings us."

Fisher shoved the car into gear, the suspension grunting in protest as they joined the bumpy track and began their slow, careful ascent through the trees.

32

ANITA SAT BEHIND the wheel, engine off, staring out across the quarry pit. Raw, scarred walls faced them from the other side of the chasm.

She had parked the car in the middle of the clearing, next to the ancient oak tree. The space was ringed by evergreens, except along one edge, where the grass ended abruptly twenty yards in front of them. Although they couldn't see it from here, Anita knew it was a sheer drop – thirty feet at least – into the waters below.

The sun was behind them, halfway to the horizon, splitting the opposite quarry wall in two. She stared at the line of shadow, the cliff face bright and colourful in the sunlight, dark and grey below. Kind of how she felt. She'd slipped from sunshine to shadow now too. Whatever fire had burned in her had gone out, the force that had driven her to this point completely spent. Clarity – that treacherous presence of mind – had seeped in, dousing all her plans, all her visions, in the icy chill of reality.

Mila sat next to her, sniffing back tears and shifting subtly, as if Anita couldn't see that she was trying to get her hands on the knot holding their seatbelts together.

Holding them together.

Forced bond.

Anita made no move to stop her. She hadn't fully decided what to do, now that she was here. Her plans — dumping Jason's body into the deep, dark quarry waters and then striking out for a new city and a new life — seemed painfully unattainable now. One look at Mila's face — a proper look, after she'd parked up and could focus on her sister — one glance at that terrified, tear-streaked expression, had told her that she was losing her.

Losing her sister.

She didn't want to lose Mila. She didn't want to be alone.

And yet, hadn't she always been alone? A lonely, silly brat of a girl.

Silly brat of a girl.

"I'm so sorry, Anita. I had no idea."

They had been sitting in silence for so long that Mila's hoarse whisper startled her. She blinked. Tasted tears and realised she was crying. When had she started crying?

Mila was watching her. She didn't look terrified anymore; her expression held something else now.

Sympathy.

"What he did to you," she said. "That man."

Silly brat of a girl. Come here! I'll straighten you out!

Anita rubbed the tears from her cheeks. She turned to stare out over the quarry again.

"Is that why you… why you…?" Mila didn't seem able to finish the question.

"Yes." She spat the word, making Mila flinch. "And it

wasn't just me. There were others. You saw."

"I'm sorry," Mila whispered.

Anita gripped the steering wheel. For a moment she remembered with horrible detail the feel of his grubby hands and smell of his sour breath, just like she did in her nightmares, dreams that all the pills and weed in the world couldn't chase away anymore. She felt again the soul-stealing sense of self-loathing he had brought to her life. She'd lived with it all these years, and she was tired. Tired of trying to chase it away.

You had to face what you feared.

You had to kill what you feared.

And when Anita had returned to Belfield, the man she had feared most in her life had transformed. No longer a towering giant. Nothing more than a frail old man. Finally, it was Anita who was the stronger of them. Not just a silly brat of a girl anymore…

* * *

Mila waited for Anita to face forward again before she tried another gentle tug at the cloth belt. The knot was getting closer, but whenever she moved it, she heard it rasping against the polyester edges of the seatbelts. Faint as it was, it made her wince every time.

Anita had stopped talking shortly after they'd arrived. She'd gone silent as soon as they'd pulled in next to the old oak tree, the tree into which they had carved their initials and made their pact all those years ago.

Even though Anita's ranting and raving had freaked Mila

out, it had been far better than the silence. At least when she'd been talking, she'd spoken about trips to other cities, plans for their future together. Now, sitting here, facing the edge of the cliff like this, Mila didn't trust her silence. She didn't like the mournful, hopeless look in her eyes. And when Anita had started wringing the steering wheel with her hands, Mila knew she needed to derail whatever train of thought she was riding. The clearing sloped gently down to the cliff here. Anita wouldn't even have to start the car. All she'd have to do would be drop the handbrake, and they'd go rolling towards the edge.

Mila had considered bringing up Edinburgh again, but the image of those photographs had popped into her head and the words that had come out of her mouth were not the words she had intended to say. But they'd felt like the right words.

"He deserved it, Mila," Anita told her softly now, still gazing across the quarry. "For what he did to us."

Mila couldn't argue with that.

Then, all of a sudden, Anita straightened, and her hands came away from the wheel. She was staring at something in the rearview mirror.

"Oh fuck!" she exclaimed. "Oh no!"

Mila turned and saw a police car emerge from the gap in the trees behind them.

* * *

"Get in front of them!" Esther said.

Fisher accelerated, putting her patrol car between the

blue hatchback and the cliff.

Esther had a clear view inside the Ford as she jumped out. She recognised Mila in the passenger seat, despite the blonde locks, and Anita Jess behind the wheel. There was no sign of Jason Laird. The sight of Mila alive made Esther's heart leap into her throat, and it was only then that she realised how far her hopes had dwindled on that front.

But her relief was short-lived. As she hopped from the patrol car, she heard Jess trying to start the hatchback; the engine wheezed, refusing to turn over. Mila looked petrified. The teenager reached down as if to undo her seatbelt, but Jess's left arm shot out to stop her. As Esther raced to the passenger side of the vehicle, she heard Mila cry out in protest.

Esther tugged at the door handle. It was locked.

"Open the door!" She smacked at the window. "Police! Mila! Unlock the door!"

Mila began fumbling with the lock. There were a couple of clicks in rapid succession. Jess had stopped trying to start the car long enough to reach over and snatch Mila's hand from the door. Mila was clutching her left arm to herself, awkwardly using her right hand to try and undo the lock. The teenager was pleading with the woman, but Jess was shrieking back at her, not relenting. Their words were hard to make out, but it sounded like Jess was shouting at Mila not to leave her. Mila fumbled with her safety belt once more, but some kind of rope held the seatbelts together.

The engine sputtered again.

Esther glanced towards the cliff edge and the quarry. She couldn't give Jess time to start that car. She began thumping at the passenger window with her elbow. A couple of blows produced a long fissure, running from top to bottom, but the glass was surprisingly resistant.

Meanwhile, PC Fisher had appeared at the driver's side.

"Open up!" she shouted. "Get out of the car!"

Jess, startled to see a uniform cop at her own door now, was pumping the clutch and turning the key in the ignition, but the car's engine refused to start.

Fisher drew her baton and began attacking the driver's window.

With Jess trying frantically to get the car started, Mila was finally able to unlock her door. As soon as she heard the lock click, Esther reached down and snatched it open before Jess had a chance to lock it again.

At that same moment, the engine turned over and Jess shoved the car into reverse. Esther grabbed the swinging passenger door as the car backed rapidly up the slope, but it was too difficult. The door slipped from her fingers, and she tumbled to the grass.

* * *

When the passenger door came open, Mila turned all her attention to undoing the belt. Anita had really hurt her last time, and her fingers shook badly, but at least she was able to dispense with discretion now in her bid to get the knot undone.

Anita was like a woman possessed – crazy and unpredictable – and any notion Mila had that she'd been getting through to her in the moments before the police showed up was blown apart by yet another total schizo freak-out. She kept screaming about Mila not leaving her, about not being alone.

She was reversing fast in the direction of the trees now, the two police officers unable to keep up.

Then suddenly she stopped.

The cops were racing towards them, the one in uniform coming straight at them while the other circled to cut off the route that led to the main road.

Anita had gone quiet again, her eyes distant once more.

"Anita, please," Mila cried, struggling with the knot. "Please, don't. Just give up."

"I can't go back there, Mila," she replied, her voice dreamy now. "Can't go back. Can't lose you too."

"You have to stop! It's over!"

Mila couldn't get her seatbelt free. Whatever Anita had done, it was tied too tightly, and Mila's fingers shook too badly to pull it loose. She was going to have to try and talk Anita down.

An idea occurred to her.

"We can give ourselves up together, Anita. Together!"

Anita turned to her then, eyes still dreamy. Her brow wrinkled. And then she smiled.

"Or we could just fly away, little sister," she murmured. "Fly away together. Like birds."

"Anita, wait! No!"

Too late. Anita slammed the car into first gear and hit the accelerator. The old Ford lurched forward, forcing the uniform cop to dive aside as they hurtled towards the cliff's edge.

33

THE FORD FIESTA stopped just short of the trees, its passenger door still hanging open. Then, all of a sudden, the wheels spun and it shot forward. It veered towards Fisher – who had no choice but to dive from its path or be flattened – and straight on past the patrol car. Esther heard Mila scream.

They were heading for the quarry pit.

Esther wasn't sure what she was doing as she ran towards the old hatchback – it's not like she was going to be able to stop it – but she ran anyway. She was still running when it reached the cliff, tipped forward with a thump, and disappeared over the edge.

She skidded to a halt at the top of the cliff, in time to hear Mila's scream cut off abruptly as the car hit the black waters with a frothy splash. They'd landed in the deepest part of the flooded section, a dozen yards or more from where the quarry floor rose at a steep angle out of the murky pool.

Fisher appeared at Esther's side, her uniform trousers streaked with mud from her roll across the grass. She began casting about for a way down.

"There!" she cried, pointing to a narrow path running along the edge of the cliff.

"Too far," Esther panted as she stripped off her jacket and began tugging at her boots.

Fisher stood gaping for a moment, then starting undoing the fasteners on her stab vest.

"No!" Esther said. "You take the path and try to find a way down. Radio in our location. Get an ambulance and divers up here."

Fisher hesitated, but Esther saw the relief in her face as she nodded.

"I've already called the location in and told the despatchers that we've found them," Fisher replied. "I'll get them to call for an ambulance. And divers." She immediately began transmitting crisp, clear instructions over the radio.

Esther, shorn of encumbrance, took a couple of deep breaths. She stared down at the dark waters, down to where the backside of the Ford Fiesta was already sinking from view. The drop to the water below was a solid forty feet.

Don't think.

She took three steps back, then bounded forward and dived.

She couldn't close her eyes. Not until the last moment. She needed a fix on where the bubbles were rising from the water, the point the car had gone in; the spume from the car's entry was already beginning to dissipate as it spread across the dark surface. The black waters rushed towards her. Esther tucked her head between her outstretched arms and squeezed her eyes shut.

The force of the collision knocked the air from her lungs. When she resurfaced a few seconds later, gasping and sucking for air, the cold hit her. She only had precious moments to do this, and already she'd lost all her bearings in the dive. She treaded water, panting, searching, but the froth of her landing was mixing with what was left of the car's impact, and she could see no trace of where it had gone in.

With little choice but to trust that she was still in the same spot she'd aimed for, she filled her lungs and tumbled in the water. She did her best to ignore the cold as she thrust forward and down, moving her arms in big, sweeping breast strokes and kicking her legs with all her might, fighting against the water's buoyancy.

At first, everything was so dark she saw nothing. Then, slowly, a shape materialized in the gloom below her. It was nothing more than a glint initially, catching what little light managed to penetrate the lake, but as Esther swam towards it, she could see it was the rear end of the car. It was still sinking.

Her lungs were already starting to burn. She had no idea how deep this water was, but it was beginning to look too deep for a second dive. Desperately, she thrust herself onward, legs pumping, hands pushing in her effort to get lower, to get closer to the car.

Then she heard it, even through the muffling effect of the water: a faint thud, as the car's front hit the quarry floor. It fell backwards in slow motion, landing on its four wheels once more.

Esther's eyes adjusted to the gloom as she swam towards the open passenger door. She took hold of the vehicle's roof and pulled herself down into the opening, where she found Mila struggling to free herself. The girl had managed to unfasten her seatbelt, but it was still tied to the driver's one, and she didn't seem able to wriggle free.

A glance across revealed that Anita Jess was alive and moving too, and similarly trapped by her own safety belt. Instead of trying to pull it loose, though, Jess seemed to be searching for something; she was bent over, pawing desperately around the footwell beneath her feet and under her seat.

Ignoring the other woman for the moment, Esther began working at Mila's seatbelt in an attempt to loosen it. It wasn't easy; in her panic, the girl was fighting against the locking mechanism. Esther signalled for her to stop pulling and let her help, when all of a sudden the shock of a third person drifting up out of the backseat sent the air from Esther's lungs and an explosion of bubbles filled her vision. It was all she could do to hold on to the passenger door and keep herself from floating away.

Jason. She hadn't seen him when they were on the clifftop.

But then she registered the sightless gaze, the pale and lifeless expression. He was dead.

The bloody carpet. It was Jason's blood.

A searing pain in her chest reminded Esther that time was running out. Jess seemed to have given up her search around the footwell. Esther attempted to get her attention as she pulled herself towards Mila again, but the woman was too busy wrestling with her own seatbelt now.

Mila had almost passed out. But as her eyes drifted closed and she grew more lethargic, Esther was able to take control of her belt. She fed it gently backward, letting the polyester strap tighten on Mila's body for an inch or so before slowly pulling it back out again, making it looser and looser.

All the while, Esther did her best to ignore the fire building in her chest. She had very little time to get Mila free of this, a mere handful of seconds before she too passed out. The girl was pawing uselessly at the seatbelt now – no help, but no longer a hindrance either.

And then suddenly Jess grabbed hold of Esther's arm. The woman opened her mouth in a gurgling, muted scream for help. Esther lost her grip on Mila's seatbelt and it began rolling slowly back into place again. She struggled free of Jess's grasping hands and pushed her away. She held up an open palm, signalled to the woman what she needed to do, but Jess wasn't paying proper attention. She just started pulling recklessly at her own belt again, futile and desperate.

Esther tried to focus. Darkness was eating at the edges of her vision. She felt her fingers growing numb. If she didn't get this done now, there were going to be four bodies down here. She took a gentle hold of Mila's seatbelt and slowly pulled it loose once more.

At last, she was able to flip the upper strap of the belt behind Mila's shoulders and pull the lower strap wide enough for her to slide her legs out. The girl, seeming to sense her sudden freedom, looked down and with slow, clumsy movements managed to do just that. Esther put her hands under Mila's arms and pulled with all her might.

Mila was free. But it was clear that, even without her injured left arm, and even if the girl could swim, she didn't have the strength to make it to the surface.

As the remaining oxygen left Esther's lungs, she thrust up and away from the car wreck, one arm around Mila. The last sight she had of Anita Jess was a glimpse of the uncomprehending terror on the woman's face, as though she couldn't believe that Esther was leaving her.

But there was no more time.

Esther kicked for the surface. Kicked towards the faint, pale square of light above.

Mila was completely limp in her arms now, and Esther's own strength was fading fast. She closed her eyes. Tried to keep kicking even as her consciousness began to wane.

When she broke the surface, it happened abruptly, and Esther immediately started sucking in air – desperate, ragged breaths – blinking the water out of her eyes and rolling so that she lay on her back. She pulled Mila up into the fresh air with her.

The quarry walls towered over them on three sides. By turning her head carefully, Esther was able to find the open end of the pit where the gravel slope rose out of the lake.

Gathering her strength, she began a careful backstroke towards that stony beach.

Mila was like a dead weight now, but Esther didn't dare waste her breath trying to get a response from the girl. It was all she could do to kick for shore.

It seemed to take an eternity. Every time Esther arched her neck to look up and back, to gauge the distance, it appeared as if she was no nearer the water's edge. After a while she gave up checking; it was too disheartening, with the minutes stretching and no sign of life from Mila.

And then, all of a sudden, there was a flurry of splashing and Imelda Fisher rose into her field of vision. Esther felt the officer's arms under her, and a moment later, she was being pulled to shore.

As soon as she sensed solid ground beneath her, Esther

tried to stand up. Fisher took Mila, dragging the girl up onto the bed of pebbles to begin CPR.

Esther was so exhausted that she needed a couple of tries to find her feet. Swaying there, with her teeth chattering and water up to her knees, she turned to look across the pit lake. She was amazed at how little distance she'd actually swum. It had seemed like hours, and yet it couldn't have taken more than a minute or two.

Fisher was crouched over Mila, administering the initial breaths. A cough and a splutter of spat-out water from the teenager told Esther there would be no need for chest compressions.

The sound of distant sirens reached her ears. The cavalry were coming, but they were too far away for Anita Jess. If Esther waited for divers, the woman would be dead by the time they got to her.

"Do you have a knife?" she asked Fisher.

The officer looked at her.

"A Leatherman or a penknife or something?" Esther insisted.

The PC fumbled in one of her pouches and produced a large Swiss Army Knife.

Esther took it and began wading out into the water again.

"Sergeant, what are you doing?"

"Anita Jess is still down there," Esther replied croakily. "I need to try."

"Wait!"

But Esther didn't wait. Mila was alive. Soon, Anita Jess would not be. She heaved a lungful of air, put the knife between her teeth, and pushed herself back out into the water.

The plunge was less of a shock this time, without the

forty-foot fall, and she no longer really noticed the cold. But her lungs hadn't fully recovered. The ache she'd felt as she'd tried to free Mila was already forming in her chest, a dull protest that was fast becoming another searing pain.

Determined, she pressed on – stroke and kick, stroke and kick.

By the time the car came into view again, her chest was ablaze. She grabbed hold of the roof and passenger door and hauled herself into the front seats. Jess wasn't moving anymore. Her eyes were closed, her hair a drifting mass of blonde.

It might have been easier with the woman unconscious, but Esther's burning lungs meant she had less time than before and she wasted none of it. Grabbing the seatbelt, she took the penknife from between her teeth and began cutting.

As she tugged away the severed belt, Esther wrapped an arm around Jess's unresponsive body and pulled her free of the car. Then she kicked for the surface once more. The effort of it sent a shock of dull pain across her chest; she imagined it was what a heart attack might feel like.

This time when she broke the surface, she was met by a lot more noise and activity. Flashing blue lights and the sound of voices and crunching gravel announced the arrival of police, as well as several search and rescue trucks and two ambulances.

It seemed as though she'd only just turned into her backstroke when a flurry of activity erupted all around her. Search and rescue personnel and police officers, chest-deep in the water, took the weight of her casualty out of her arms.

Esther nearly collapsed with relief. She had no option but to let two volunteers carry her from the water. They brought her to the back of an ambulance, where a paramedic threw a silver foil blanket around her and began to check her over.

Esther found she could only mumble answers to the simplest of questions, but it was mostly because her eyes were searching for Mila. It took a few moments to find the girl in all the bustle. She was sitting in the back of the other ambulance, clad similarly in silver foil, with another medic hunkered down in front of her.

"Can you tell me your name again?" Esther's paramedic asked her.

"Esther," she replied thickly, through violently chattering teeth.

"Esther what? Can you remember your surname?"

Although she felt vaguely annoyed by the stupidity of the question, it actually took her a moment to remember. Longer than it should have.

"Penman," she mumbled hoarsely.

The paramedic ripped open another package and shook out a second silver blanket, placing it around the first.

Esther turned, foil rattling, to stare at two more paramedics who were administering CPR to Anita Jess on the pebble shore nearby. They were giving her chest compressions. A policeman hurried over with a defibrillator.

"Are you a police officer?" Esther's medic asked.

"A detective," Esther replied. She couldn't raise her voice above that rasping mumble. "Belfield CID."

The paramedic checked her temperature, then explained that he was going to go and find her something warm to drink in one of the search and rescue trucks and that he would be back in a moment.

Esther watched the paramedics work on an unmoving Anita Jess. The automated voice of the defibrillator was issuing instructions. Shouts of "keep clear", followed by a mechanical announcement that a shock had been administered, and they were in again for more chest compressions, more mouth-to-mouth.

Esther leaned against the ambulance door and closed her eyes.

EPILOGUE

MILA WAS SITTING up in the hospital bed, her knees tucked up to her chest, wearing the same plain grey sweater and tracksuit bottoms as Esther. These were the outfits doled out to prisoners in custody whenever police had to seize clothing as evidence. Someone – PC Fisher, perhaps – had had the presence of mind to get a crew to run a couple of sets from the police station to the hospital for Esther and Mila. They were pretty awful-looking – Esther had pulled her leather jacket on over hers in a futile effort to hide it – but at least they were dry.

Mila's top had been cut away at the left shoulder, a thick cast encasing her upper arm and the crook of her elbow, her forearm supported by a foam sling. She was examining a dark mark on the inside of her left wrist. A pentacle tattoo, exactly like Katie Wilde's. The doctors were still working on Anita Jess – who'd been rushed to ICU on arrival – but Esther was pretty sure that if they looked they'd find an identical tattoo on her wrist too. All three girls had scars on their palms as well.

"Hey," Esther said, by way of greeting, her voice still a little raspy. "How are you doing?"

Mila regarded her through long, dark lashes.

"You're the one who saved me."

It was more a statement than a question.

Esther shrugged. "Just doing my job. If I hadn't jumped in, PC Fisher would have, but she was wearing far too much clobber."

"Thank you," Mila said. She said it simply, shyly even, her gaze slipping back to the tattoo on her wrist.

Esther opened her mouth to say it was nothing, but stopped. It wasn't nothing, and they both knew it. Instead, she said: "Your parents are on their way down."

Mila didn't reply or look up, but she did stiffen slightly.

Esther put her plastic bag of wet clothes on the ground and sat down on the end of the bed, positioning herself within Mila's line of sight.

"Is there anything you want to talk to me about, before they get here?" she asked, realising as she said it that it sounded like she was questioning the girl. A lawyer would rip her a new one if they thought she was trying to wheedle information from a suspect – a juvenile suspect, at that – without representation. But PC Fisher and the paramedics had got a rough idea of the girl's ordeal during the ambulance ride to hospital. Mila Rose was primarily a victim in all this, *not* a suspect; at least, that was what Esther intended to tell anyone who tried to pull her up for this little meeting. Because she wanted to make sure Mila wasn't a victim of anything else. Before the Roses got here.

"They're going to kill me," Mila mumbled.

"Who? Pastor Rose? Has he ever been violent to you?"

Mila looked up sharply then, her eyes wide as she realised what Esther was implying.

"No," she said, shaking her head. "I don't mean, like, *literally*. Tim has never... He wouldn't..." She trailed off and shook her head again. "He's not like that. I just mean"—she sighed—"I just mean he's going to be furious."

"Oh, I don't know," Esther replied. "I think they'll be too relieved to be angry."

The girl left off thumbing her tattoo. She began picking at a loose thread in the lining of her cheap custody trousers instead.

"Why'd you run away?" Esther asked.

Mila shrugged. "Fed up. Sick of being treated like a child. Tim might not be violent, but he's strict. And he never stops ramming Bible stuff down everyone's throat. He can't just let me be *me*." She sighed again. "It's hard to explain. Seems silly when I think about it now. I feel so stupid. But Anita made it seem..." Her eyes filled with tears, and she trailed off.

"They're still working on her," Esther said. "She's in ICU."

Mila nodded and wiped her eyes. "Imelda told me."

"You know, I ran away too, when I was about your age," Esther said.

Mila glanced up at her through those dark lashes. "Oh yeah? Bet you didn't end up in some weird cult, though."

Esther chuckled, eliciting a small smile from Mila.

"No," she replied. "I didn't end up in a cult."

Mila's smile was replaced by an earnest expression.

"What happened when you got home?" she asked.

"I didn't go home," Esther said.

Mila blinked. She hadn't expected that answer.

"My mum was an alcoholic," Esther explained. "It was just the two of us and life in that house was… difficult. The men she would drag home…" She shook her head. "It was tough being a teenage girl in that environment, I can tell you. We used to argue all the time. Though I suspect the language my mother used was a bit more colourful than anything Pastor Rose might say. There were shouting matches, things thrown. Police were always getting called to our door because of domestics."

"Sounds a bit like how my mama and I lived in Lithuania," Mila replied, studying Esther closely now. "It seems less bad the more time that passes, but I know things were not good when I was small."

"Time plays tricks on everyone's memory," Esther told her. "But I do remember one thing pretty clearly: the last argument we had, my mum and I, just before I ran away… that was a big one. Lots of names and accusations flung about, and then… well, I just left. Ran away to London. Got a job, found somewhere to live. Started out fresh." She hesitated; this wasn't quite the direction she had meant to go when she began speaking about her own experience. But since it wouldn't have been true to say she regretted running away, she fudged. "When I look back now, I wish I hadn't cut her off so completely," she said. "I regret that."

"So, you, like, *never* went back?" Mila asked. "Like, *ever?* Have you not seen her since?"

"We made amends. Last year. Just before she died. She had cancer."

"I'm sorry."

"Thank you. But I was lucky. I got to know her again. Got to spend some time with her before she passed. A lot of people don't get that." She fixed Mila with a steady gaze. "I know you lost your mum when you were young. And I guess what I'm trying to say is that the Roses might piss you off something awful at times – you're a teenager, lots of things are going to do that, especially parents – but I'm sure they're trying. All relationships need a little give and take. A little leeway. A little forgiveness. Your relationship with your parents is no different. And it's worth the effort. Believe me. No one doubts you're your own person, Mila. You have your own mind. But maybe there's a better way to go about showing it. Maybe cut them a bit of slack, yeah?"

Mila lowered her eyes. She nodded mutely, a touch of colour rising to her cheeks.

Esther caught the sound of Jared's voice from the hallway, growing louder. She reached out and put her hand on Mila's bare foot, the only part of her she could reach.

"Are you ready?" she asked.

Mila swallowed, but then raised her head and nodded.

"Just remember what I said, Mila," Esther told her, keeping her voice low. "Don't make the same mistake I did."

She held the girl's gaze a moment longer, and then slipped off the bed.

"Mila?" It was Jared, talking gently.

"We're both in here, Jared," Esther replied. "You can come through."

The curtain was pulled aside to reveal Jared, along with

286

Tim and Vera Rose.

Vera, already trembling and teary-eyed, broke down as soon as she saw Mila. She rushed forward and flung her arms around the girl. Esther was glad to see that Mila didn't hesitate in hugging her back.

Pastor Rose was a different matter. He hesitated, though his eyes were full of tears too, tears he let roll down his cheeks unchecked.

After a flurry of kisses and a great deal of relieved sobbing, Vera finally settled herself on the bed next to Mila. Esther noticed that she held the girl's good hand tight, as if she might never let go of her again.

Mila was crying, but she was smiling at the same time. They both were. When Timothy stepped forward, her smile faltered. She half-glanced at Esther before she fixed the pastor with a steady gaze.

"I'm sorry," she said, looking from the pastor to Vera to include both of them in the apology. "I'm sorry for making you both worry so much."

"I'm sorry too, Mila," he said. "We can do things better. *I* can do better. I promise."

Vera was sniffing back tears while she stroked Mila's hair with her free hand.

"You've changed your hair," she said.

Mila wrinkled her nose. "Yeah, I'm not sure about it. I think I prefer it dark."

Vera pulled Mila close and kissed her forehead. "Whatever you like, dear," she said. "Whatever you like."

As the pastor sat down on the edge of the bed with his wife and daughter, Esther looked at Jared and gestured towards the door. She pulled the curtain as they left, giving the reunited family a bit of privacy.

"She seems to be recovering well," Jared mused as they stepped out into the corridor.

"She'll be okay," Esther replied. "How's Anita Jess doing?"

"Stable," he said. "Doctors reckon she'll pull through. We'll have to keep her under guard at the hospital for a few days before we can take her into custody. That means we'll need to hold the crime scenes. It'll chew up a lot of resources over the next week or so. Uniform commanders won't be happy, but there's no way around it."

Esther nodded. "I'll get Liz and Kyle to start working on an interview plan in the morning."

"Are you okay?"

It was the first time she had been able to speak privately with Jared, and he didn't bother hiding his concern.

"I'm fine," she told him. "The medics have checked me over, filled me with hot chocolate. I'm good. Apart from the husky voice and the dodgy outfit."

Jared smirked as he looked her up and down. "You'll blend in with Belfield's finest down at the courthouse." His smile faded. "PC Fisher told me what you did. It was incredibly brave. And incredibly stupid."

Esther tossed a hand at the remark. "I'm a good swimmer. I was fine."

"Well, that family in there have you to thank that they're still together. Search and Rescue wouldn't have pulled either girl out in time."

"Just doing my job," Esther said. "Fisher would have done the same if I wasn't there."

"I don't think so," he replied. "She told me she can't

swim for shit. Said she'd probably have ended up at the bottom with them."

"Well," Esther said, shifting uncomfortably under Jared's inscrutable gaze, "right place right time for me, then, I guess."

"And Mila." Jared's expression was indecipherable. "And Anita. And Vera and Tim."

Esther conceded that addendum with a nod. She glanced down the corridor toward where a crew of nurses were rolling someone along on a trolley. The hospital wasn't as busy here as the emergency department downstairs, with only a handful of people moving about the corridors, but the sight of hospital workers in scrubs made her think of Triona. She looked at her watch.

"I've got to dash," she said. "Triona's parents are catching a train to the airport shortly. If I don't go now, I'll miss them. You okay to stay here for a bit?"

"Of course. I'll speak to the Roses before I go, and get an update on the Jess girl. And Esther?"

She hesitated.

"Well done."

Esther couldn't quite read the odd expression on Jared's face as he said it, but the words were sincerely meant.

She nodded. "Thanks, Jared."

* * *

Belfield's main train station wasn't that far from the hospital, but Esther was still cutting it close as she hurried up the steps to the main concourse. Rush hour was well underway, the place full of commuters crowding the entry points to the platforms.

As Esther slowed to scan one of the overhead display boards, she heard Triona calling her name. Her girlfriend stood with her parents beside the queue to Platform Four. Her smile slipped a little when Esther hurried over to them, her brow pursed as she looked her up and down.

The custody tracksuit.

Before Esther could explain, Cormac spoke.

"We saw you on the telly," he announced brightly. "Very smart. Very professional."

"We watched your press conference earlier," Triona explained. "Did you find that girl? The missing teenager?"

"We found her," Esther replied. "She's safe and sound now."

"Well, isn't that good news!" Cormac declared, still beaming. "You've had a busy day of it, I suppose?"

Esther nodded. "You could say that."

"Well, we'll not keep you, so," Áine declared. "We've only a few minutes left to board, so we'll say goodbye now." She held out her hand. "It was nice to meet you, Esther. Thank you for having us."

Esther shook her hand, her smile fading slightly in the arctic front of Áine's farewell. Áine barely met her eyes. She simply gave a curt nod, lifted her bag, and leaned in to give her daughter a quick peck on the cheek. "We'll let you know when we arrive home, dear."

With that, she turned and joined the queue filing onto Platform Four. She already had her ticket in hand.

Cormac turned to Esther, his smile apologetic. Esther

half-raised her hand as though to shake his too, but he took her by surprise by putting his arms around her and giving her a hug. Esther hugged him back.

"It was so nice to meet you finally, Esther, after all Triona's told us about you." He said the words quietly, for Esther's ears alone. "You've made my little girl happier than I've seen her in quite a long time. I'm glad she met you."

He pulled away from her then. He was still smiling, though his eyes were a little moist as he turned to Triona and gave her an even longer hug. Again, there were words for his daughter that were just for her. It seemed he might go on hugging her forever if it wasn't for Áine's impatient command from the other side of the security fence for him to hurry up.

Cormac finally broke away, wiping away a tear discreetly as he waved them both goodbye. He pulled his ticket from his pocket and went to join his wife.

"Thanks for coming," Triona murmured to Esther, as they watched her parents walk down the platform. "I'm sure you were up to your eyes."

"It's fine," Esther replied. "I wanted to come."

Áine was marching onto the train without a backwards glance. Cormac stopped to wave again. Esther and Triona waved back.

"Your dad's lovely," Esther said.

"He's a legend," Triona replied, and then sighed. "Sorry, again, about my ma."

"Don't be," Esther said quickly. "She's your family. Can't change your family. Besides, I'll win her over yet."

When Triona turned to her then, there was such a look of gratitude in her eyes that Esther couldn't help kissing her, a long kiss that attracted more than a few stares from passersby. Esther wasn't able to pretend that she was getting used to the stares, but she was getting better at ignoring them.

They parted to watch the train begin pulling away from the platform.

"You'll have to tell me what the story is with that get-up," Triona said, glancing sideways at the custody tracksuit. "Long story, I suppose?"

"Long story," Esther agreed.

"You want to talk about it?"

"Maybe later," Esther replied. "But since we have the house to ourselves again, maybe you can help me out of this 'get-up' first."

Triona laughed her sparkling laugh, and it was only then that Esther realised she hadn't heard that laugh in days.

"Come on," Esther said, taking her by the hand. "Let's go home."

PENTACLE

ABOUT THE AUTHOR

I spent over ten years as a frontline police officer in the UK. It's a job unlike any other, a job that exposes you to aspects of life and society that most people never get to see. It changes your perspective on the world. My time in law enforcement made me want capture that perspective, to write crime fiction with an authentic voice, raw and unvarnished. Detective Esther Penman is the product of those efforts – I hope you enjoy her stories!

— J.K. Flynn

jkflynn.co.uk

Made in the USA
Las Vegas, NV
22 June 2025

23925542R00177